PRAISE FOR

All We Could Still Have

"A deeply moving story."
—Suzanne Redfearn, #1 Amazon bestselling author of *In an Instant*

"Diane Barnes is a masterful storyteller . . . Readers will fall in love with *All We Could Still Have* from the very first page."
—Barbara Conrey, *USA Today* bestselling author of *Nowhere Near Goodbye*

"[Barnes's] story will leave you with the most redemptive emotion of them all: hope."
—Alli Frank and Asha Youmans, authors of *The Better Half* and *Tiny Imperfections*

"I read this book in one night, holding my breath until the very last line."
—Ann Garvin, *USA Today* bestselling author of *I Thought You Said This Would Work*

More Than

Ippy Awards 2020: Silver Medal: Best Adult Fiction Ebook
Indies Today 2020: Best Book of the Year Finalist
NYC Big Book Award—Distinguished Favorite Women's Fiction
Ms. magazine favorite book to curl up with for the holidays
Selected by BookTrib as a novel that celebrates women's midlife transitions
"Peggy is an inspirational character."
—Chick Lit Central

"A story that is truly inspired and truly inspiring!"

—Indies Today

"A book chock full of heart!"

—Annie Hartnett, award-winning author of *Rabbit Cake* and
Unlikely Animals

"A pace that keeps the pages turning."

—Jennifer Klepper, *USA Today* bestselling author of *Unbroken
Threads*

"Fresh, crisp, and real."

—Kelly Stone Gamble, *USA Today* bestselling author of *They Call Me
Crazy*

Mixed Signals

"A snappy tale with sweet undertones . . . Barnes has written another
charming, funny romance that keeps its plot rolling while capturing
workplace dynamics."

—*Kirkus Reviews*

"Clever, honest, and endearing."

—Chick Lit Central

"Completely relatable and so well written."

—Chick Lit Club

Waiting for Ethan

"Fans of romantic beach reads will find that this book's charismatic heroine makes it an engrossing page-turner."

—*Kirkus Reviews*

"The novel is written in a breezy fashion and is likely to keep you furiously turning the pages until the back cover is reached and you find yourself hungry for more."

—*Worcester Magazine*

"I didn't want to put it down."

—Chick Lit Central

"This is a great romantic read."

—Chick Lit Club

The Mulligan Curse

ALSO BY DIANE BARNES

All We Could Still Have

More Than

Mixed Signals

Waiting for Ethan

The Mulligan Curse

A Novel

DIANE BARNES

LAKE UNION
PUBLISHING

Published by Lake Union Publishing, Seattle

www.apub.com

Amazon, the Amazon logo, and Lake Union Publishing are trademarks of Amazon.com, Inc., or its affiliates.

ISBN-13: 9781662518362 (paperback)
ISBN-13: 9781662518355 (digital)

Cover design and illustration by Kimberly Glyder

Printed in the United States of America

For Michael, Maria, and Susan: my first and forever friends.

Michael, you still owe me five dollars.

Chapter 1

Mary's finger cramped as she scrolled down to her birth year on the online form. Numbers zoomed by. The twenty-first century became the twentieth. The 1990s turned to the 1980s. Her vision blurred as she reached the '70s. Once she'd finally made it to the 1960s, the teenage boy sitting next to her in the dentist's waiting room bumped her arm, knocking her hand off the tablet's keyboard. *Dang it.* She had to start all over again.

She didn't mind using technology, but she would have preferred to type in her birth date. Honest to goodness, her birth year appeared so far down the list, she felt as if she'd aged a decade while scrolling to reach it.

"Mary?" A dental assistant standing by the reception desk called her name. "Mrs. Amato?" The dark-haired girl smiled and waved. "So nice to see you. I didn't realize you were a patient here."

Mary squinted. The girl looked familiar, but she couldn't place her.

"Lindsey Harrington. I'm a friend of Kendra's."

"Of course. Good to see you, Lindsey." An image from a decade earlier of Lindsey and Mary's daughter, dancing around the living room and singing Taylor Swift songs, popped into Mary's head. The two girls had been freshmen in high school then. All that scrolling to reach her birth year had made Mary feel old, but the fact that this girl was all grown up and one of her health care providers made her feel ancient. It also reminded her that Kendra, too, was all grown up and didn't need her anymore. Mary's friends used to marvel at how close the two of them were. More like sisters than mother and daughter, but that all changed when Kendra took the job at the ad agency. Now she was too busy to spend time with her mom. In the spring and summer, Mary's sense of loneliness heightened because her husband, Dean, spent most of his free time on the golf course, leaving her alone almost every weekend. A flash of pain streaked through the back of her mouth. She brought her hand to her face. "My back teeth have been killing me."

"Let's find out what's going on." Lindsey strode down the hall. Mary trailed behind.

The distinct smell of the dentist's office—clove oil, formaldehyde, and a disinfectant—filled her nostrils as she walked into the exam room. She imagined she was breathing in tooth dust from the patient before her and coughed. Once settled in the big chair, she stared out the window at a pink flowering dogwood. During spring in Massachusetts, the landscape put on its own fireworks show with an explosion of colors that made suffering through the cold, dingy gray winter almost worth it.

Lindsey adjusted the dental chair. "How long have your teeth been bothering you?"

"Since last Thursday." Mary remembered the exact moment she'd first felt the pain. She was standing in line at the supermarket checkout when she spotted Liz Collins, her former coworker and nemesis, now the anchor of *CBS Evening News*, on the cover of *People*. Above Liz's smiling face, the headline read, "America's Most Trusted Broadcaster."

That should be me. Before Mary could process the thought, a searing pain had streaked through her mouth, causing her knees to buckle.

Here in the dentist's chair, as she pictured Liz's face on the cover of that magazine, all her muscles tightened. She was better than Liz. Everyone said so. If only she hadn't turned down that promotion, she'd be a famous newscaster today instead of a bored housewife whom no one noticed, not even her husband or daughter. When she'd tried to talk to Dean about how seeing Liz on the cover of that magazine had made her feel like she'd wasted her life, he'd dismissed her with an awkward laugh before running out the door for the golf course.

"Relax your jaw," Lindsey said. As she poked around Mary's mouth with the mirror and probe, Mary struggled to keep her tongue out of the way. In the room next door, a drill started, and a patient shrieked. Mary's grip on the armrests tightened.

Lindsey finished her exam and settled on a stool in front of the computer. "So weird. Your wisdom teeth are coming in. We usually see that in younger patients."

Kendra had had her wisdom teeth removed junior year of high school. Mary had bought her daughter milkshakes every evening for almost a week, and they binge-watched *Downton Abbey* together until Kendra recovered. Mary smiled at the memory, happy to think about a time when Kendra needed her and giddy that whatever was wrong with her was most commonly associated with younger people. She'd been feeling so old lately. That day at the grocery store when she'd seen the magazine with Liz on the cover, she'd also run into an old classmate, Debbie Berger. Debbie had spotted her from the other side of the frozen food aisle, and Mary wondered who the old woman waving at her was. She wanted to cry when she figured out that the woman was someone she'd grown up with and was actually a few months younger than she was. Of course, Mary had long ago accepted that she was no longer young, but at that moment she'd realized she wasn't even middle aged anymore, not unless she lived to 108. Her life was getting away from her, with more time behind her than in front of her, and she'd done absolutely nothing with it.

She heard a quick knock on the door, and the dentist entered. "We didn't have a chance to meet before Dr. Goldberg retired. I'm Dr. Montari." He shook Mary's hand. With his boyish face, big brown eyes, and rosy cheeks, he looked more like a model for OshKosh B'Gosh than a dentist, and Mary wondered if he could possibly be as skilled as his predecessor.

He turned his attention to Lindsey. "What's going on?"

"She's complaining of pain in the back of her mouth. It looks like her wisdom teeth are coming in."

Dr. Montari smiled. "Really?" He slid his hands into gloves. "Let me have a look." The excitement in his voice suggested he expected to see a third row of teeth growing in Mary's mouth, and she basked in his attention. No one had found anything about her this interesting in years, decades even.

She concentrated on not gagging as his latex-covered finger slid over her gums. "Amazing." He clicked his tongue as he pulled his hands back and snapped off his gloves. "I've read about patients in their fifties whose wisdom teeth suddenly erupt, but it's so rare that I never imagined I would treat one."

A blast of heat rushed over Mary. She felt as if she were burning from the inside out. Sweat pooled above her lips and along her clavicles. *Not another hot flash. Not here. Not now.* She fanned herself with her hand.

Lindsey gave her a paper cup filled with water, and Mary guzzled it down.

"Here's the issue," Dr. Montari said, stroking his chin. "Your wisdom teeth are only partially emerged, and they've made a pathway for bacteria to get to the gums. Because they're so hard to reach when brushing, there's ample opportunity for the bacteria to grow, increasing the likelihood of gum disease and infection. There's already some inflammation. I recommend taking the teeth out."

Mary breathed in the odor of the room—which, come to think of it, smelled like pain, not tooth particles—and thought about the patient next door shrieking. Maybe her discomfort would end as suddenly as it had started. "I need to think about it."

Dr. Montari frowned. "Don't take too long, and if the pain gets worse, give us a call right away."

~

Mary rushed through the parking lot of the restaurant where she was meeting her cousin Darbi for their monthly lunch. Inside, a large group of men crowded the hostess stand, laughing as they waited to be seated. She squeezed her way around them and scanned the dining room.

A loud, piercing whistle came from a high-top near the bar. "Mary, over here." Darbi waved her arms over her head.

In front of the table, the two women hugged. As usual, Darbi smelled like a combination of tangerine and patchouli from the essential oils she used as perfume to keep calm.

"Where have you been, girl? I had to start without you." Darbi pointed to the remains of a margarita.

"Stuck in traffic."

"Well then, you need one of these, pronto."

"One? After my morning, I need several. In fact, let's get an IV going."

"What happened?"

Mary lifted her hand to her mouth. "My wisdom teeth have been killing me. The dentist says they have to come out."

Darbi's eyebrows shot up her forehead, and her grin widened. "You must have been sprinkled with Mulligan magic too. Good for you."

"What are you talking about?"

The server, a woman with streaks of pink in her hair, approached them. "Are you ready to order?"

The menus sat stacked on the corner of the table, untouched. Mary picked one up and handed it to Darbi. "We haven't even looked yet."

"I'll come back."

"Bring two more of these, please." Darbi tapped her glass.

"What do you mean by 'Mulligan magic'?" Mary asked.

Darbi slowly turned her head to the left and right as if she was making sure no one could overhear her. "You'll have a hard time believing what I'm about to tell you. I didn't believe Uncle Cillian when he told me. You heard about him, right?"

"My dad always referred to him as his crazy relative in Ireland."

"That's what I thought. Until it happened to me."

Mary leaned across the table toward her cousin. "What happened to you?"

The group of boisterous men who had been waiting by the door passed by, trailing the hostess. She sat them at three long tables pushed together along the back wall.

"How do you think they all know each other?" Darbi asked.

Mary shrugged. "Maybe they work together."

"Are there no women in the company?"

"Of course there are. Not all women stay home to take care of their kids." Her words came out harsh, and she realized she was scolding herself for her long-ago decision to give up her career to stay home with Kendra. "Sorry."

"That was my point," Darbi said.

"Forget that. Finish what you were saying."

Darbi opened her menu. "Let's figure out what we're eating first."

The server returned with their drinks and took their order. After she left, Darbi spoke. "Some of us Mulligans have a magical gene that causes our wisdom teeth to erupt when we start having serious regrets about a past decision. The gene can only be passed on from fathers, but they can pass it to their sons and daughters. I have it. Uncle Cillian had it, and you might have it t—"

Mary interrupted. "Almost everyone gets their wisdom teeth, and almost everyone has regrets. The two are not related." Like subtitles scrolling across the screen during a foreign film, a list of Mary's regrets flashed through her mind: not taking the job in Iowa, quitting work after Kendra was born, not trying harder to find a job after Kendra left for college, not doing anything special with her life, not leaving her mark on the world. Someone had once told her that at the end of their lives, people regretted the things they hadn't done, not the things they'd done. Mary definitely believed it was true.

"Let me finish." Darbi took a big sip of her margarita, her lips twisting as she swallowed. "When we Mulligans with the magical gene have our wisdom teeth removed, we wake up from the procedure the same age we were when we made the choice we regret, and we get to reconsider our decision and choose differently."

A busboy on the other side of the restaurant dropped a tray of dirty dishes. The group of men at the long tables burst out laughing, and somewhere nearby a baby started to cry. Mary's mouth fell open, but no words came out. She'd been expecting Darbi to say something about how having her wisdom teeth removed would hurt so badly that she'd forget about her regrets, or she thought Darbi would explain that without wisdom teeth, she'd become the wisest version of herself. She certainly hadn't thought Darbi would come up with a story as ridiculous as the one she was telling her now.

Darbi rested her elbows on her place mat and perched her chin on the back of her fists. The table tilted toward her. "I was thirty-two when my wisdom teeth came in. Hurt like the dickens. I had them removed and woke up from the procedure as my twenty-five-year-old self."

Mary tapped Darbi's margarita glass. "How many of these did you drink before I got here?"

"Like I said, I didn't believe it until it happened to me."

Mary bit down on her lip as she stared at Darbi. "You want me to believe that you and I have some kind of magical gene that allows us to time travel?"

Darbi shook her head. "I didn't say anything about time travel. I woke up on the very same day I had the procedure, only I was seven years younger and everything that had happened during those last seven years had been erased."

"If you're saying I can be seven years younger by having my wisdom teeth out, I'll pull them out right now." Mary reached toward her mouth.

Darbi laughed. "It's the best thing that ever happened to me. I got to undo my biggest mistake."

"What was that?"

"That's a story for another day. I want to tell you what it will be like for you if you get your teeth out. First . . ." She trailed off as the server dropped off the food: a salad for Mary and a crab cake sandwich for Darbi.

After she left, Darbi continued speaking. "People won't remember you as . . ."

"Stop." Mary held up her fork as if it were a shield that could block out the rest of Darbi's fabrication. Usually she enjoyed Darbi's stories about the Mulligan side of her family because Mary's father had rarely spoken about them, unless to talk about how nuts they were. Mary hadn't even known she'd had a cousin her age until Darbi had unexpectedly shown up fresh off the plane from Ireland. This story was too bizarre to enjoy, though. Besides, they had more important things to talk about today, like the remodel of Celebrations, the gift shop Darbi's wife had bought a few months ago and that Darbi worked at three days a week. "Tell me how Jacqui is. Are the renovations at her store finished?"

Darbi bit into her sandwich. Once she'd swallowed, she cleared her throat. "Women your age don't suddenly develop issues with their wisdom teeth."

"That's true," Mary admitted. "The dentist looked at me as if I were a unicorn."

"It's Mulligan magic." Darbi pointed at Mary. "Admit it. You've been second-guessing a past decision."

Mary shifted on her stool. Her napkin fell from her lap to the ground. She bent under the table to retrieve it because she wanted to get away from Darbi. She didn't believe a word her cousin had said, but Darbi was right. Ever since Mary had seen Liz on the cover of that blasted magazine, she'd been having second thoughts about her life. No, that wasn't right; the second thoughts had started years before, when Kendra moved away to college. Without her daughter to take care of, Mary had found herself with nothing to do. She'd tried to get a job as a journalist again, but the only offer she'd received was to be a receptionist at the *Metro West Daily News*. She was so bored that she took that job, but nine months later, they downsized her out of a position. For the last five years, she'd been a girl Friday for her husband, doing his laundry, packing his lunch, cooking his dinner, booking his haircut appointments, even shopping for his socks and underwear, for crying out loud. She picked up the napkin and returned to her stool.

"Tell me what your regrets are. You must have a big one," Darbi insisted.

Mary swallowed hard, uncomfortable that her cousin seemed to know or at least suspect that she was questioning her life choices, regretting her long-ago decision to give up her career in broadcasting. "Well, you know that Liz Collins and I used to work together at Channel 77. What you might not remember is that job in Iowa that launched her career. They offered it to me first, but I said no." Mary felt the same pang of regret she'd had lately whenever she thought about that decision. A sharp pain streaked through the gums over her wisdom teeth, and she winced.

Darbi chewed on a french fry, appearing to consider Mary's words. "So is that your regret, not being a newscaster?"

Hearing it said back to her made it sound like it was no big deal, but it was. "I want people to know who I am. When my life is all said and done, I want it to have mattered."

Darbi drowned a french fry in ketchup. "You don't have to be on the news or be famous to matter. Of course you matter."

Mary's life didn't matter, not compared to Liz's. No one outside her immediate circle knew who she was. She had turned down the anchoring job, and Liz had accepted it. Now Liz was a celebrated journalist whom the entire country admired, and Mary was a mild-mannered housewife, doing unimportant things like picking up her husband's dry cleaning. Even some of the neighbors living on her street had no idea who she was. If only Darbi's story were true, she'd go back and take that promotion.

"How old were you when you got the job offer?" Darbi asked.

"Twenty-four."

Darbi sucked in a quick breath and fingered her bracelet. "Oh dear."

"Yeah, it was a long time ago."

"You definitely do not want to undo that decision." A stern tone had replaced the previous playfulness in Darbi's voice, piquing Mary's curiosity.

"Why not?"

"If you get your wisdom teeth out, you'll be twenty-four again when the procedure is over."

Mary studied her cousin. With her frizzy silver hair styled in corn-rows, a gold stud in her nose, and a purple knotted rope bracelet around her wrist, she stood out from all the other women in their fifties whom Mary knew. Darbi's eccentricities were one of the reasons Mary loved her. Still, carrying on with this ridiculous story was bizarre behavior even for Darbi. Was she trying to play a joke, or was she having some kind of mental breakdown?

"Why didn't you take the job?" Darbi asked.

Why didn't I? "I was dating Dean. He made it clear he wasn't coming with me, and he wasn't interested in a long-distance relationship. I really liked him, so I stayed."

"So you chose Dean over your career?"

"I guess I did." She hadn't known it at the time, but that was exactly what she'd done. She drained the rest of her margarita.

"And knowing what you know now, would you choose the job or Dean?"

Would she choose a career like Liz's over Dean? Lord help her, right now she would. She needed her life to have meaning. The tequila was leaving a nasty taste in her mouth. She gulped down water to wash away the harsh flavor. It wasn't that she didn't love Dean. She did. Her wedding had been one of the happiest days of her life—the happiest until she'd given birth to Kendra—but she'd never imagined that staying in Massachusetts to date him would limit her career. After she'd turned down the position in Iowa, her boss had assumed she didn't take her job seriously and started giving her less fulfilling assignments. By the time she left the station for maternity leave, she didn't have a compelling reason to return.

Darbi tapped her foot against the leg of the table. "Well? Would you choose Dean again?"

Mary squirmed. While she and Dean had once been madly in love, they barely spent time with each other anymore. He was always golfing with his friends while she was stuck puttering around their house by herself. *No, I don't think I would.* She couldn't say those words out loud. She couldn't admit that to her cousin. She wasn't even comfortable admitting it to herself. "Of course I would."

Darbi raised her chin. "Well then, for the love of everything holy, leave your wisdom teeth alone."

Chapter 2

The first thing Mary noticed when she returned home after lunch was Dean's glass from the night before sitting on the coffee table. It was where he always left his cups if he'd had a drink while watching television. Usually, seeing the glass there didn't bother her, but today it infuriated her. She snatched it up and slammed it into the top rack of the dishwasher. After returning to the living room with a damp cloth, she scrubbed the ring the glass had left on the wood with so much force her knuckles turned red. She was his wife, not his maid, for Pete's sake.

She collapsed on the couch, wishing she'd never had lunch with Darbi today. Their conversation had spoiled her mood. Her cousin's crazy story about Mulligan magic had forced Mary to think about how unhappy she really was, something she tried hard not to think about. And what was with that story? Did Darbi really believe it, or had it been her attempt at a joke? Driving home, Mary had thought about calling Jacqui to ask if she'd noticed any strange behavior in her wife, but Jacqui already had so much on her mind with the store that Mary didn't want to worry her unnecessarily. She'd keep an eye on Darbi, and if she noticed anything else that seemed off, she'd talk to Jacqui about it.

The *People* magazine with the picture of Liz on the cover rested on the arm of the sofa. Mary picked it up and turned to the article. She'd read it so many times by now that she practically had it memorized. Now as she read, she substituted her own name for Liz's. When she reached the end, she had a huge grin on her face, wishing somehow, some way, the nonsense Darbi had spewed at lunch were true. She pictured herself sitting behind the anchor desk, Kendra and Dean in the studio, watching her with riveted attention. When the news ended, the three of them would go to dinner together. Of course they'd get the best table in the restaurant, and people would stop by to ask Mary to be in pictures with them.

The garage door rumbled open. Seconds later, Dean rushed through the breezeway into the living room. He held his tie and a small white bag in one hand and unfastened the buttons of his untucked dress shirt with the other. Pausing in front of the couch, he handed her the bag. "Went to Davio's for lunch and snagged you a couple of popovers."

She stuck her nose in the bag and took a deep breath in, almost tasting the buttery, eggy flavor. She couldn't wait to sink her teeth into one. "How was your day?"

Dean swayed from side to side. "Long."

"I had lunch with Darbi. You'll never believe . . ."

His phone rang, and he pulled it from his pocket, looking at the screen. "Sorry, been waiting for this call." He walked toward the stairway. "Murph, my man." Before he'd made it to the top step and out of earshot, he said, "What time are we teeing off Saturday?"

He returned wearing black wind pants and a blue Addison Heights Golf Club quarter-zip pullover. Without saying a word, he raced by Mary toward the backyard, where he'd installed a putting green years ago. She felt a hollowness in her chest, wishing he had taken a moment to ask about her day. She wanted him to be interested in her life. Then again, nothing about it was interesting lately. At least today she could tell him about Darbi's bizarre behavior. *We'll talk at dinner,* she thought as she started to cook. When the pasta was ready, she stepped onto the deck and called Dean's name. "Time to eat."

He held up his index finger, bent at the waist, and struck the ball with his putter. The ball skirted to the right of the hole. He whacked his club on the ground and looked up at Mary. "I'll be a few minutes. Don't let your food get cold."

Mary sighed. He wouldn't come in until he'd made thirty consecutive putts. It was his nightly ritual, weather permitting. Usually, he didn't start until after dinner. Sometimes he putted in the black of night with the floodlights shining down on him. When Kendra still lived with them, she would challenge Dean to putting contests a few times a week. Mary would sit on the deck with a book while they played, smiling every time they laughed and feeling content. Watching Dean practice in silence tonight, she felt an emptiness that brought tears to her eyes. Before Kendra moved out, the three of them had always sat down for dinner together, and the meals would be punctuated with lively discussions and hearty laughter. With just Mary and Dean at the table, the kitchen had gone quiet, and Mary wondered if their daughter had been the glue holding their marriage together.

She took her plate to the living room and settled on the sofa with the nightly news to keep her company. Liz Collins's familiar voice poured out of the surround sound speakers. "Crowds are expected to rally in cities all over the country this weekend, demanding stricter gun control laws."

Mary repeated the words out loud in her best broadcaster voice, varying her inflection. She studied her old coworker's unlined face and tried to imagine herself sitting in that anchor chair. Back when she and Liz had worked together at Channel 77, people regularly mistook them for sisters because they looked so much alike. They both had brown wavy hair, square faces, and almond-shaped eyes. Mary's were bright green, while Liz's were powder blue. Over the years, Liz had added highlights to her hair, easier to hide the grays, and today it was much lighter than Mary's, which was in desperate need of a color to cover up her roots.

If people saw us together today, they'd probably think I was her mother.

Well, maybe she was being too hard on herself. Her old colleague had had cosmetic fillers injected in her cheeks and lips and regularly underwent Botox treatments. Liz had admitted as much in the *People* article.

Mary knew her cousin's story about erasing years off her age was malarkey, but for fun, she let herself imagine that Darbi was telling the truth. If she could do it all again, she wouldn't let anything get in the way of her career aspirations. Heck, if she could be twenty-four again right now, she'd work her butt off to dethrone Liz Collins as America's most trusted broadcaster. She imagined filling in for Liz on weekends and holidays. Viewers would grow to love Mary more than Liz. They'd flood social media with posts demanding Mary get increased airtime. #MoreMary #LessLiz.

Dean finally came inside. Mary had no idea how he could entertain himself for so long hitting a stationary ball. How utterly boring. The microwave beeped. A few minutes later, he joined her on the couch with his reheated macaroni and a glass of wine. "Sorry. Needed to get my putting right for the tournament. I'll make it up to you tomorrow. I'll take you to Welly's for dinner."

Mary shook her head. "We're going to James's concert with Jenni and Rick tomorrow." How could Dean forget about James's show? The man was a superstar, and he was Mary's friend. How many people actually knew a rock legend? *Rolling Stone* had once referred to James as America's Rod Stewart, and Mary had cut out the article and had it framed, wanting everyone she knew to know she and James were tight. She'd lived in the apartment above James's in Framingham all those years ago when he was just starting out. The two had been as close as a drum and drumstick back then.

"I thought that was next Friday," Dean said.

"Nope. This Friday." The tickets had been hanging on the refrigerator for over three months. Dean had been excited about the idea of seeing James. The two men used to golf together when Dean and Mary had first started dating.

Dean put his dish down. "I'm sorry. I got the date wrong. I can't make it."

Mary narrowed her eyes. "Why not?"

"I can't be out late on Friday night. The tournament's this weekend."

Mary clenched her teeth. He played in a golf tournament almost every weekend from April through October. "It doesn't start until Saturday."

"My tee time is at eight thirty. On the Cape." He picked up his fork. "I'm sorry. If it were any other tournament, I'd be able to go with you."

"I really need you to come with me." She sat up straighter, determined to make him understand. "I don't want to be a third wheel with Jenni and Rick."

"Rick's more likely to feel like the third wheel with you two. Poor schmuck won't be able to get a word in."

"I thought you were excited to see James."

"Any other weekend, I'd be thrilled to see him." Dean's gaze wandered from Mary to the TV, where Liz was saying good night. "Liz looks great."

Mary snapped off the television. "We've had these plans for months."

"I'm sorry I mixed up the weekend."

"Skip the tournament." Mary wanted to pat herself on the back. She'd told Dean exactly what she wanted him to do. Usually, she'd drop hints, and he'd pretend he didn't understand what she wanted.

"I can't let the guys down, especially Anthony. We've played in this together since I was fourteen."

"So you don't want to let your brother down, but it's okay to let me down?" Her voice cracked. She hated herself for being so emotional.

"I don't understand why you're so upset. You'll have fun without me."

He'd once been so disappointed whenever she'd make plans with her friends that didn't include him, but after twenty-six years of marriage, they'd increasingly started doing things on their own. She stomped across the living room to the front door and slammed it behind her. The motion lights snapped on as she stalked down the stairs and across the walkway. A cold wind blew, and she wished she had grabbed her coat. There was no way she was going back inside to get it, though.

With the flashlight from her phone leading the way, she set off down the street, walking fast to try to calm down. These days, she was used to being a golf widow and always found ways to keep herself busy. She'd even planned a full weekend starting with Friday's concert. On Saturday, Kendra was coming over for a rare visit. The two planned to walk the bike trail and then have lunch, and on Sunday, she and Jenni were attending an author talk at the local bookstore. She only needed Dean to be with her for a few hours on Friday night, and he couldn't even do that.

She kicked a stone and watched it skip down the road. Earlier, she'd felt guilty for thinking she would choose her career over Dean if she could do it all again. In this moment, she regretted not choosing her career the first time. As she returned home, the pain in the back of her mouth became almost unbearable.

Chapter 3

In the parking garage, Rick raced around the car to open the door for Jenni. The two of them leaned into one another, holding hands and giggling as they strolled toward the auditorium. They'd been dating for only a few months and were still in the couldn't-get-enough-of-each-other phase. Mary trailed behind, trying to remember the last time Dean had held her hand, but she drew a blank. Well, she and Dean had been together for almost three decades. The romance had long ago evaporated, but for many years, they'd gone overboard with their romantic gestures. Early in their marriage, whenever they ate at a restaurant with karaoke, Dean had insisted on performing Rick Astley's "Never Gonna Give You Up" and always made a big show of dedicating his performance to her. Once on their anniversary, he'd had twelve different florists deliver a single red rose at different times throughout the day because one rose signified true, undying love. To this day, instead of signing cards with the word "love," he wrote "SRR" for "single red rose."

On their first Valentine's Day as husband and wife, she'd sent a box of a dozen red golf balls to his office. He'd once told her that one of the things he missed most about living at home was his mother's gravy, which Mary later learned was pasta sauce, so, unbeknownst to Dean, she had spent an afternoon at his parents' house learning to make his mother's famous tomato sauce and then surprised him with homemade manicotti on his birthday.

When Kendra was born, their attention had rightfully shifted from one another to the baby. What Mary hadn't expected was that they'd never return to how they'd once been. Now that Kendra was out on her own, they struggled to find common interests. Listening to live music had always been something they enjoyed doing together, but tonight Dean's interest in golf had even trumped that.

Once inside and seated, Rick rested his hand on Jenni's thigh. Mary eyed the empty seat next to her, silently cursing Dean, who had changed into his lounge pants before she'd even left the house that evening. She would bet right now he was sprawled out on the sofa, watching a rerun of some long-ago tournament on the golf channel.

Rick whispered something in Jenni's ear, and Jenni burst out laughing. Mary jumped to her feet. "I'm going to get something at the concession stand."

"I'll go." Rick stood. "Peanut M&M'S, right?" He squeezed by the women sitting next to him and stepped into the aisle without waiting for an answer.

"Looks like things are going really well with you and Rick," Mary said.

Jenni's eyes sparkled. "He's almost too good to be true. I keep waiting for him to lose his temper, belittle me, or do some other awful thing Scott used to do."

Mary shook her head. "Rick is not Scott, and after all those years in a miserable marriage, you deserve to be happy. Enjoy him."

Jenni leaned toward Mary and gave her a quick hug. "I don't think I would have ever had the courage to leave Scott if it weren't for you."

Mary's face tightened. "Me? What did I do?" In the twenty-five years that Mary and Jenni had been friends, Mary had often been appalled at the way Jenni's husband talked to his wife, but she'd never mentioned anything about her disdain for Scott, or encouraged her friend to leave him. She would never interfere in someone else's marriage.

"You're always so supportive. You helped me realize I'm not the incompetent idiot Scott made me think I was. You made me see I deserved better."

"I'm pretty sure you figured that out on your own."

The women on the other side of Jenni all stood. Rick shuffled into the row past them, handing Mary and Jenni each a bag of chocolate. The lights dimmed, music started to play, and Mary got lost listening to James sing and forgot all about what she and Jenni had been discussing.

~

After the concert, an usher led Mary, Jenni, and Rick backstage to James's dressing room. He sat on a couch drinking a bottle of sparkling water. His short salt-and-pepper hair was damp, and he had changed out of the black leather pants and tight red shirt he'd worn during the show and was now dressed in jeans and a black T-shirt. When he saw Mary, his smile shone brighter than the spotlight that had followed him around the stage all night. While Mary and James spoke on the phone and texted a few times a month, they hadn't seen each other in over a year because he lived on the other side of the country.

"Mary Mulligan!" James rushed across the room, lifted her off the ground, and spun her around. "You gorgeous thing. Time has stood still for you. You look exactly like you did the day we met."

Feeling as giddy as a schoolgirl, Mary giggled. She knew his words weren't true. She'd aged more than thirty years since they'd met. Life's ups and downs had carved a road map of fine lines over her face. The skin on her neck sagged. Her hair had thinned, and her waist had thickened. Still, she beamed. James had always made her feel good about herself. "You were amazing tonight."

"I'm amazing every night, honey." He winked.

"She danced the entire show. Didn't sit down once. I got exhausted watching her," Jenni said.

"Watching her?" James exaggerated curling his lip in mock disapproval. "Why weren't you dancing with her? Speaking of which, where is that brawny husband of yours? Why wasn't he dancing with you?"

Mary's jaw tensed. She still couldn't believe Dean had refused to come tonight. "Home sleeping. He has an early-morning tee time on the Cape tomorrow."

"Oh my, has he turned into an old fart?" James had witnessed the beginning of Mary and Dean's relationship, teased her about the way Dean looked at her with moony eyes, and predicted Dean would propose long before he did.

Leaning against the doorframe, Rick laughed.

James's attention turned to him. "Why, hello." A lopsided smile broke out on his face. "Who is this beautiful specimen of a man?"

"Rick Zeller." Rick offered his hand. James ignored it and pulled him into a bear hug.

"Sorry, James. He's spoken for," Jenni said.

"All the good ones are." James flung his arm around Mary's shoulders and led her out the stage door to an alley.

"So, tell me what's going on in your life," Mary said.

James told her about new music he'd recorded. "Covers of songs from when we were growing up."

"Music that's on the oldies stations now," Mary said. Long ago, she'd watched James ease into the business at local bars, covering musicians from the seventies and early eighties. He later made a name for himself by performing songs he'd written. His big break came after Springsteen had asked him to open. While James could never sell out stadiums such as Fenway and Gillette like Bruce did, he regularly performed in front of capacity crowds at thousand-seat venues like the Shubert Theatre and Melody Tent when performing in his home state.

Mary glanced over her shoulder to make sure Rick and Jenni were behind them. The two were holding hands, giggling, seemingly unaware that anyone else lived on the planet with them.

"So I saw that Liz Collins is the country's most trusted journalist, " James whispered, as if he were letting Mary in on juicy gossip.

Her tongue stuck to the roof of her mouth. She considered telling James about the funk she'd been in ever since seeing Liz on the cover of *People*. It was the exact kind of thing she would have been able to confide in him when she was in her early twenties and they saw each other every day and told one another everything, but she feared that confessing those feelings to him now would make her seem insecure. "Good for her." She hoped her words didn't sound as bitter as they tasted in her mouth.

James pulled her closer to him. "'For everyone at *CBS Evening News*,'" he said, imitating Liz's highly affected voice, "'I'm Liz Collins. Thank you for joining us and have a good night.'"

"Hey, where are we going?" Jenni asked.

"Just a little farther," James said.

A few blocks later, he stopped in front of a popular Irish pub and held the door open. A hostess led the party of four to a table in the back. Some of the patrons recognized James and asked for an autograph or to take their picture with him. Mary served as the photographer. As James and the customers smiled brightly, Mary's own smile dimmed. James, like Liz, had achieved his dreams and made a large impact on the world, but what had Mary done with her life? Cooked meals for her husband and daughter, did their laundry, kept the house clean, volunteered for the PTA and school fundraisers, and carted Kendra and her friends from one activity to the next. Today, she had nothing to show for it. *This isn't how it was supposed to be.* Twenty-four-year-old Mary who thought she would dominate the broadcasting scene would be ashamed of her fifty-something self. The gums above her emerging wisdom teeth throbbed, and she grimaced.

Finally seated, James ordered Captain Morgan and Cokes for the table. "For old times' sake," he said as he tapped his glass against Mary's. The taste of the spicy rum on Mary's tongue brought her back to the top of the staircase at her old Framingham apartment, where she and James used to sit and talk about their dreams with the moon shining down on them. They always picked a star to wish on. She could see him in his baggy postal uniform, strumming his guitar while she yammered on and on about a news story she'd covered that day. Back then, anyone who had known them would have bet on her achieving her goal, not him.

"What do you mean, Mary launched your career?" Rick asked.

Hearing her name, Mary realized she hadn't been paying attention to the conversation at the table and tuned in.

"She encouraged me to sign up for an open mic night. I ended up getting a regular gig, and one night an executive from Red Label Music heard me. The rest is history."

"One way or another, you would have been discovered," Mary said.

James shook his head. "Without you, I never would have gotten my big break. I wouldn't have ever stepped foot into the Skunk. That place should have been condemned. What a dump."

Mary's memory of the bar didn't match James's at all. The old wooden tables had scars that added character. Generations before them had worn out the sticky old oak floor while standing around enjoying each other's company, and the bartender who'd made the drinks in those flimsy plastic cups was always quick with a smile.

"Do you remember Flannel Shirt Guy, who always sat at the bar next to the pole?" James asked.

"You asked him out, and he showed you a picture of his wife," Mary said.

"Pretty sure it was the photograph that came with the wallet." James laughed. "I wonder if he's come out yet."

Mary and James reminisced, laughing so hard that tears streamed down their faces. At two, the bar closed, and they reluctantly ended their night. As Mary climbed into the back seat of Rick's car for the ride back to Hudson, her feet ached, her voice was hoarse, and her ears rang, yet she felt more alive than she had in years.

At home, she had trouble fitting her key in the lock. The door swung open. Dean stood on the other side, circles under his eyes and a wrinkle in his brow. "It wasn't locked."

"Whoops." Mary giggled, still on a high from her night with James.

Dean bit down on his lower lip. "It's three in the morning. I was sure you'd been in an accident. You didn't answer my texts or calls." He pulled her into his arms.

Even this time of night, he smelled like a combination of cut grass and suntan lotion, as if he had just walked off a golf course. Mary rested her head against his chest, breathing in his scent. It warmed her like a fleece blanket on a chilly night. She felt awful for worrying him, but she felt even worse because she hadn't thought about him once all night long.

Chapter 4

"Mom."

At the sound of Kendra's voice, Mary jerked awake. Her head pounded and her mouth felt as if she'd swallowed a bucket of sand. Downstairs, the front door banged shut. Mary squinted at the clock. The red numbers blurred together. She blinked and looked again. 10:07. She wondered how she'd managed to sleep through Dean showering and leaving for his golf tournament on the Cape.

Quick footsteps climbed the stairs. Mary sat up, resting her back against the headboard.

"Mom?" Kendra, her lips curling downward at the corners, stood in the doorway of the bedroom, watching her. "Are you sick?"

"Why are you here so early?" They had plans to walk the bike path together at noon.

"I'm a half hour late."

Mary reached for her glasses on the nightstand and looked at the clock again: 12:27. "Oh, my!" She giggled. She hadn't slept this late since her college days. Her internal clock had reset itself as she'd aged. Each year, she woke up thirty minutes earlier than the year before. These days, she was usually up before seven.

Kendra crossed the room and plunked down on the edge of the bed. "You look kind of green."

"I had a little too much to drink last night. Captain Morgan and Coke." Mary raised her chin, hoping her daughter was impressed. *See? Your mom is not such an old fuddy-duddy.*

Kendra's dark eyebrows shot upward. "You're hungover? And since when do you drink rum and Cokes?"

Mary smoothed the bunched-up blanket. "When I was your age, it was my signature drink."

"Signature drink?" Kendra wrinkled her nose. "Who are you, and what have you done with my mother?"

"I saw James in concert. After the show, we went to a trendy bar in the heart of the city. I didn't get home until three in the morning." She felt strangely proud of this, as if staying out late proved she could still keep up with the young crowd.

"Dad stayed out that late?"

The mention of Dean sucked all the joy out of the moment. No doubt if he'd been at the show last night, he wouldn't have wanted to go out after, and he would have made them all leave before James had played his last song so they wouldn't get stuck in a slow line leaving the parking garage.

"Your father refused to come. He had to wake up early for golf."

"Are you too tired to walk?" Kendra retied her long, dark ponytail as she spoke. "We can do something another day."

Mary shook her head. The slight movement made her woozy. "No way." After Kendra had graduated from college and moved into an apartment in Boston, Mary had imagined her daughter coming home every Wednesday night to do her laundry and have dinner. She pictured meeting Kendra on rainy weekends at the old movie theater in West Newton, and she was certain she and Dean would drive into the South End on Sunday mornings in the winter to take Kendra to brunch. In the two years since Kendra had moved to the city, none of that had happened. Instead, Mary could count on one hand the number of times her daughter had come home to visit. While Kendra would make time to play a round of golf with Dean, whenever Mary asked her to do something, she was busy.

"Give me a few minutes to get dressed," Mary said. She was eager to find out why her daughter had invited her to go for a walk today.

~

After Mary dressed, she found Kendra in the backyard practicing her putting. Kendra was six years old when Dean taught her how to golf. Mary was glad their daughter had taken to the sport because Dean finally stopped pestering her to learn how to play. Over the years, though, she'd sometimes felt left out when Dean and Kendra spent long afternoons together at the club or rehashed highlights from their eighteen holes at the dinner table.

Now as Mary stood on the porch watching Kendra make putt after putt, her eyes watered in the bright sun, so she went back inside to retrieve her sunglasses. They were on the bench in the breezeway next to Dean's battered royal blue baseball hat, the "good luck cap," as he called it. Kendra had given it to him years ago for Father's Day. Since then, he'd worn it to every tournament he played in. He must have forgotten it today, because there was no way he would have intentionally left it behind. Mary sometimes wondered if Dean loved golf more than he loved her, but she had no doubt he loved Kendra more than anything else in the world. She couldn't have picked a better father for their daughter, and seeing the sweet way he treated Kendra had made her love him even more than she had at the start of their marriage.

~

On the rail trail, Mary and Kendra set out at a fast pace, weaving their way around other walkers. Occasionally, bikers or runners would shout "On your left!" as they passed.

"You should have seen how James got mobbed at the bar," Mary said. "And he was so gracious, posing for photo after photo."

"Were they all middle-aged women like you, reliving their youth?" Kendra teased.

Reliving their youth. Mary pictured the throngs of women like herself packed into the theater. Were the ninety minutes they'd spent singing, dancing, and screaming out how much they loved James a way to revisit their heyday? Did they all miss their younger days as much as she did? If only Darbi's crazy story were true, she would go back to being twenty-four again right now. "If you could redo a part of your life, would you?" she asked.

"No way," Kendra said. "The best is yet to come."

Mary missed believing the best was still in front of her. Kendra had so much to look forward to—building her career, getting married, having children. Every day she lived with the excitement of wondering how her life would turn out. She had plenty of possibilities. Mary, on the other hand, had no possibilities. She knew exactly how her life had turned out. Not at all as she'd planned. If everything had gone how she'd wanted it to, she'd be on the cover of that magazine, not Liz.

"Speaking of 'the best is yet to come,'" Kendra said, "I have some exciting news, but I'm afraid of how you're going to react."

"Oh my God, you're pregnant." Mary would have preferred Kendra to be married before having kids, but her daughter did seem to be in love with her current beau, Nate. They would figure it out. She tried to imagine herself holding her grandchild. Her neck stiffened. She wasn't sure she was ready for that. Not yet. It would mean she was old enough to be a grandmother. A grandmother!

Kendra laughed. "I'm definitely not pregnant, Mom."

"Whew." Mary relaxed. "Then what's the news?"

"The ad agency is opening a new branch. They asked me to manage it."

"Oh, honey, that's wonderful. Congratulations." Mary wrapped her arm around her daughter's shoulders and pulled her closer. "Why would you be worried about how I would react to that?"

Kendra swallowed hard. "The job's in London."

Mary's stomach roiled. She swore she could hear all those drinks from the night before sloshing around down there.

"It's a great opportunity. A lot more money."

"You're moving to England?" Kendra lived only a little more than thirty minutes away now, and Mary rarely saw her. If she moved overseas, they would never see each other.

"I'll be a plane ride away. Dad's already planning a trip. He wants to spend time in Ireland too. There are a bunch of courses he wants to play there."

"Your father knows about this?" Mary's skin prickled as she imagined Kendra telling Dean as they drove around the golf course in one of those silly little carts.

Kendra's cheeks reddened. "I told him last weekend at the club."

"He's known for a week?"

Kendra licked her lips.

A young dad with a baby strapped to his chest and holding his wife's hand approached from the other direction. The man and woman both smiled at Mary. She watched them until they'd passed by. "What about Nate? I thought you really liked him."

"He encouraged me to apply."

Of course he did, Mary thought, remembering Nate telling her his parents were originally from the London area, Tottenham. Nate's mother and younger sister had moved back a few years ago, after his father's death. How could she have forgotten? Well, maybe because with his blond hair and blue eyes, Nate reminded her of the traditional all-American boy next door. "He's moving back and asked you to go with him. That's why you applied for the job."

"I love him, Mom."

"When are you leaving?"

"June tenth."

Mary felt her body go rigid. "That's next week."

Kendra placed a hand on Mary's shoulder but didn't say anything else.

"Let's turn around. I'm not feeling well." Mary reversed direction without waiting for Kendra, walking at twice the speed she had on the way out. Kendra was moving to London. No doubt she'd marry Nate. They'd have beautiful children together, whom they would raise in Bexley or Chiswick or some other posh London suburb. Mary's grandchildren would have proper British accents. She would never see them. They wouldn't know her. A moment before, she'd wanted no part of being a grandmother, but now she mourned not being able to spend time with her adorable imaginary grandchildren with the English accents.

Mary and Kendra walked in silence until they reached the top of the stairs to the deck in Mary's backyard. "Do you not want me to go?" Kendra asked.

Mary froze. *No, I do not want you to go.* Her throat burned the way it always did before she cried. She looked up at the cloudless sky. If she told Kendra to stay, her daughter would end up resenting her. Besides, Mary knew what it was like to give up your dream, so she'd always encouraged her daughter to follow hers. She couldn't stop now, no matter how much it would hurt not to have Kendra nearby. She couldn't be that selfish. She swallowed hard. "I want you to be happy."

Kendra embraced her mother. Mary clung to her tightly, wishing she could hold on forever.

～

From the living room where she was watching television, Mary heard the garage door rumble open. She ran to the breezeway. Dean slunk in. After a day in the sun, his face and arms were a bronzy gold.

Mary watched him with her hand on her hip.

He yawned and stretched. "I played like crap today."

"I can't believe you didn't tell me about Kendra."

He turned his back to her to hang his fob on the wall hook.

She fought the urge to grab him by the shoulders and shake him. "You've known for a week." His not telling her made her feel like an outsider in her own family. Did he and Kendra have other secrets?

Dean let out a deep breath and turned toward her again. He picked up his baseball cap from the bench. "Realized I didn't have this with me right after I got on the highway. I should have circled back to get it. I played awful without it."

"How could you not tell me?"

"I had to take a provisional off the first tee." He shook his head. "Knew it would be a long day after that."

Mary ripped the hat from his hands and flung it toward the bench. "Our daughter is moving to London."

Dean watched his hat sail through the air with a shocked expression. He exhaled loudly and softened his voice. "She asked me not to tell you. Swear to God." Using his index finger, he drew a cross over his heart after he spoke, something he always did when he said the word "God." "She knew you'd be upset and wanted to talk to you about it herself."

"Why would she think I'd be upset?"

Dean raised an eyebrow.

Well, of course she was upset. What mother wouldn't be? "Did you try to talk her out of it?"

He scrubbed his hand over his jaw. He hadn't shaved that morning, and Mary noticed several gray hairs mixed in with the dark ones.

"Of course not. It's a great opportunity."

A great opportunity. A flash of pain streaked through Mary's mouth so sharp that she flinched.

Dean stepped toward her. "Are you okay?"

As quickly as the pain had come, it subsided, and she dismissed him with a wave of her hand. "She's moving there because of Nate, not the job. She admitted as much to me."

Dean nodded.

Something about the casualness of his gesture irked her, as if it were no big deal that their daughter was willing to uproot her life and move to another country, another continent, for Nate, a boy she'd known for only a few months. Mary's dissatisfaction with Dean had boiled into anger, and now she understood the root cause of that anger. It wasn't because he'd skipped dinner to practice putting. It wasn't because he'd stood her up for James's show. It wasn't even because he hadn't told her about Kendra's plans to move. Darbi had stirred those old feelings of resentment Mary had tamped down long ago, when Dean refused to go to Iowa with her. There was no reason he didn't go other than he didn't love her enough.

"You refused to come to Iowa."

Dean blinked and stared at her with a confused expression.

"You wouldn't move to Iowa with me." She said it louder this time, and her voice broke.

"What's in Iowa?"

She gasped and her hand flew to her chest. "My. Great. Opportunity."

"What are you talking about?"

Mary's nostrils flared. She bared her teeth. How could he not remember that she'd sacrificed her career for him? "I could be America's most trusted newscaster."

Dean rubbed the back of his neck. "You're talking about the broadcasting job in that rinky-dink town in the middle of nowhere?"

"The CBS affiliate."

"You turned it down because you didn't want to move away from your family and friends."

"I said no because of you."

"I encouraged you to take the job."

"But you wouldn't come with me."

"You never asked."

"You knew I wanted you to come."

The cords in Dean's neck bulged. "Why are we talking about this now? It was so long ago."

"Because Liz took the job, and now look at her."

Dean's eyes widened, and he slowly shook his head. "You think you'd have Liz's job today if you took that job?" He spoke much slower than usual.

Mary balled her hands into tight fists. "I'm better than her. That's why they offered the job to me first."

Dean put up his hand. "You were better than her at the time, but Liz has improved through the years." He yawned, his mouth hanging open for several seconds. "I'm too tired to talk about this now." He squeezed her shoulder as he passed her on the way to the stairs. A few minutes later the shower came on.

Mary's wisdom teeth throbbed. Her heart raced. She took long deep breaths to try to calm down. If only Darbi's story were true. She'd go back and do it over again. She'd show him she was still better than Liz.

Chapter 5

Usually Mary enjoyed hosting parties, but she dreaded today's barbecue. It was a bon voyage party for Kendra. Mary suspected the only reason Kendra had been willing to make time for the cookout was because it was Dean's idea. He seized any opportunity to show off his mammoth grill. Soon after he'd bought it, she'd overheard him telling his brother about it on the phone. "Six burners, a smoker box, and a built-in refrigerator. A real bad boy." As he went on and on about the grill's attributes, Mary had watched him with a bemused expression. "What?" he'd asked after he hung up.

"Honestly, the way you boast about that thing, I'd think you'd given birth to it."

"That thing? His name is Gus, and I just about did give birth to him." He'd needed three weeks to put the grill together. In the end, Rick had come over to help because Jenni was tired of listening to Dean complain about how hard it was to assemble every time she came over to see Mary.

Now, Dean stood in front of it, wielding tongs in one hand and a giant metal spatula in the other. Smoke billowed through the backyard, carrying the scent of mesquite-flavored steak tips, burgers, and chicken. The guests stood in small groups, laughing and clutching red Solo cups filled with sangria.

Surrounded by friends, Mary should have been happy, but she felt the burning in her throat that let her know she was on the verge of tears.

She glanced down at Kendra, who was talking with her girlfriends and Nate. They stood in a circle on the side lawn in the shade provided by the maple tree that Dean had planted the day Kendra was born. In all the years since, they had called it "Kendra's tree." Mary's eyes watered. She'd already broken down crying three times today.

Her outbursts weren't only because she'd miss her daughter. She was mourning the past she'd never had.

Ever since Darbi's crazy story and her night out with James, Mary couldn't stop wishing she could be in her twenties again. She wanted to be younger, with most of her life in front of her rather than behind her. For a moment, she let herself imagine today was thirty years ago and that the cookout was for her. She was leaving for Iowa the next day. She pictured herself at the airport. In her mind, she saw Dean running through the terminal and finding her just before she slipped through the gate to board her flight. "Of course I'm coming with you." He picked her up and spun her around. She felt herself smiling.

A burst of laughter by the grill jarred Mary from her daydream. Dean's brother, Anthony, the head pro at Addison Heights Golf Club, and his latest girlfriend, a curvy young blonde in a skort with a ball-shaped bulge in her pocket, sleeveless top, and a visor, were talking to Dean. The young woman had clearly come straight from the golf course, and Dean stared at her with a goofy expression as if he were in a trance.

Mary trudged up the stairs of the deck, trying to remember the last time her husband had looked at her—or anything other than a great golf shot—like that. Maybe if she dressed in cute golf outfits and carried a seven iron around the house, Dean would look at her the same way. She stepped between Dean and Anthony's girlfriend, mostly to give the girl breathing room. Dean was practically standing on top of her. "I'm Mary."

"Jessica."

"Jessica has a ten handicap." Dean grinned like a horny teenager meeting a pinup model. "A ten."

Jessica reached around Mary to touch his arm. "We should play together sometime."

"Let's do it," Dean said. "I'll make a tee time for tomorrow."

Mary elbowed him. "We're taking Kendra to the airport tomorrow."

"Another time then," Dean said.

The scent of patchouli and tangerine floated in the air. A moment later, Darbi's jovial voice called out, "Drumroll, please. Darbi and Jacqui Mulligan have arrived."

Mary watched as they climbed the stairs to the deck. They were a most unlikely couple, Darbi with her pale freckled skin and Jacqui with her rich dark complexion, Darbi with her crazy gray cornrows, and Jacqui with her stylish textured pixie, Darbi with her tie-dyed T-shirt and khaki shorts, and Jacqui in a designer yellow sundress.

When the two women reached the top stair, Darbi thrust a tin-foil-covered paper plate at Mary. "We brought brownies."

Mary cocked her head. "Are they special brownies?"

"Try one and find out." Darbi winked.

Jacqui put a reassuring hand on Mary's elbow. "They're fine. I made them myself."

Kendra and Nate joined the crowd on the deck. Kendra hugged Darbi and then Jacqui. "I swear you get more beautiful every time I see you," Jacqui said.

Dean wrapped an arm around Mary. "She looks just like her mom at that age."

That's a lie, Mary thought, but still she smiled. At the most unexpected times, her husband of almost three decades resembled her young groom, which made staying angry at him difficult.

When the food was ready, Mary led the guests to tables set up under a canopy on the lawn.

"Dean, you're an amazing chef," Jessica said.

Dean puffed out his chest. "When you have a great helper like Gus, it's easy."

"Who's Gus?" Anthony asked.

"Dean named the grill." By the way Mary said the words, everyone knew she thought naming a grill was ridiculous.

"It's not just any grill," Dean said. "It's the crown jewel of grills."

"Must have been a beast to assemble," Nate said.

"You have no idea." Dean launched into a story about how he'd struggled to put it together. With his thumb and index finger, he demonstrated how short some of the screws were. "And there were—"

"Kendra," Anthony cut in. "Tell us about your new job and where you'll be living."

A ray of sunlight struck the top of Kendra's head, and she appeared to be glowing. "We're opening a new office in Canary Wharf. I'm responsible for managing it, scheduling projects, keeping it organized, ordering office supplies, overseeing the administrative staff."

Mary watched her daughter with a sense of pride. Kendra had inherited the best parts of her and Dean and none of their faults. She had Mary's big heart and Dean's sense of adventure. Her face, mouth, and eyes were the same shapes as Mary's, but she had Dean's Sicilian coloring. Like him and his family, she talked with her hands. She motioned with them now, imitating the queen's wave, and like a sucker punch to her gut, Mary realized again that Kendra was moving to another country, a different continent. Would Nate know how to make chicken soup with acini di pepe when Kendra got a bad cold? If he made it with rice instead of the pasta, she would refuse to eat it. Would he make sure she kept an emergency twenty dollars in the glove box of her car and didn't spend it on coffee? Would he turn up the radio and sing along with her when Taylor Swift's "You Belong with Me" came on the radio? Would he remind her to call home?

From across the table, Darbi winked at Mary, pulling her from her thoughts. Today was the first time the two women had seen each other since their lunch. Mary wondered what had ever possessed Darbi to make up that story about Mulligan magic.

I should have my wisdom teeth out on the off chance the story is true.

The thought popped into her head without warning. She batted it down, unable to believe she'd given any credence to the possibility that she could erase years off her life by having her wisdom teeth extracted. The sangria must have been stronger than Dean usually made it.

Her skin began to tingle. She felt grossly hot. Sweat streamed down her back. Perspiration pooled above her lips. She mopped her forehead with a napkin.

"Are you okay?" Jessica asked.

All the guests turned toward Mary. She brought her hand to her chest as her heartbeat accelerated. *Damn hot flash.* "I'm fine."

"You don't look fine. You're flushed," Kendra said.

Everyone stopped speaking. Chirping birds made the only sounds in the backyard.

Mary managed a smile. "I said I'm fine."

She wasn't fine, though. This particular hot flash was not a flash at all. It felt more like a prolonged wildfire. Jessica, Kendra, and Kendra's friends stared at her. *Yes, ladies, this is what you have to look forward to. So, enjoy your youth while you can.*

Mary had to get out of there. She rose from her seat like an erupting volcano. "I'm getting some ice water. Does anyone need anything?" Without waiting for an answer, she sprinted toward the house. Halfway across the lawn, her foot got caught on a tree root. She fell, scraping her knee on the ground.

She pushed herself up to a sitting position. Blood dripped down her shin. Footsteps raced toward her. Dean lifted her to her feet and escorted her to the house. Inside the quiet sunroom away from the wide-eyed stares of her guests, she broke down in tears.

"Poor baby," Dean said, wrapping her in a tight hug.

She knew he was trying to be sweet. Any other time she would have taken comfort in his embrace, but for the past few weeks, she'd felt imprisoned by the choices she'd made long ago. Today, as they celebrated Kendra's departure, those feelings of imprisonment were peaking, so she pushed herself away from Dean, not wanting to be held in place, and sank into the love seat.

Dean sighed and left the room. He returned with a facecloth wrapped over ice and held it to Mary's knee. "What's going on?"

Her chin trembled as she answered. "How is this my life?" She buried her face in her hands. "How is this my life?" she asked again.

"What's wrong with your life?"

"I'm fifty-four years old. How did I get to be fifty-four?"

Dean scratched his head. Water from the melting ice dripped on the tiled floor.

"I was just twenty-two," Mary continued. "Moving into my first apartment, with my whole life in front of me."

"Kendra's just a plane ride away."

Mary used the back of her hand to wipe away the tears running down her cheeks.

"That's what this is about, right?" Dean asked. "Kendra leaving?"

"How am I old enough to have a daughter who's old enough to move away? I was just hosting birthday parties for her at Roller Kingdom."

Dean chewed on his lower lip.

"Yoo-hoo!" Darbi's voice drifted in through the screen door seconds before it slid open. "Go join the guests. I'll stay here with Mary."

Dean nodded and raced out of the house as if it were on fire.

His quick escape didn't surprise Mary. She was so cranky these days that she irritated even herself. She needed to mix things up. She needed something to look forward to.

Darbi plopped down in the recliner across from Mary. "It's a hard time with Kendra leaving, but don't make any rash decisions."

"Like what?"

"Like having your wisdom teeth out. The pain will subside when you stop thinking about your regrets."

"Today's not the day for a crazy story."

Darbi picked up a throw pillow and hugged it to her chest. "I know it's hard to believe, but Mulligan magic is real."

"Stop."

"Why would I make up something like that?"

"You tell me."

Laughter from the guests outside drifted in through the sliding screen door.

"I wouldn't. I'm not that imaginative. I'm telling you, it happened to me. Just before I left Ireland."

Mary's mouth throbbed, and despite what Darbi said, she doubted her wisdom teeth would stop hurting without medical intervention. The Mulligan magic story was utter nonsense, but for a little while, Mary could pretend it was true. Thinking she could be twenty-four again might even lift her out of her funk, and it would certainly give her the courage she needed to make an appointment with Dr. Montari. She sprang to her feet, forgetting all about her sore knee. "I'm calling the dentist Monday morning."

"Listen to me," Darbi said, but whatever else she was about to say, Mary didn't hear. She raced out the door to join the other guests.

Chapter 6

In the car on the way to the dentist's office on Wednesday morning, the earliest they could get her in, Mary tried calling Kendra. She'd left messages on Monday and Tuesday, but Kendra had never returned them. Instead of being worried, Mary simmered with anger because Kendra had spoken to Dean both days while he was at work.

At the sound of Kendra's outgoing message now, she slammed her phone down. It fell off the passenger seat, landing on the floor mat below her.

Dean glanced at her, dropping his hand from the steering wheel to her thigh to soothe her. "Don't be mad. It's just the time difference."

"She has no trouble finding time to talk to you."

"Only because she needed money."

Mary should have been grateful for his white lie, but it outraged her that Dean had to make excuses for their daughter. Clearly, Kendra didn't want to talk to her.

"We'll call from my phone when we get to the dentist."

His words were like a sucker punch to her gut because they confirmed her worst suspicion. "So you do think she's intentionally avoiding my calls."

Dean lowered his window, even though the air conditioner blasted cool air on them.

"Is she mad at me?" Mary asked.

He twisted in his seat as if trying to work out a kink in his back.

Mary turned off the radio. "What did she say?" There was no point in asking if Kendra had said something to him. Mary knew she had by Dean's constant fidgeting. He leaned his shoulder against the driver's door as if he were trying to bump it open so he could roll out to the street and avoid this conversation.

"You might want to give her a little space." It was his gentle tone, the one he used to break bad news.

"Give her space? She's an ocean away."

"She just . . ." He rubbed his temple. "Don't smother her right now is all. Let her get settled and used to being there."

"She said I smother her?"

He stepped on the gas as if he could race away from this conversation. "That's my word, not hers."

The hurt and angry feelings festering in Mary ever since she'd learned Kendra was moving exploded, and the shrapnel pummeled Dean. "Smother" was not his word. It was Kendra's. Mary was furious at him for lying, even if his fib was intended to spare her feelings. How dare her husband and daughter talk about her parenting style behind her back. "She can have all the space she needs. I won't call her again. The two of you can talk all you want. When you visit her, I'll stay here."

Dean turned into the dentist's parking lot without letting up on the accelerator. The car's tires squealed. Momentum threw Mary against the door. Her elbow banged against the door handle, triggering her funny bone. A vibration-like feeling shot down her arm into her fingers.

Instead of parking, Dean brought the car to a stop in front of the entrance. "Call me when you're done."

Mary knew he'd had enough of this conversation. Of course he'd realized she was bluffing. She'd never refuse to talk to Kendra or stay behind if Dean went to visit her. She'd said those things to make him understand she was hurt, to try to persuade him to take her side instead of Kendra's for once.

"Aren't you coming in with me?" This probably wasn't the best time to pick a fight with him. She usually didn't mind going to medical appointments by herself, but today she wanted someone with her. Between the dentist's reaction when he'd seen her wisdom teeth erupting to Darbi's outlandish story about Mulligan magic, everything about this procedure seemed out of the ordinary.

Dean pointed across the street to the sign for the driving range. "I thought I'd hit a bucket of balls while I wait."

Mary pushed open the passenger door without saying anything. Dean grabbed her arm. She thought he'd changed his mind or would at least wish her good luck. "Don't forget your phone." He reached toward the floor to retrieve it.

"If you call Kendra while I'm in there, don't tell her about our conversation. Don't mention me at all."

"Come on, Mary. You're being too sensitive."

"I mean it." She slammed the door and huffed up the stairs to the entrance. Before walking into the building, she glanced back at Dean. He gave her a small wave, but his furrowed forehead let Mary know he thought she was overreacting.

∽

Mary's leg bounced up and down as she waited in the reception area. Maybe she shouldn't go through with this. She could manage her tooth pain with Orajel or Anbesol. To distract herself and forget about the procedure and the fact that her daughter had complained to Dean that she was smothering her, Mary pretended Darbi's story was true. She imagined what she would do if she woke up from the procedure thirty years younger.

She'd start by visiting one of her old haunts, Clarke's Bar and Restaurant in Faneuil Hall. *Is that place even still around?* In her twenties, she and her friends had spent most Saturday nights sitting at the bar there. She'd had such a crush on the bartender, Eoin, with his ginger hair and freckled skin. He spoke with a brogue that had turned Mary into a puddle.

Her phone vibrated with a text message.

Darbi: Mulligan magic is real. Don't get your wisdom teeth out.

Mary sighed and tapped out a response. I've never been so excited about a dentist appointment.

Her cell shook again, this time with a phone call from Darbi. She eyed the sign above the reception desk asking patients to turn their cell phones off while in the office and hit the red ignore button.

A moment later, another text came in. Remember you always used to tease me for forgetting how old I am?

Mary slid her phone into her pocket. She wanted to go back to daydreaming about cute bartenders and being in her twenties, but her cousin's last text gnawed at her. Darbi did get confused about her age. Unlike many women who claimed to be younger than they were, Darbi claimed to be older. When she'd moved to the States, she'd told everyone she was thirty-two. One day Mary saw her passport and discovered Darbi was really twenty-five, the same age as her. Mary asked Darbi why she'd lied about her age. Darbi had paused for an uncomfortable minute, wringing her hands. Then she'd grinned. "I look amazing for thirty-two. Not so much for twenty-five."

The receptionist called Mary's name. She grabbed her purse and followed the woman. Her entire body hummed. Could Darbi's story be true? Of course not. Her nerves about this procedure were making her loopy. Music played in the hallway, Laura Branigan singing "How Am I Supposed to Live without You." To calm her nerves, Mary softly sang along. She'd always loved this song.

In the exam room, Lindsey and Dr. Montari both greeted her with enthusiastic smiles. Mary didn't smile back. Her stomach twisted and turned as she climbed into the chair. She wiped her sweaty palms on her jeans. The shiny silver dental instruments gleamed on the tray in front of her, reminding her of the unused tools on Dean's dusty workbench in the basement. She stared at the forceps and imagined Dr. Montari using them with the same ineptitude that Dean used pliers. She flinched as if she could feel the pain.

I should leave now.

On the ceiling, a few of the tiles had been replaced with a mural of a hot-air balloon floating through a cloudless bright-blue sky. Thinking about being in that balloon made her more nervous. She was terrified of heights.

"Are you ready?" Lindsey asked. Without waiting for an answer, the girl lowered the chair until Mary was practically upside down. Blood rushed to her head, and her knuckles turned bright white as she hung on to the armrests for dear life. "Bring me up. Now!"

As Lindsey raised the chair, she and Dr. Montari exchanged a look.

"I'm going to give you a little something to help you relax," Dr. Montari said.

Yes, bring on the drugs, please.

He picked up a needle and began to fiddle with it. "There's nothing to worry about. You'll take a nap. When you wake up, your wisdom teeth will be gone, and you'll feel as good as new."

Mary took a deep breath in and closed her eyes. She'd never been the best patient.

A needle pricked her arm. "Count backward from ten," Dr. Montari said.

Her muscles loosened as she counted. The balloon floated across the sky. Mary felt as if she were riding in it. The Laura Branigan song ended, and now REO Speedwagon sang about not being able to fight a feeling. Mary had loved this song back in high school too. She was surprised music from the eighties was playing in this office with all the young people, but then she realized they'd probably put the oldies station on for her.

Something was burning. *Is the office on fire? No, it's my mouth.* Her gums radiated heat. Her tongue tasted like singed popcorn. Her skin itched where the needle had poked it. She tried to scratch the spot but couldn't lift her arm. A force held her back. The chair spun in circles around the room, each revolution bigger than the last. She thought about one of her first dates with Dean. They had gone to a carnival set up in a grocery store parking lot, and she had thrown up all over him on the Tilt-A-Whirl. She didn't think he'd ever call her again. When he did call, she knew their relationship had staying power.

Dr. Montari said something. He sounded as if he were in a wind tunnel, and she couldn't make out the words. She tried to speak. Her jaw wouldn't move. She tried to open her eyes, but it was as if elephants were sitting on her eyelids. REO Speedwagon stopped singing, and Mary could no longer fight the feeling.

Chapter 7

A loud beeping woke Mary. Her jaw ached, and there was a terrible taste in her mouth. *What happened to me?* She turned toward Dean's side of the bed and jolted upright. Not only was he not lying beside her, but the mattress was much smaller than her California queen. This wasn't her bed. She jumped up and looked around. *Where am I?* Her mind felt groggy, making it impossible to think clearly.

A sense of déjà vu overwhelmed her. She'd been here before. Maybe? The light-gray walls didn't jibe with her memory. They'd been eggshell the last time she was here. The gingham-striped blackout curtains had been sheer pink panels, and the hardwood floor had been a dingy oatmeal-colored carpet. The layout of the space was the same, though. Sloped ceiling, windows on the walls to the left and right of the bed, and a tiny closet on the opposite wall.

Outside, clanking metal replaced the beeping. A dumpster being emptied? Yes, that annoying commotion had woken her every Wednesday morning for the four years she'd lived in the apartment in Framingham. Why was she dreaming about her old apartment? Maybe because she'd seen James recently?

The last thing she remembered was Dean dropping her off at the dentist. She rolled her tongue over the empty sockets in the back of her mouth, and Darbi's crazy story came rushing back. That's why she was dreaming about the place she'd lived in during her early twenties. The thought bothered her. It seemed too reasonable for a dream. She raced across the room toward the mirror. When she saw her old, or rather young, face staring back, she blinked hard and leaned closer to the image. *This is not possible?* She squeezed her eyes shut and opened them again. Her crow's-feet had vanished. Her forehead was unlined. Her laugh lines weren't as deep. Thick golden-brown hair without a strand of gray hung to her shoulders. Her neck was smooth. Even her teeth were whiter.

"No, no, no. This can't be." Her heart thumped, and she couldn't catch her breath. A panic attack! She hadn't had one in so long. They'd plagued her through her early twenties but had stopped after she'd married Dean.

Dean! She glanced down at her hand. Her wedding ring was gone. Instead of her usual french manicure, her fingernails were painted an aqua blue. A fitness tracker around her wrist had replaced the silver Cartier watch Dean had given her on their tenth anniversary. She pressed a button on the Fitbit's side, and the device lit up, revealing it was ten o'clock on Wednesday, June 12, the exact day, time, and year of her appointment to have her wisdom teeth removed.

She couldn't swallow, and pain streaked across her chest. *Calm down. It's only a dream.* She took a deep breath in through her mouth and slowly released it through her nose. Usually dreams had at least one bizarre element that made no sense. She had to find something nonsensical to let her know this was a dream. She would look out the window and see a Caribbean beach instead of a street in Framingham. *Yes, that's it.* She pushed back the curtain. There was no ocean or sand, just the plaza with the pizza shop, drugstore, and bank that had stood there for years. She watched as the garbage truck that had emptied the dumpster pulled out into traffic.

Maybe a group of penguins would be camped out on the sofa, watching television. *Yes, that would be crazy.* She left the bedroom, headed down the hall, and descended the three small steps into the sunken living room. A sofa, coffee table, and television crowded the area. She didn't remember the space being so small, but maybe she'd been spoiled by the Wang Theatre–size living room in her and Dean's Hudson home.

The first time she'd moved into this place, she had swelled with pride when she signed the lease—$325 a month, a bargain because it was an attic apartment with a thirty-eight-step wooden staircase leading to its only entrance. Still, it was her very own home. She'd finally felt like a grown-up. Why in the world had she been in such a rush to become an adult?

Her stomach growled. *Is it possible to have hunger pangs in a dream?*

The kitchen walls had a fresh coat of gray paint, the cabinets had been refaced with cherry stain, and the appliances were modern versions of the older ones that she had used when she'd lived here. She rubbed her temples. This dream was more logical than any other one she'd ever had. Memories washed over her as she ran her hand over the dark-gray laminate countertops. Her parents had been alive when she'd lived here. Once a month on Sundays, she'd make them brunch, usually coconut-encrusted french toast with hash browns but sometimes omelets with sourdough toast. It wasn't the food that was special about those mornings. No, it was the stories her parents had shared about their lives. She'd learned so much about them after she'd grown up and moved out of her childhood home. Her mom had been a high school track star, and her dad had been president of the student council and voted most likely to succeed. They'd stopped coming to Mary's apartment after her father's stroke because he could no longer climb the long staircase that led to her door. Her eyes filled with tears. If she was dreaming she was young again, why couldn't it be the 1990s, when her parents were still alive?

A red wristlet resting on the kitchen table caught her attention, and she rushed across the room to examine it. When she unzipped it, credit cards, coins, and dollar bills spilled out onto the floor. As she gathered them, on one of the plastic cards she noticed the blue-and-white logo of Channel 77, the Independent Cable News Network, along with a picture of the face she'd just seen in the mirror. For a long moment, she studied the photo.

She looked like she was trying to stop herself from laughing. When she was really twenty-four, every time she'd looked at her picture or reflection, she'd found faults with herself. Her eyes were too close together. She had a horrible cowlick. Her pores were like sinkholes. Her lips were too puffy. Looking at this picture of her young face now, her fifty-four-year-old brain realized that twenty-something Mary had been beautiful. She even thought she resembled Olivia Wilde. Yes, she most definitely did.

Her eyes moved from the image of her young self to the name on the card, Mary Mulligan. She'd been Mary Amato for so long that seeing her maiden name was like seeing the name of an old friend she'd lost touch with and couldn't wait to reconnect with.

The last name Mulligan also made her think of Darbi. Was it possible she'd been telling the truth? No! Of course not. But holy moly, if this wasn't a dream . . .

That badge must mean she worked for Channel 77. She laughed out loud, not believing she was actually considering that this all might be real and not a drug-induced dream in the dentist's chair. But oh, if it was real, she could change her entire life, wipe away all her regrets. She'd be the best reporter to have ever worked for the Independent Cable News Network. Everywhere she went, people would know her and rave about her work. The station would offer her a promotion. This time she'd accept it, and the entire trajectory of her life would change. She'd return to her fifty-four-year-old self as the country's most trusted broadcaster, working for ABC or NBC. Liz could keep her job at CBS. Mary wanted to knock off one of the men so two women would be anchoring the nightly news. Dean could compare her with Liz in real time, watching Mary on the television and Liz on his laptop, or maybe using that screen-within-a-screen feature with Mary on the larger screen. He'd see she was better.

Outside, a motorcycle drove by, startling her. The sound had been so lifelike. Usually loud sounds in dreams woke her. Not this time. Maybe this wasn't a dream. She didn't know whether to celebrate or curl into a fetal position and hide under the table. She would do neither. Instead, she'd find her cousin so Darbi could explain what was going on.

Chapter 8

A Toyota key hung from a hook by the door. Mary grabbed it and hurried down the long narrow wooden staircase outside her apartment, feeling lighter on her feet than she had in decades. A light-blue Corolla with a Channel 77 parking permit stuck to the windshield was parked behind the house. She'd had an older version of that same vehicle the first time she was in her twenties, and seeing the newer model in the driveway gave her the same off-kilter feeling she'd had inside the apartment.

She steered the car down the street toward Darbi's. As she turned onto Old Connecticut Path and crossed the bridge over the Mass Pike, her heart pounded. What if in this dream—or whatever it was—Darbi didn't live nearby? Mary's throat went dry. She reached for a can of diet soda in the cup holder and broke out in a coughing fit as the hot flat cola slid down her throat. *How long has that been there?* The light turned green. Her foot shook as she stepped on the gas. *Please let Darbi be there. Please.* She chanted it in her head until she turned onto her cousin's street.

Everything about Darbi's Campanelli ranch looked exactly as it did in Mary's real life. The house was painted a turquoise color better suited for the Southwest than New England, pink and white daisies bordered the crushed-stone walkway, and a rainbow flag flew above the mailbox. Darbi's yellow Volkswagen Bug was even backed into its usual spot in front of the garage with the top down.

The sound of Steely Dan's song "Do It Again" drifted out of the backyard. Mary sprinted across the freshly mowed lawn toward the music. With each step, she expected her knees to creak and her feet to protest in pain, but they didn't. She unlatched the fence and pushed open the gate. "Darbi, Darbi!" They were the first words she'd spoken out loud since waking up young, and she barely recognized the perky, high voice as her own.

Wearing a reddish-orange bikini and an enormous sun hat, Darbi floated on an inflatable unicorn in the in-ground pool. "Who's here?"

Mary rushed toward the diving board. "Mary."

Darbi sprang up to a sitting position and pulled off her sunglasses. For a moment, she sat perfectly still. Her lips quivered. She laughed, softly and controlled at first, but her laugh soon erupted into a roar. Mary knew it was Darbi's nervous laugh, the inappropriate one that sometimes slipped out at funerals or whenever she was uncomfortable. The fact that she was laughing that way now made Mary think Darbi had been telling the truth and that, by having her wisdom teeth removed, Mary had entered an alternate world where she was twenty-four again. No, what was she thinking? That wasn't possible.

Darbi slipped off the unicorn into the water. Her hat drifted away, leaving her gray cornrows bobbing on the surface. Her arms and legs fluttered as she dog-paddled to the pool's steps and reached for a towel.

She waited until she dried herself off before speaking. "I really wish you had listened to me."

Mary drew in a deep breath. "This is a dream. It has to be." She sank into a lounge chair, realizing—too late—its cushions were wet. The back of her sundress got soaked. *Would I be able to feel the wetness if this were a dream?* She slapped her face, hoping the slap would wake her. Her skin stung, but she was still in the lounge chair by Darbi's pool. She whacked herself again, harder.

"What in the world are you doing?" Darbi's shadow grew larger as she approached Mary's chair.

"Trying to wake myself up from this dream."

Standing in front of Mary now, Darbi unwound the towel from around her waist and snapped it against Mary's bare legs.

"Ouch." Mary rubbed her stinging skin.

"You felt that because this isn't a dream. It happened because you had your wisdom teeth removed." Darbi squeezed her eyes closed and shook both fists in the air. "I warned you not to get your teeth out. Why didn't you listen?"

The strong scent of chlorine coming off Darbi made Mary's nose itch. She sneezed. "I entered an alternate universe where I'm young again because I had my wisdom teeth out?"

Darbi's face was tight with anguish. "You erased the last thirty years of your life is what you did."

The air in the backyard seemed to thicken, and Mary struggled to breathe. "Tell me exactly what's going on."

"I can't explain it any better than that." Her entire body shook.

"Try."

Darbi took a long, calming breath. "It's . . . ah, geez. We need alcohol for this." Her flip-flops slapped against her heels as she made her way to the pool bar. "Run inside and get the chips and salsa."

Mary's legs felt weak as she stood. She didn't want food and drinks. She wanted to know what was going on. Inside, a photo hanging on the sunroom's wall of her sitting alone on a large boulder brought her to a dead stop. For over a decade, a picture of her, Dean, and Kendra standing beneath the marquee for *Beauty and the Beast* at the Boston Opera House had hung in that exact spot. A chill ran down her spine. If she was twenty-four again, what had happened to Kendra and Dean in this universe?

By the time she returned with the snack, Darbi was perched on a barstool sipping a giant strawberry margarita. A full glass rested in front of the empty stool next to her, and the scent of patchouli hung in the air. Mary placed the bowls of chips and salsa between her cousin and herself. "Tell me what's going on." Her words came out in a rush.

Darbi pointed to the drink. With a shaky hand, Mary lifted the glass by its cactus-shaped stem. The thick, creamy red liquid spilled over the edges onto the bar top as she sipped. The spicy tequila burned her throat. She lowered her drink toward the coaster, but Darbi slid a hand under the bottom of the glass and pushed it up. "You're going to need more."

Mary emptied half her cup. Darbi began, her voice a hoarse whisper: "The last thirty years of your life have been erased."

The hot sun beat down on the back of Mary's head. Sweat rolled down her neck. Her brain felt as if it were on fire, about to explode. She didn't know what she'd expected Darbi to say, but she wanted to hear something that made sense. Then again, how could anyone make sense of this? "What do you mean?"

"I don't know how else to explain it."

"What happened to my other life?"

Darbi sighed and looked toward the fence separating her yard from the neighbor's, where a bronze sun sculpture hung. She stirred her drink with her straw and slowly turned back to Mary. "The last thirty years of the life you knew never happened." Darbi paused and placed her hand over Mary's as if she was trying to comfort her. When she spoke again, sorrow tinged her voice. "None of it."

Something about Darbi's touch and the way she'd said those last three words chilled Mary to the core. She folded her arms across her chest and rocked back and forth, trying to warm herself. In her mind, she heard Father Carbone announce her and Dean as man and wife, felt the weight of Kendra in her arms in the delivery room. Her eyes welled up with happy tears as she remembered those life-changing occasions. Of course the last thirty years of her life had happened. "If it never happened, why do I remember everything so clearly?"

Darbi reached for the pitcher and topped off their glasses. "I don't know. The memories are what make this painful, make it a curse sometimes instead of a blessing."

Mary wanted to ask Darbi what she meant by a curse, but the words stuck to the roof of her mouth. She was afraid to ask. She stared into her drink, trying to remember the woman she'd been before meeting Dean. An insecure girl, struggling to find herself in the world. She'd fit perfectly by his side and in the family they'd created together. If she'd never married him, then Kendra wouldn't exist and Mary would have missed out on the purest, most all-encompassing form of love known, and the world would have been cheated out of the most compassionate person Mary had ever met.

"When it happened to me, the only people who remembered my other life were me and Uncle Cillian," Darbi said. "I expect you and I will be the only ones with memories of your past."

Mary couldn't focus. The harder she tried to concentrate, the more confused she became. She wasn't sure if the hot sun, the alcohol, the bizarre situation, or all three were to blame. The only thing she knew was that what Darbi was saying was entirely impossible. Years couldn't be erased from a life. Those drugs Dr. Montari had injected into her vein must be causing her to hallucinate. She stood and stretched, trying to clear her mind. Returning to her stool, she decided to poke holes in Darbi's story, prove this was all a dream. Like earlier, her rationality frightened her. She wouldn't be so reasonable if this was a dream.

"What about your parents? They must have noticed you were younger."

"They never saw me after I had my wisdom teeth out. A few days before I had the procedure, I came out to them, and they disowned me." Darbi looked up at the sky and wiped away a tear.

"Was that your regret, coming out to them?"

"No." Darbi bit into a chip. "I married a man I didn't love because that's what was expected of me."

Mary sat up straighter. "You were married to a man?"

"Sean McDaniel, a good guy, but there was no chemistry. There couldn't be. I'm not wired that way." Darbi stared off into the distance.

Mary imagined her cousin was seeing the old Darbi, side by side with Sean. For the life of her, she couldn't picture what this person would look like, couldn't envision Darbi with any man. Couldn't imagine anyone other than Jacqui with her cousin.

"At that time, divorce wasn't allowed in Ireland."

"What do you mean it wasn't allowed?"

"It was illegal until 1996, when the people voted to allow it, but just barely."

Mary squirmed on her stool, picturing her friend Jenni, miserable and emotionally beaten down, still getting belittled by her ex-husband if divorce were illegal in the United States. There must have been lots of women like Jenni in Ireland.

"Every day, I regretted my decision to marry Sean more," Darbi said. "My wisdom teeth started to hurt, and Uncle Cillian told me if I got them removed, I could erase my past. Of course I thought he was a senile old man, but I had the teeth extracted because they hurt like no one's business. I woke up seven years younger and, most important, single. I packed up and moved here because, back then, Americans were more tolerant of my lifestyle." A fly hovered over the bowl of chips, and Darbi shooed it away. "Did you know it was a crime to be gay in Ireland until 1993?"

So many things about what Darbi was saying made no sense. Having years erased from life by removing wisdom teeth, divorce and certain types of love being illegal. Mary was convinced again that she was dreaming or hallucinating. Any minute now, she'd wake up in the dentist's chair. For now, she'd play along.

"Does Jacqui know? About, about, um, years getting erased from your life?"

Darbi shook her head so fast that waterdrops flew off her hair. "It's hard keeping this extraordinary thing that happened to me from her. She'd understand me a lot better if I told her, but she'd never believe me." She stopped and fixated on Mary. "Promise me you'll never talk to anyone about what happened except me."

"No one would believe me."

"You'd end up committed." Darbi dunked a chip in salsa. "There is one very important rule you need to follow, no matter what."

The way Darbi said the last three words caused the hairs on the back of Mary's neck to stand. She pushed her drink away and leaned closer to her cousin, sharpening her focus.

"No seeking out people from your past." Darbi pointed at Mary with a chip. "That means don't look for them in person or on the internet."

"Not even Dean?"

"Especially Dean."

"Why?"

Darbi rubbed her temples. "Just believe me. Bad things will happen. To you." Her voice softened. "And him."

Mary swayed on her stool, her sense of unease growing. "What kind of bad things?"

"Trust me, you don't want to find out."

Mary's heart hammered. She was starting to think being twenty-four again wouldn't be as great as she'd originally thought. No matter; this was just a hallucination. She would go with it until she woke up. In the meantime, she'd have fun.

"It's funny," Darbi said. "We get our wisdom teeth removed and go back to being our younger selves. But during these do-overs, without our wisdom teeth, we have more wisdom than we ever had before. We've learned from the mistakes of our old lives and get to use that knowledge and experience in our new ones."

Out front, a car door slammed. Mary turned toward the gate, expecting to see Jacqui.

"It's just the next-door neighbor," Darbi said. "Always gets home about this time."

"What's going to happen when Jacqui sees me? How will I explain that I'm thirty years younger?"

A hummingbird fluttered by the feeder, drinking up the sugar water. After a few seconds, the magical creature flittered off. "That bird flew backward, and we didn't think anything of it," Darbi said. "Jacqui will think nothing of you being younger. She won't have any memories of the other you, only of this one."

"But I don't have memories of this version of myself."

"It's a little tricky at first, but as you interact with people, your mind fills in the blanks. Somehow, you're able to pull up memories and make sense of things."

"What if I can't?" Mary's cheeks twitched as she imagined herself bumbling through her new life. Hallucination or not, this was all getting to be too much. She tried to take a deep breath but felt a sharp pain across her chest. She sucked in air, certain she was about to have a heart attack.

"Relax," Darbi commanded. "Somehow it all works out. The only thing you need to figure out is what you'll do differently this time so that you don't end up with the same regrets, or any regrets." She settled back on her stool. "It's like you pressed a magical undo button for your life. Tell me what you'll do to make the most of this opportunity."

Mary took a big gulp of her drink, savoring the sweet taste of strawberry. She was twenty-four again with a chance to correct the biggest mistake of her life. A warmth spread across her chest. There was nothing to be afraid of. This was exactly what she had wished for, a chance to do it over to focus on her career. Her heart rate slowed. The pain in her chest went away. She closed her eyes and imagined a picture of herself on the cover of *People* under the headline "America's Most Trusted Broadcaster."

"I'm going to be the anchor for a major television network."

Chapter 9

Back at the apartment, a red Jeep Wrangler with the roof and doors removed was backed into the driveway next to Mary's parking space, the spot that used to be James's. For the briefest moment, she let herself believe the vehicle belonged to James, that he still lived here, and would help her navigate her new life. On some level, she knew he couldn't still be here. He lived on the West Coast and was an international superstar. Besides, he didn't even have a license anymore. He'd let it expire because his chauffeur drove him everywhere in a black Mercedes SUV. When James lived in the apartment below hers, he'd driven a fifteen-year-old rusty blue Renault Le Car with a hole in the floorboard on the passenger side. Watching the road zoom by below her as they drove around MetroWest together, Mary had always felt as if she were on the fast road to success. Boy had she gotten that wrong. Her old life had gone nowhere.

The door to the first-floor apartment swung open. A man who most certainly was not James but most definitely resembled Lady Gaga's handsome ex-boyfriend, Taylor Kinney, the actor who played a Chicago firefighter, stepped onto the landing, a large black dog with a white diamond-shaped fur patch on his chest following behind. Mary shut her eyes, more sure than ever she was hallucinating. When she opened them again, the man, presumably her downstairs neighbor, was still there, walking toward her car. Not only did he resemble the *Chicago Fire* actor, but he wore a gray T-shirt with a fire department insignia. He grinned at her like no handsome twenty-something man had in quite some time, and Lord help her, that made her feel powerful. She was so used to being invisible to young men.

He stood by her driver's side door, waiting for her to climb out. By the way he was smiling at her, she was certain she was supposed to know him, yet he was a stranger to her. For several seconds, she remained rooted behind the steering wheel, afraid to interact with him. Surely he'd realize there was something off about her, that she wasn't a typical twenty-something. Finally, she slid out of the car and stepped onto the driveway. The dog rushed to her side and leaned against her. She reached down to pat him. As her hand traveled over his silky hair, she had the inexplicable urge to belt out the lyrics to "My Way," a song she'd never liked.

"How's our resident Savannah Guthrie today?" her neighbor asked.

At the sound of his low-pitched teasing voice, she stumbled and had to grab on to the side mirror to steady herself. Was she really so lucky that she had a job at Channel 77 and that this Taylor Kinney look-alike lived below her? And was he flirting with her? She hoped this hallucination wouldn't end anytime soon.

"Why are you looking at me like that?" he asked. He stepped closer, the scent of his sharp, zingy cologne filling the air between them. "I hope you're not still embarrassed about last weekend."

What happened last weekend? She waited for memories to fill in like Darbi said they would. Nothing came to her, not even his name. *How will I get by if people know me and things about my life but I don't know anything about them—or even myself?* She forced herself to silence her inner dialogue and engage with the neighbor with the sexy, manly stubble outlining his jaw.

"Are you embarrassed?" he asked again.

She waved her hand as if dismissing his suggestion. "I've already forgotten all about it."

"You haven't. You just don't want to talk about it, but I think we should."

Her mind raced, trying to think of something that might have happened between them.

He kicked at the ground. A small stone skidded across the pavement and bounced off the front tire of her car. "I don't want things to be awkward between us."

No, no, no! She drew in a deep breath. Did she sleep with him?

"I'm hoping we can still be friends." He looked so earnest as he said it that she was almost certain they'd been together. A wave of guilt washed over her. She'd never cheated on Dean. Had never even thought about it. So, why was she dreaming about this guy?

A woman walking a yellow Lab passed on the sidewalk in front of the house. The black dog bolted from Mary's side down the driveway toward them.

"Frank," her neighbor yelled. "Get your butt back here."

Mary felt a jolt to her temples, and the driveway seemed to move as if it were a treadmill. Her grip on the mirror tightened as memories came to her, just like Darbi had promised. The dog's name was Frank Sinatra, and he had belonged to the downstairs neighbor's grandfather, who had moved to an assisted care residence that didn't allow pets. Her firefighter neighbor had insisted on taking the dog so he wouldn't end up at a shelter. While she was certain the information was true, she had no idea where it had come from and no recollection of this guy's name. Still, the memory dump reassured her that other details of her new life would emerge.

The Taylor Kinney look-alike whistled. Frank Sinatra reversed direction and trotted back to his side.

"You're still coming to Belli's birthday party Saturday night, right?" he asked.

Mary waited for information about the hot firefighter or Belli to come to her just like it had for the dog, but it didn't. Belli was probably his girlfriend. Gabriella or Isabella. Whatever her name was, Mary didn't want to meet her. Not if what she thought had happened with him had happened. "I don't know."

"Because of last weekend?"

She looked into his bright-blue eyes, wishing she knew what had happened and really hoping she hadn't slept with him. Just thinking about it made her feel like a dirty old woman. She'd never identified with Mrs. Robinson or wanted to be a cougar.

"Let's go inside and talk," he said.

"No." The last thing she wanted to do was talk about something some other version of herself had done. "I'm on my way out."

He cocked an eyebrow. "You just got here."

She bolted for her car.

"Come on, Mary," he called out. "Let's be adults and talk about this."

The tires kicked up dust as she peeled out of the driveway.

~

Mary's entire body vibrated with nervous energy as she drove off. She pulled over to the side of the road to collect herself but couldn't stop shaking. What was happening to her felt too real to be a hallucination, and she certainly hadn't been hallucinating when Darbi had told her about Mulligan magic at lunch that day. She'd been telling the truth. Somehow by getting her wisdom teeth out, Mary had entered another dimension where she was thirty years younger. All she'd wanted was a chance to work at a news station again. Instead, she'd broken her marriage vows to Dean with a boy Kendra's age. And she was living in a world where Kendra didn't exist, which made it a less happy place than her real world. Mary shook her head. It had been fun to look in the mirror and see her young self, but it was time to get back to her husband and daughter. She stepped on the gas and sped across town to Darbi's.

Like earlier, Darbi floated around the pool on the unicorn. This time, Jackson Browne singing "Somebody's Baby" blasted from the wireless speakers.

Mary raced toward the diving board. "How do I get back?" She shouted to be heard over the music.

Darbi, who had been lying on the float, pulled herself up to a sitting position. "What happened?"

"I slept with my neighbor." The words left a nasty taste in Mary's mouth. She wished she had a mint.

"In the thirty minutes you were gone, you had sex?"

Mary kicked off her sandals and plopped down on the diving board, wincing as the hot plastic scorched the backs of her bare legs. The pool's bluish-green tiles reflected off the water, making it the color of the Caribbean Sea. She dipped her feet below the surface. Her entire body cooled. "Before I got here."

Using her hands to paddle, Darbi maneuvered to the deep end and reached for the edge of the pool below Mary's dangling feet to anchor herself. "You're not making sense."

"You told me I'd be able to pull up memories, but I met my downstairs neighbor, and nothing came to me. I think we slept together." She splashed water over her arms as if trying to wash the neighbor off her skin.

Darbi bit down on her lip. She had a gleam in her eyes that let Mary know she was trying not to laugh. "Why would you think that?"

"The things he said."

"Is he attractive?"

An image of his face with his square jaw and plump, kissable lips popped into Mary's head. "Extremely."

Darbi cocked her head. "Maybe you want to sleep with him."

"No, I don't." Her cheeks flamed as she thought about undressing in front of another man. Dean had looked at her with wide-eyed wonderment the first time they'd been together. "You are so beautiful," he'd said, his voice breaking with emotion. Even now, after all this time, on the occasions they were together that special way, he still looked at her as if he was amazed she was with him, making her feel like the girl she used to be instead of the beyond-middle-aged woman with the saggy body she was. "The only man I want to sleep with is Dean," she said.

Sorrow replaced the gleam in Darbi's eyes. Mary didn't understand why. It wasn't as if she would never be with Dean again. She just couldn't be with him while she was twenty-four.

"What exactly did your neighbor say?" Darbi asked, her voice flat, with none of the teasing from before.

"He asked if I was embarrassed about what happened last weekend. Said he didn't want things to be awkward between us and hoped we could still be friends."

"'Awkward'? Yikes." Darbi rolled off the float and disappeared underwater.

Mary squirmed. That word had triggered the same reaction in Darbi as it had in her. "What should I do?" she asked when Darbi emerged in the shallow end.

"There isn't anything you can do."

Mary hung her head. "I hope that memory never comes to me. It would make things really uncomfortable with Dean when I return to my real life."

Darbi's face turned ghostly white. "Return to your other life?"

Mary nodded.

Darbi stared at her for several seconds. A few times, her lips parted as if she was about to say something, but then she snapped them closed.

"What?" Mary asked.

"Forget about Dean. Forget about the neighbor. You're here because you wanted to anchor the news. You need to do that."

Mary fidgeted, and the diving board bounced in response. Darbi was right. She couldn't waste this magical do-over opportunity. All she had to do was stay here long enough to be offered the promotion. She would say yes, and voilà, she'd return to her real life as a famous anchor. The Independent Cable News Network ID badge she'd found in her wallet let her know that dream was within reach.

"You told me memories of my new life would come to me, but not all of them are. Why is that?"

Next door a dog barked with an insistence that made Mary wonder if he'd been eavesdropping and had the answer she needed.

Darbi covered her ears with her hands. "I don't know." She pulled herself up the ladder and hustled across the pool deck to a small table with her suntan lotion and her essential oils. She sprayed the oil on her wrists and took three deep breaths.

Mary wondered what had made her uncomfortable and why she needed a calming spray when she'd been relaxing by the pool all day. Well, of course, this crazy situation must be the reason.

"I never had to worry about filling in the blanks because I moved here right after it happened to me. Uncle Cillian lived his entire life in the same tiny village, so he went through it. He sent me letters that explained some of his experience."

Mary jumped to her feet. "What did they say?"

Darbi shrugged. "I never read them."

"What?"

"This whole thing makes me so uncomfortable." She sprayed some of the oil on her neck. "I wanted to put it out of my mind and live a normal life. Before I left, he told me he was going to write, give me advice. I asked him not to." She scrunched up her face. "It infuriated me to see his chicken scratch on those international envelopes."

"Oh, Darbi."

"I kept them, just in case I ever needed them, but can't remember where I put them. I'll keep looking."

The familiar jingle of an ice cream truck played out front.

Darbi glanced at the clock hanging above the pool bar. "It's getting late. You should go. Jacqui will be home soon. We have to act like everything's normal so she doesn't suspect anything. I don't think we're ready for that."

"What if I can't figure out what's happening at work tomorrow?"

"You will."

"How do you know?"

They walked toward the fence gate in silence, the glare from the June sun making it hard to see in front of them.

"Because somehow you already know you have to work tomorrow."

Chapter 10

By the time Mary returned from Darbi's, the red Jeep was gone from her driveway. As she passed the neighbor's window on the way to the stairs to her apartment, the dog barked, probably because he wasn't used to her coming and going. The thought caused her to freeze on the staircase. What had happened to the person who lived here in her other life? Where did they live now? The whole world was out of kilter. She felt dizzy and tightened her grip on the handrail so she wouldn't fall. Once inside, she called Darbi.

"Now what?" her cousin asked.

"What happened to the person who really lives in this apartment?"

"What do you mean, 'really lives' there?"

"The person who lives here in my other life?"

"The only life you need to care about is this one." Pots and pans clanked in the background. "If you start thinking about it, you'll go mad. Just live. That's what I did. It's why I didn't open Uncle Cillian's letters."

Mary put the phone down and massaged the back of her neck, trying to figure out this alternate universe. It made her head hurt to think about it, so she decided to take Darbi's advice. Who lived here wasn't important. If she really wanted to know, she could always look up the information when she returned to her other life. For now, she needed to focus on getting that promotion so she could be a famous newscaster when she got back.

In the kitchen, she searched for something to make for dinner. There were three boxes of Kraft macaroni and cheese on a shelf in a cabinet. She used to love that stuff, but she hadn't had it in years because Dean thought it tasted disgusting.

As she sat on the sofa eating a bowl of it, she gagged. He was right. The homemade version she made with his mother's recipe was gourmet compared to this crap.

At nine o'clock, Mary went to her room, hoping to get a good night's sleep before going to work the next day. She had the entire bed to herself but confined her body to the right side, where she usually slept. The empty space next to her crowded her thoughts. Who was Dean sleeping with? What had become of him in a world without her? He'd probably married Michelle, his high school girlfriend who still pined for him. Thinking of them together made Mary's right eyelid twitch.

She switched her train of thought to working at the news station instead. Now both eyes twitched. Would she still be good? She flipped from her stomach to her side. Would she know how to use the equipment? Surely it had changed over the years. She flipped to her back and glanced toward the empty space next to her. Usually when she tossed and turned, Dean reached for her hand, and the feel of her palm against his was a calming balm, slowing her racing thoughts and allowing her to fall asleep.

She lay awake for most of the night, staring up at the glowing star decals on the ceiling that she hadn't noticed before.

~

The rectangular brick building that was home to the news station looked like all the others in the industrial park nestled alongside the highway. The only hints that it housed a television station were the satellite dishes and the white vans with the Channel 77 ICNN logo parked behind them. Mary's entire body vibrated with excitement as she turned into the lot and pulled in next to one of the vans. The gateway to the career she had missed out on stood a mere hundred feet in front of her. So many people fantasized about getting second chances, but she, Mary Mulligan, was actually getting one.

She took a deep breath before stepping out of the car and heading toward the entrance. At the glass door, she swiped her badge and bounced on her toes as the door clicked, unlocking. The interior of the building had been redecorated since she had been there last. The dingy off-white walls she remembered now sparkled a vibrant blue. The stained threadbare gray carpet had been replaced by a glossy premium-grade charcoal version.

The station's most famous alumni smiled at her from inside picture frames as she made her way down the hallway. Brent Campbell, the sports director when she'd been there the first time, now addressed national audiences from his prime-time show on ESPN. Dylan Whetly, the morning meteorologist who'd joined the station shortly before Mary left, had spent the last nine years forecasting the weather on *Good Morning America*. Mary paused in front of a photograph of a stern-looking man, Cory Atkinson. She recognized him from *Dateline* but hadn't realized he had started his career at Channel 77. When she reached the end of the gallery of past employees, she turned back to study the wall. Just like when she'd looked at the picture of herself in Darbi's sunroom, a chill ran down her spine. Something was off. She racked her brain, but nothing came to her. She continued down the hall with a feeling of unease until she reached the pictures of the present-day anchors, Alex Mason and William Casey. She bounced up and down on the balls of her feet. Someday soon she'd be sitting behind the anchor desk with one of them.

As she turned the corner and entered the newsroom, the room started to spin. She felt as if she were on that ride at an amusement park that rotates and then the floor drops out. She grabbed onto a nearby chair to steady herself.

"Are you okay?" a broad-shouldered man with a pointy chin asked.

"I felt a little lightheaded, but I'm okay now."

"You didn't eat breakfast, did you? Probably saving your appetite for today's assignment." He laughed. "That's what I would do."

Today's assignment? Mary fidgeted with her necklace, sliding the small microphone charm up the chain and then back. She'd found the silver chain in a jewelry box on her dresser that morning. The sight of it had brought tears to her eyes. Her parents had given her a similar necklace the first time she'd started working for Channel 77. She'd lost it while skiing at Sunday River a few days after she'd turned down the Iowa job, and she'd always felt losing it at that time had been a sign that she'd destroyed her career.

"Make sure you interview the vendors and not just the attendees," the man said.

She nodded, though she had no idea what she was agreeing to. She had to get her eyes on the list of today's assignments.

"Talk to a kid or two."

She listened to the man, wondering who he was. Someone important, that was obvious. She could tell by the authority in his voice, or maybe the clipboard he carried made him look as if he was in charge.

He had stopped speaking and now studied Mary with one eyebrow raised. Had he figured out that she had no idea who he was or what her current assignment was? Why weren't memories filling in? She'd never be able to fake her way through conversations without them.

"Any thoughts?" he asked.

She had none. Her face heated up. It had probably turned fire-engine red the way it always did when she was embarrassed, the curse of Irish skin tone.

"Don't forget to have some ice cream yourself," the man said.

A metallic taste filled Mary's mouth, and her temples throbbed. Images of the man she was talking to flashed through her mind. They were much more vivid than the ones of her neighbor's dog. The man grilled her from across a large oak desk, interviewing her for the job. He led a brainstorming discussion on story ideas. He sat at the head of a table, addressing a group of reporters. He critiqued one of her news stories. The pictures kept coming, as if someone had plugged a flash drive into her head and was uploading videos. They had to be memories from the version of herself that had been here before yesterday.

"Mitch Wise, news director." She blurted it out, excited she knew who he was. "I'm covering the Scooper Bowl today."

He folded his arms across his chest. "Are you sure you're okay?"

"Why wouldn't I be?" Mary beamed. The jitters she'd been experiencing ever since walking into the newsroom were gone. Darbi was right. Her memories would fill in.

The corners of his mouth bent downward. "Because no one calls me Mitch. It's Mitchell."

~

Waiting by the rear exit, the cameraman had his back to Mary as she walked down the hall toward him, her legs like Jell-O. After almost twenty-five years, she was going out on assignment. Would she remember what to do? Of course she would. It would be like riding a bike.

The cameraman's head swiveled toward her so she could see his face. Something about him seemed familiar. She squinted, trying to figure out who he was. As she got closer, she noticed a faded oblong scar under his nose, a scar that had been much angrier the last time she'd seen it, days after he'd had a mole removed. "Carl! You still work here?" In the other version of her life, they'd started their careers together, twenty-two-year-old kids, green in the field, figuring it out together one assignment at a time.

"Still work here," he repeated with an irritated tone. "Not even a little bit funny. I'm not in the mood for old guy jokes today." His voice sounded just as gravelly as she'd remembered, as if his vocal cords had been run through a shredder.

He was a skinny kid when she'd last seen him, still growing into his body. If they'd had time after an assignment, he would steer the news van through the drive-through window of Wendy's, always ordering double burger patties with extra cheese, large fries doused with salt, and a chocolate Frosty. The fast-food meals had taken a toll on his body. His large belly hung over the belt on his jeans. His mop of blond hair had thinned and turned yellowish white. Fine lines wove across his forehead. His shoulders had started to round.

If she'd seen him from time to time over the past few decades, the changes in him might not have seemed so pronounced, but after having no contact for twenty-five years, she almost couldn't believe he was the same person. Growing old was a privilege but also a curse with the damage it did to a person's body. She touched the side of her mouth, grateful her wisdom teeth had reversed her damage, at least for a little while.

Something about Carl's presence at the news station comforted her. Having him there was like having a lifeline back to her old life, where she was fifty-something. "I'm so happy to see you." She opened her arms, intending to hug him.

"What are you doing?" He took a step backward, and Mary froze. "Were you about to hug me?"

His rejection wounded her. Then again, Carl had no idea that she hadn't seen him for decades. As far as he knew, they'd seen each other earlier in the week. They also were no longer peers. He was a thirty-year grizzled veteran, and she was a twenty-something kid trying to make a name for herself.

"Let's go." He pushed open the heavy metal door to the loading dock, hurrying outside. On the way down the steps, he stumbled.

Mary gasped, remembering Darbi's warning. *No seeking out people from your past. Bad things will happen.* He was from her past, but she hadn't sought him out. He had just been there.

His hand flailed through the air. Somehow, he managed to grab hold of the railing, keeping himself upright.

Mary exhaled, wondering if Carl's stumble was a reminder not to look for people she had known in her other life. She stared into the parking lot, wondering what Dean was doing now and how Kendra was back in the other universe, or whatever it was.

~

Mary stood on the walkway at City Hall Plaza, smiling as she took in the scene. Long lines of men and women, some dressed in shorts and T-shirts and others in business attire, waited in front of white tents. A few waved paper fans or their hands in front of their faces, trying to get relief from the scorching June sun. Inside the tents, sweaty workers frantically scooped ice cream into small cups, trying to keep up with demand. Crowds of people, most lifting white plastic spoons to their mouths, stood in small groups off to the side.

The Jimmy Fund Scooper Bowl, an annual all-you-can-eat ice cream charity event for the Dana–Farber Cancer Institute, was the perfect first assignment for Mary version 2, as she had come to think of her new young self. She felt at home at the festival. Back in the nineties, she had covered it twice. After that, she, Dean, and Kendra had attended it every year until Kendra graduated high school. Dean and Kendra would compete to see who could eat the most, and the rest of the night they would both complain about having stomachaches. Mary glanced around to look for Dean but then stopped herself, remembering Darbi's stern warning and Carl's stumble on the loading dock. Anyway, she would see him soon enough in her much-improved other life.

"Where to?" Carl asked.

Mary pointed to a red-and-white sign that read FRIENDLY'S. "There." It was the same place where they'd filmed her first story on the Scooper Bowl all those years ago.

He hoisted the camera onto his shoulder and wove his way through the throngs of people, with Mary practically skipping behind him she was so excited. Only days ago, the most important thing she'd had to do was pick up Dean's shirts from the dry cleaner. Today, she was working as a reporter interviewing Bostonians at a beloved charity event. People all over the commonwealth would see her on television tonight. This alternate life was too good to be true.

When she and Carl reached their location, she studied faces, trying to choose a person to talk to first. To her right, a small boy collided with a man holding five single-scoop cups stacked on top of each other. The top cup tumbled off the man's tower. He left it where it had fallen on the brick-covered ground. The ice cream instantly melted into a brown puddle that a woman in pink open-toed sandals stepped in. As Mary watched it happen, her own toes felt sticky.

"Mary." Carl beckoned her to where he stood, talking to a group of twenty-somethings standing in a circle under a tree. They were all employees from State Street, a local financial services company, on their lunch break. A stocky White man in Ray-Ban sunglasses holding a stack of cups agreed to be interviewed.

Carl gave Mary the microphone. For a beat, she stood motionless, looking down at it as if she had no idea what it was.

"Ready?" Carl asked.

Beads of perspiration collected above her lip. Her hands trembled. Her throat felt dry. She needed to excel at this, not only to get a promotion but to prove to herself that she hadn't misremembered anything. She had been a darn good journalist. She sucked in a big breath. She was going to crush this.

"How much ice cream do . . ."

Music blasted from a nearby tent, where a band started to play, startling Mary midquestion. She flinched, sure the pounding of the drum was coming from inside her head it was so loud. The screech of the electric guitar pierced her eardrums.

Carl led them to a spot away from the noise. They could still hear the song, but the racket wasn't as distracting in the new location.

"Whenever you're ready, Mary." Carl breathed heavily, as if hauling the camera equipment through the thick, humid air was too much for him. His face glowed red, and a ring of sweat circled the collar of his navy Red Sox T-shirt. When Mary had last worked with him, his energy was endless, and she'd had trouble keeping up with him.

"The sooner we finish, the sooner we can get back into the air-conditioned van," he said.

The microphone felt slippery in her clammy hand, so she tightened her grip, holding on to it for dear life. "Can you tell me your name, and spell it for me?" she shouted.

The man in the Ray-Bans stepped backward as if the volume of her voice had pushed him away. "Patrick Boyle," he said. "P-A-T-R-I-C-K B-O-Y-L-E."

"Why are you here?" Her tone was all wrong. She was trying to disguise her nerves and in the process had implied he had no business being there.

He stood straighter. His biceps tightened. "Because I like ice cream, and it's a good cause." He said the words slowly, as if he was talking to someone he thought was an idiot.

His attitude unnerved Mary. She swayed left and right, fidgeting with the microphone. She'd annoyed the man, and now she had to fix it. She flashed a shy smile. "Sorry, it's my first day. I'm nervous."

Carl mumbled, "Your first day? Please."

Patrick Boyle relaxed. "It's okay. We've all been there."

"So how much do you think you'll eat today?" Mary's voice sounded conversational, much friendlier than when she'd started.

The man pointed to the tower in his hand. "I'm working on cup fifteen right now. But you better believe, I still have a lot in me."

Mary pumped her fist. The quote was great. She knew she'd use it in her story.

A tall thin Hispanic woman with long dark hair who was nibbling on vanilla ice cream dotted with chips and nuts passed by them. Mary thanked Patrick Boyle and bolted across the walkway toward the woman. "Excuse me. I'm covering the Scooper Bowl for Channel 77," she shouted.

The woman stopped. She flattened the collar of her blouse and straightened her skirt before agreeing to be on camera.

"Why did you come to the Scooper Bowl today?" Mary asked.

The woman laughed. "I'm on a mission to try every flavor here."

"What's your favorite so far?"

"Mint chocolate chip."

Carl gave her a thumbs-up. Mary moved on to a bald Black man who looked to be somewhere in his thirties. "Why did you come here today?"

The man gave her a wistful look. He glanced up toward the sky. When he met Mary's eyes again, his were watering. "I had lymphoma. Doc gave me nine months to live. That was six years ago." He swallowed hard. "Dana–Farber saved my life." The man took a deep breath and puffed out his chest. "So if they want me to choke down some ice cream to support them, who am I to say no?"

Mary smiled, glad the man was okay. Her nerves had finally settled, allowing her to enjoy being a reporter again.

After she'd interviewed a half dozen more people, including two children and a few workers scooping ice cream, Carl said they had enough footage.

"Let's talk to one other person." She was having so much fun that she didn't want to be done. How foolish she'd been to quit this job. Being here interviewing people made her feel important, like what she did mattered.

"Let's do the wrap-up." Carl positioned her in a spot where he could film the heart of the festival behind her. "On three," he said. "One, two, three."

Holding up a cup of fudge swirl ice cream, Mary smiled. "I'm Mary Amato, reporting live from City Hall at the Dana–Farber Scooper Bowl." She slid an overflowing spoon into her mouth.

Carl peeked out at her from behind the camera. "Who the hell is Mary Amato? Did you get married and not tell anyone?"

Mary's face heated up. "I, I . . ." After twenty-six years of being Mary Amato, she was having trouble thinking of herself as Mary Mulligan again.

Carl waved a dismissive hand and pointed the camera at her again. "Get your name right this time."

Chapter 11

Mary yawned as she pulled into Darbi's driveway. The excitement of the day and being on her feet under the blazing sun all afternoon had exhausted her. If she hadn't been so hungry, she would have driven straight to her apartment to go to bed. Earlier in the day, she'd called Darbi to tell her that she'd been able to make sense of things at the station and figure out who everyone was. Darbi had insisted Mary come over for dinner to see what would happen with Jacqui. "I'm going crazy thinking she's going to know something's off. We need to get your first meeting over with so I stop worrying," she'd said.

The scent of grilled meat hit Mary as soon as she stepped out of her car, and her stomach grumbled. Other than a spoonful or two of ice cream, she hadn't had anything to eat since breakfast.

Across the street, a shirtless thirty-something neighbor mowing his lawn waved at her as she walked to Darbi's front door. She was so surprised by his friendliness that she froze midstep with her mouth gaping. In all the years middle-aged Mary had visited her cousin, the guy had never acknowledged her presence.

Darbi's voice coming through the screen door pulled her from her thoughts. "Don't be so surprised. You're young and beautiful again. No longer invisible."

Mary cringed because her cousin spoke the truth. Middle-aged women were invisible. Jenni had once told her the clothing store Chico's, which targeted older women, intentionally sold clothes with bright colors and attention-getting patterns so that the women who wore them would be noticed. Mary wasn't sure if the information was true or something Jenni had made up. Either way, though, she believed the sentiment.

"Just wave back," Darbi said.

Wave? Mary wanted to give the guy the finger on behalf of all women older than thirty-five. Instead, she blew him a kiss, something she would never had had the chutzpah to do the first time she was in her twenties.

"Come get it while it's hot!" Jacqui's rich voice called out from somewhere inside the house.

Mary tried to step through the open door, but Darbi grabbed her arm while blocking her path. "Be careful when you're talking to Jacqui," she whispered.

"What do you mean?"

"Don't say boo about Dean or Kendra. She doesn't remember your other life and has no idea who they are." Darbi's forehead creased. In this alternate world, she looked much older to Mary.

"I looked for Dean today at City Hall," Mary said. "He loves the Scooper Bowl. Next year, I'm going to go with him. Maybe Kendra will be back by then too."

Darbi's grip on Mary's forearm tightened, and her face blanched. "Don't you under—"

A loud clanking sound came from across the street. Mary and Darbi both jumped. The neighbor had hit a rock with the lawn mower.

Jacqui emerged from the kitchen, walking up behind them. "What's all the whispering out here?" She whacked Darbi in the butt with a dish towel.

Mary's muscles tightened as she felt Jacqui's appraising gaze on her. *Does she notice I'm thirty years younger? She must.* Mary reached for the finger on her left hand to spin her wedding ring, a nervous habit she'd had for decades, but of course the diamond band wasn't there. She left her thumb there on the empty spot, realizing this day would have been even better if she'd been able to tell Dean and Kendra about it. She pushed the thought away and slid the microphone charm on her necklace back and forth.

Jacqui narrowed her eyes. "You two are up to no good. I can tell." A hint of amusement tickled her voice.

"Not us," Darbi said. She raced inside the house and disappeared down the hallway.

In her real life, Mary never ran out of things to talk about with Jacqui, but standing alone with her now, she didn't open her mouth, fearing anything she said would give her secret away. She bolted for the dining room, with Jacqui on her heels. They sat in chairs on opposite sides of the table. Was Jacqui looking at her strangely? Yes, she most definitely was.

"I like that dress. Is it new?" Jacqui asked.

Was it new? Mary had no idea. She fiddled with her silverware. "I found it in the back of my closet." That was true.

Jacqui laughed, and the familiar sound put Mary at ease.

Darbi joined them, reeking of patchouli.

"Pee-yoo." Jacqui pinched her nose. "Why did you douse yourself with essential oil before dinner? Are you nervous the food won't taste good?"

Darbi paused before answering. "That loud boom across the street startled me. My heart's been pounding ever since."

Jacqui raised an eyebrow. She handed Mary the salad bowl. Mary tried to meet Darbi's eye to signal for her to calm down. Everything was fine.

"Your story on the Scooper Bowl was great. We just watched it," Jacqui said. "Are you sure you're going to have an appetite? I bet you ate a ton of ice cream today. I sure would have."

"I didn't know I would be covering the Scooper Bowl, so I didn't have my pills with me."

Darbi sat up straighter and thrust the plate of steak at Mary. "Have some."

"What pills?" Jacqui asked.

Darbi jabbed at a piece of meat with her knife. "That right there is cooked medium well, the way you like it." She dropped the beef strip on Mary's plate.

"For my lactose intolerance."

Darbi cleared her throat. "What do you want to drink?"

Jacqui's eyebrows squished together. "Since when are you lactose intolerant?"

"Wine!" Darbi shouted. "Jacqui, will you pick out a bottle that goes with dinner from the rack in the dining room? A nice red."

As Jacqui stood, her attention turned to Darbi. "You're extremely jumpy tonight, hon, even with your calming spray."

Darbi waited for Jacqui to leave, then hissed at Mary, "Fifty-four-year-old Mary was lactose intolerant, not twenty-four-year-old Mary."

Mary had been in her early forties when her intolerance to dairy products began.

"It happens to many women as they age," her doctor had explained. "There's increasing evidence that shifting hormones during perimenopause and menopause are the cause."

"Darn, I would have had a much better time at the Scooper Bowl if I'd remembered that," she said. Thankfully, she'd be back in her other life long before Mary version 2 reached perimenopause. She didn't want to go through that again.

~

Darbi was unusually quiet through dinner, and Mary was too scared of saying something wrong, so Jacqui carried the conversation, explaining the products in her store that customers liked most. At one point, she stopped speaking, eyeing Darbi and Mary. "You ladies are quiet tonight. Something going on that I don't know about?"

Darbi and Mary made fleeting eye contact. "It's exciting hearing you talk about the store," Darbi said. To Mary, her cousin's voice sounded forced, as if she was mimicking the normal way she spoke.

After they finished eating, while Darbi did the dishes, Jacqui and Mary settled in the living room to watch *Jeopardy!* Mary finally let herself relax. In her real life, she watched the game show with Jacqui whenever she ate dinner there. The one difference tonight was Dean's absence. He usually sat in the recliner, trying to yell out the answers before Jacqui did. Mary glimpsed toward the chair and could almost see Dean sitting there wearing a golf shirt with a beer in his hand. She blinked hard to clear the water collecting in the corners of her eyes. She'd only been here for two days, and she missed him already.

Jacqui turned on the television. There were still a few minutes before the show was scheduled to start, and the news was ending. A dark-haired woman sat behind the anchor desk.

Mary leaned forward on the sofa.

"For all of us at *CBS Evening News*, I'm Nora O'Donnell. Thank you for watching."

"Who's Nora O'Donnell? Where's Liz?" Mary asked.

"Who's Liz?" Jacqui said.

The sound of a pot clanking against the sink came from the kitchen. Darbi raced into the living room. "Mary, could I get some help, please?"

Jacqui placed a hand on Mary's leg. "She's a guest. She doesn't have to clean. Now, who is Liz?"

"I could really use some help," Darbi insisted. She caught Mary's attention and bobbed her head in the direction of the kitchen.

"I don't mind." Mary followed her cousin out of the room. "What's going on? Why isn't Liz on the news?"

Darbi held her index finger over her pursed lips and yanked on the faucet so that the sound of the streaming water filled the room. "Liz is not the anchor of *CBS Evening News* in this version of your life," she whispered.

There in Darbi's kitchen, Mary pictured the Hall of Fame wall at Channel 77 and figured out what was wrong with it. Liz's photo was missing. Dang. How had she not realized that? The dinner she'd just eaten twisted and turned in her stomach. A sour taste filled her mouth. "Why not?" She braced herself for Darbi's answer, almost regretting asking. Something horrible must have happened to Liz for her not to be the CBS anchor or pictured on the news station's Hall of Fame wall, and Mary couldn't help but wonder if her being here was the cause.

"Ladies, I don't enjoy watching alone," Jacqui called.

"Let's not talk about this when Jacqui's around."

"Just tell me what happened to Liz."

"I'll explain later. In the meantime, remember what I told you. Bad things happen when you look up people from your other life."

In the heat of the kitchen, Mary shivered. Was Darbi trying to warn her that she'd inadvertently changed the paths of the people she'd known? She bit down on her lip, determined to do a better job at work so she'd be offered a promotion and return to her real life sooner rather than later.

Chapter 12

The next day at work, Mary typed Liz's name into Google's search bar. Before she hit the return key, Darbi's warning ran through her mind. While Mary was living in this alternate universe, she had to trust her cousin. She hadn't believed what Darbi had said about having her wisdom teeth removed, and look what had happened. Mary would follow Darbi's advice to a T. Everything here was too unpredictable not to, and she didn't want anything bad to happen while she was here because of something she'd done. She tapped on the backspace button until all the letters in Liz's name disappeared.

"I'm waiting on you." Carl's grumpy voice came from behind her. They were heading to a nursing home in Burlington to cover the 105th birthday party of one of the residents. Mary loved covering feel-good stories like that, but she wondered if they would be enough to get her the promotion she needed to return to her other life as a success. She'd have to volunteer to cover harder news, no matter how much she disliked it, just like she'd had to last time.

In the news van, she tuned the radio to Oldies 103.3 and sang along to "Careless Whisper," by Wham! In her new body, she enjoyed listening to songs from her high school and college days because they reminded her of a time when anything was possible, and, being twenty-four again, she felt that way now.

Carl glanced over at her. "This is what you listen to? Would have figured you more for a Taylor Swift or Beyoncé fan."

Mary's face reddened. Twenty-somethings didn't like music like this. Kendra hadn't even known who George Michael was on that sad Christmas Day he passed away. Mary had played "Freedom," and Kendra had scrunched her nose, unimpressed. Music was yet another thing Mary and her daughter didn't bond over.

The brake lights of the car in front of them came on. "Watch out!" Mary yelled.

"Relax, I'm nowhere near them," Carl said.

He was, though. He was riding their bumper. She would have preferred to drive, didn't like riding with other people, except Dean. He always left at least a car's length of space between them and the car they were behind, making her feel safe. Without him behind the wheel, she felt vulnerable.

~

Mary had a blast covering the old man's birthday party. It aired at the end of the six o'clock news, a happy story to leave viewers in a good mood. She drove home feeling exhilarated and watched the story again on the station's website. She briefly considered forwarding the URL to Dean's email with a message that said *Told you I was good at this* but decided against it, thinking again of Darbi's warning.

Often on Friday nights, Dean and Mary ordered takeout and watched a movie together. He always let her choose which one, but she rarely picked the rom-coms she loved because when she did, he spent the night looking at his iPad, or he'd fall asleep within the first twenty minutes. Alone in her apartment tonight, she queued up *Bridget Jones's Diary* and watched it guilt-free while munching on microwave popcorn, which wasn't nearly as good as the old-fashioned stuff Dean popped on the stovetop and drowned in butter.

The next day, Saturday, she woke up from a deep sleep to the sound of incessant barking. Her eyes popped open. For a second, she lay there groggy and disoriented, trying to remember where she was.

"Hush, Frank," a voice called out, and the barking stopped.

Mary's mouth fell open as the events of the last three days came crashing back. Lying alone in her bed, she broke out laughing. She really was twenty-four again, working at a news station. How did she get so lucky? She felt a tad guilty for enjoying her new life without Dean and Kendra but then realized if she were back home, she wouldn't be spending time with them anyway. Kendra was in England, and no doubt Dean was playing in a golf tournament this weekend. They wouldn't even miss her while she was here vying for the promotion.

She jumped out of bed, eager to start the day, thinking she'd go for a walk. Just as she was finishing dressing, the doorbell rang. Darbi stood on the landing, hunched over at the waist, gasping for air and holding a bag that smelled like onions.

"Those damn stairs will be the death of me."

Mary remembered how walking the hill along Broad Street on the Hudson section of the rail trail always left the fifty-something version of herself winded and was glad she had a twenty-something's stamina to deal with the climb leading to her apartment. Poor Darbi, having to deal with the staircase at her age. "Come in and sit down."

"Jacqui's working at the store. I have to be there by noon to help with the register. Figured this is the only chance we'll have to talk for a few days." She dragged herself into the kitchen and collapsed into the nearest chair. As she waited for her breathing to slow, her eyes wandered around Mary's new home, and the corners of her mouth ticked downward. "Your house in Hudson was palatial compared to this."

Like a long-forgotten movie, memories of the first time Dean had visited the Framingham apartment played through Mary's mind.

"I've putted on greens that are bigger than this place," he'd said.

Her shoulders had stiffened, and she'd told herself to relax. He was joking and hadn't meant to hurt her pride. "Just wait until you see my next place. It's going to be magnificent." The confident tone she'd spoken with sent its own message: *I'll show you.* She'd firmly believed she would be enormously successful, living in either a bungalow in Malibu overlooking the Pacific Ocean or a penthouse in Manhattan with views of Central Park. Maybe she'd be bicoastal, own both homes.

Dean had pulled her in for a hug. "I hope your next place is my next place too," he'd whispered.

The idea of living with him had thrilled her. She hadn't known it at the time, but his suggestion had poked the tiniest of holes in the boat she was sailing to chase her dreams, because she was starting to care about him more than her career ambitions. Over the next few months, he'd poke bigger holes with his sweetness, and the boat would take on too much water to stay afloat and reach its destination.

She'd realized she loved him during their first argument. Mary had told Dean she was leaving, because she didn't want to fight with him. He'd wrapped his arms around her waist. "We're not fighting. We're trying to clear up a misunderstanding."

She'd started to cry because his response was so reasonable. She and her previous boyfriend had had ugly shouting matches as they tried to work out differences.

Later, when she'd told Dean that was the moment she knew she'd loved him, he'd cocked his head. "If I'd known that's what it took to get you to fall for me, I would have picked a fight much sooner."

The sound of the paper bag crinkling pulled Mary from the memory. Darbi slid out a bagel wrapped in parchment paper.

"Technically, it's my first apartment. Of course it's small," Mary said.

"Someday you'll be a famous anchor, and they'll feature your mansion on HGTV."

"I wonder where we'll live when I go back?"

Darbi's movement became twitchy. "I'm surprised to hear you talk about going back. I thought you were enjoying being young." She knocked the bag off the table, and an envelope spilled out.

Mary reached down. "Is this one of Uncle Cillian's letters?" She held up the envelope.

Darbi shook her head. "I swiped it from your neighbor's mailbox. Looks like a credit card offer."

"You stole his mail?"

"I was only going to look at it. Find out his name, but he saw me standing on his stoop. Asked what I was doing there. I dropped the mail in the bag before he saw it so he wouldn't know I was snooping. It was awkward, so I offered him a bagel. Yours."

Mary stared down at the name typed across the front of the envelope and read it aloud. "Mr. Brady Zecco." She closed her eyes, hoping she wouldn't remember them sleeping together. Even thinking about it made her feel icky. "Nothing's coming up." *Phew.*

"At least you know his name now." Darbi busied herself unwrapping the bagel. The pungent odor of onions wafted through the room.

"You're supposed to tell me why Liz isn't the anchor of *CBS Evening News,*" Mary said.

"I have no idea." Darbi averted her eyes, turning her head and staring out the door.

Mary sighed. She knew her cousin was lying. "You told me you would explain." She sounded like a petulant teenager.

"Don't you use that tone with me." Darbi pointed a finger at Mary. "Remember, I'm your elder now."

Mary rolled her eyes.

"I told you before. I don't have all the answers." Darbi stood and went to the refrigerator.

The fact that her cousin was uncomfortable sitting across from her and couldn't look her in the eyes reinforced Mary's belief that Darbi was lying, but why?

Darbi pulled a Diet Coke from the refrigerator and snapped the can open. "Erasing thirty years of your life may have had unintended consequences."

"What do you mean?"

Darbi took a gulp of soda. "Think about all the interactions you had with people during those years. Those interactions never happened. None of them."

None of them. Mary's stomach dropped with the reminder that she was living in a world without Kendra. She shot up from the table and filled a glass with cold water. What if, in addition to becoming a famous anchor, she made other changes to her real life by being here?

Darbi watched Mary drink, her face emotionless. "Something you did helped Liz get that job at CBS."

"That's ridiculous." Mary and Liz had competed against one another.

Darbi shrugged. "The only thing that should be different in Liz's life is that she doesn't know you."

Mary and Liz began their careers at Channel 77 on the same day in early September, two newbies being assigned the stories no one else wanted. At first, they'd been friends, good friends, collaborating on projects and enjoying each other's company outside of work. The news director even referred to them as the Bobbsey Twins.

"Maybe she learned from you," Darbi said. "Or maybe you inspired her without knowing it."

Perhaps that was true. After a few months, they'd started to compete against each other for better stories and to fill in behind the anchor desk. First the competition was friendly, but soon they'd stopped confiding in one another. Before too long, they no longer trusted one another. As Mary's distrust grew, she became more determined to beat Liz and worked harder. Maybe Liz had done the same for the same reasons.

Sitting in the kitchen with Darbi now, Mary realized that she and her archnemesis Liz Collins had been good for each other. How about that? Her unease returned as she took the thought one step further. Would she be able to succeed without Liz pushing her?

Chapter 13

After Darbi left, Mary went for a long walk on the bike path. It didn't exist the first time she'd lived in Framingham, and being on it today reminded her of the last time she'd walked the Hudson trail with Kendra. Her heart ached when she remembered Kendra asking, "Do you not want me to go?" Thinking back on it now, Mary wished she'd been more supportive of Kendra's news instead of making her feel guilty. Wasn't it parents' responsibility to raise their children to have the strength and courage to set off on their own? Kendra had left for London thinking she'd disappointed Mary. The ache in Mary's chest intensified. As soon as she returned to her old life, she would make sure her daughter knew how proud of her she was.

Mary picked up her pace. Above her, the sky was a magnificent shade of blue, without a cloud in sight. The temperature was comfortable, somewhere in the midseventies, and there was no humidity. No doubt Dean was at Addison Heights today, playing a round of golf. His life probably hadn't changed too much without her. Maybe he had a new wife, and she played with him. She pictured him riding in one of those carts with a fit blond woman. The two of them laughed as they searched for a wayward ball. She felt a prickle of jealousy. *Don't get too comfortable with her, Dean. I'll be back.*

She passed a crew of landscapers, and two of the men whistled at her. She stopped to do a pirouette. When she was really in her twenties, catcalls had enraged her. A woman should be able to walk down the street without being harassed. Now, though, she relished the attention. Soon enough, she'd be back to her fifty-something body, invisible again.

As she crossed Old Connecticut Path to the other side of the bike trail, her thoughts turned to Liz. Mary didn't know what to make of her supposed impact on Liz's life. She'd like to believe she'd played a part in Liz's success, but she doubted she had. Other than Dean and Kendra, she couldn't imagine her absence would affect anyone. The thought saddened her. She'd done so little with her life and affected so few. Sitting behind that news desk was the one thing she'd done that had made her feel like she mattered.

She'd reached the part of the trail that went under the road. She didn't like walking through the tunnel by herself, so she turned around.

Back at the apartment, her neighbor, Brady, was setting up cornhole in the yard.

"Hey there." Was it her imagination, or had he said those two words suggestively?

She raced to the staircase so she wouldn't have to talk to him.

Before she reached the top, he hollered up to her from the bottom: "You'd better come tonight, or I'll toss you over my shoulder and carry you down."

~

Car doors started slamming at eight. By eight thirty, vehicles spilled out of the driveway and lined both sides of the busy street. A few pickup trucks and SUVs were parked on the grass beside a stone wall. Groups of men and women huddled on the lawn, drinking from beer cans and plastic cups. Every now and then, Frank Sinatra dashed across the yard, chasing a ball. Mary watched all the action from her living room window, wondering if she should join the crowd. On one hand, she wanted to stay as far away from Brady as she could. On the other, she had nothing else to do tonight. She also wasn't sure she could spend all evening with twenty-somethings without giving herself away. While she now inhabited the body of a twenty-four-year-old, her mind still worked like that of a woman in her midfifties. What would they talk about? A ridiculous television show that she'd never watched or a band she'd never heard of? Her heart raced and her breathing accelerated, so much so that she was on the verge of hyperventilating.

An image of Kendra walking next to her on the bike path popped into her head, and she felt herself relax. She could carry on a conversation with people in their twenties. She and Kendra and Kendra's friends had always had fascinating discussions—when her daughter bothered to come around, that was. Kendra had been particularly passionate about debating whether soulmates existed. She had argued that the person you were meant to be with was predestined. Mary had disagreed. She said the idea of there being only one person meant for you in a world of seven or eight billion people and that person being born in the same century and geographic area as you was preposterous.

At the start of the conversation, Kendra had been reclining in her chair with her splayed hands resting on her thighs. By the end of Mary's diatribe, Kendra was standing, her arms crossed against her chest and her tightly clenched fists tucked beneath her underarms. "How can you think that when you're one of the lucky ones who's found your soulmate?"

"There is no such thing as a soulmate," Mary had reiterated. "Love takes hard work, and if you're not willing to do the work, no relationship will last."

"So you don't think Dad's your soulmate?"

On the day Kendra had asked the question, Mary was miffed at Dean for spending the afternoon at the club golfing instead of relaxing on a beach with her. "He's my husband, so I'm committed to doing the work to make our relationship last."

Kendra had just celebrated her twenty-second birthday, but the way she rolled her eyes reminded Mary of the thirteen-year-old girl Kendra once was. "Of everyone you ever met in your life, you recognized something special in Dad and chose him to be your person. That makes him your soulmate."

Mary had conceded that when she'd met Dean, she'd felt a connection with him that she hadn't felt with anyone else. On their first date, she'd told him her favorite novel was *A Prayer for Owen Meany*. By their second date, he'd read it, and they'd held their own two-person book club about it over dinner. One year on her birthday, he'd gifted her a ticket to a conference where her idol, Barbara Walters, was the keynote speaker. Once when she was sick at home, he'd stopped by unexpectedly with his mother's homemade chicken soup and a video he'd picked up at Blockbuster for her, *Tootsie*, which was her favorite movie. "Why did you choose this?" she'd asked, holding up the box.

"Figured it was right up your alley," he'd said, and through her flu-like haze she'd recognized that he got her in a way that no one else ever had.

From the front lawn, Brady stared up at her, his black dog by his side with a tennis ball in his mouth. Brady lifted his hand above his head and motioned for her to come downstairs.

~

By the time Mary joined the party, most everybody had made their way inside the house, except for four guys playing cornhole with beanbags that glowed in the dark. As she walked past the game, a player wearing a Red Sox cap called out to her. "Hey, you're that girl on the news."

She felt as if she were floating. In this version of her life, she was someone people recognized.

The guy's friend swatted him in the arm. "Worst pickup line ever, bro."

"No," Mary said, stopping beside them. "I am on the news. ICNN 77."

"Is Belli's birthday party going to be on TV?" the guy in the baseball cap asked.

He sounded so excited by the idea that Mary considered lying. She looked down at the cornhole board, noticing the red, white, and blue stars and stripes. The sight of the flag painted on the game board on this hot summer night a few weeks before the Fourth of July grounded her in her new reality like nothing else had. She was not in her midfifties anymore. She was in her twenties at a party surrounded by people her new age, getting a second chance at life.

"I'm not working," she said. "I'm here to have fun." She picked up a beanbag from the ground and tossed it across the lawn toward the other board. It landed with a resounding thump before skidding up a white stripe and dropping into the hole.

~

Neon-pink strobe lights rotated around the living room, illuminating a large crowd dancing to music Mary didn't recognize. A lone spotlight shone on a tall sweaty man in an Uncle Sam hat dancing by himself in the corner. Frank Sinatra lay balled up under a table with a keg set up on it. Mary briefly considered joining him or hightailing back up the stairs to her apartment. This wasn't like any party she'd attended in decades. She was used to more intimate social gatherings, where the guests stood in small circles sipping expensive wine while caterers passed around trays of hors d'oeuvres.

The first time she was twenty-four, she wouldn't have been comfortable going to a party where she didn't know anyone. Over the years, though, she'd attended enough of Dean's work functions to perfect the art of conversing with strangers. She pretended she was a reporter on assignment to get the person's story. She threw her shoulders back and walked away from the door into the heart of the party. An enormous **HAPPY BIRTHDAY BELLI** banner hung from the wall on the opposite side of the room. A few feet in front of it, a glass bowl dangled from the ceiling. Because the bowl looked as out of place as she felt, Mary fought her way through the mob to get a closer look. Was it a prop in some game she didn't know about? When she finally reached the bowl, her hand flew over her open mouth. A lone orange fish swam in circles in a small aquarium suspended from the ceiling by bungee cords. A strobe light struck the glass, turning the water pink. The fish jerked to its right and switched directions. The strobe light hit the bowl again. The fish jerked left. Mary reached up toward the cords, intending to take the aquarium down. That poor fish had to be scared out of its mind.

"Whoa, whoa, whoa," a muscular guy in a Villanova Wildcats T-shirt said. "What do you think you're doing?"

"I'm taking this little creature someplace safe, away from the loud noise and flashing lights. It's too much for him." She stood on her tip-toes but couldn't reach the aquarium. "Help me get him down."

"He needs to stay right where he is. With a bird's-eye view of his party."

"Mary!" Brady's voice came from behind her. He handed her a beer. "I was getting ready to come up there after you." He winked. "Glad you came down."

What did that wink mean? And the way he was grinning at her made her feel skeevy. She looked away, lifting the flimsy plastic cup to her mouth. She sipped, breathing in a foul sulfuric odor. Yuck: a skunky taste filled her mouth. She hadn't drunk beer in decades, preferring trendy cocktails and malbec or cabernets. Still, she didn't remember beer being so gross. She wanted to spit it out.

"She's trying to take Belli down," the guy in the Villanova shirt said.

"He stays where he is." Brady pointed at the fish. "At least until we sing happy birthday and cut his cake."

Mary's head jerked backward. "That's Belli?"

Brady raised an eyebrow. "Who did you think it was? His twin?"

"You're throwing a birthday party for a fish?"

"Were you drinking before you came down? I've been planning this for weeks. You watched me MacGyver this." He snapped one of the cords, and the fishbowl swung back and forth.

She'd watched him set up that contraption? Was that when it had happened between them? Had it happened right here on the rug under the fishbowl? Her skin itched all over, and she scratched her arm. "I don't think it's safe or good for the fish to be hanging like that."

"We're all betting on whether Belli survives to see the day after his first birthday," Villanova T-Shirt Guy said.

"He's having the time of his—"

A woman in a burnt orange sundress flung herself at Brady. She had to be close to six feet tall. "I'll throw a hissy fit if you don't keep your promise to dance with me." Her southern drawl caught Mary's attention because that kind of accent was rarely heard in New England.

The woman's eyes landed on Mary. "You're the upstairs neighbor." Was there accusation in her voice? Mary gulped.

"I'm Brady's girlfriend, RaeLynn." She broke away from Brady and now loomed over Mary.

Was this woman going to kick her butt? "Mary." She took a step backward. The woman's height alone intimidated her.

"I know exactly who you are."

Mary had slept with Brady, and he had a girlfriend. Had he told Mary about this girl? No, no version of herself would sleep with a man who wasn't single. What a sleazeball this guy was. And perhaps she was no better. She had a husband, albeit in another universe.

In a flash, the woman's hands came toward Mary's neck. She was going to die at twenty-four, beaten to a pulp by a jealous girlfriend. Making it even worse, she had no memory of what had happened with Brady. Technically, it wasn't even her, at least not this version of her, who had done something with him.

The woman's hands thumped down on Mary's shoulders. She jerked Mary toward her, embracing her in a big bear hug. "I can't believe I'm meeting a celebrity. Brady and I watch you all the time. I made him take me to the Scooper Bowl after watching that story. You're so good."

Mary exhaled. The woman—what was her name again?—wasn't going to kill her. She was a fan. Mary had a fan! "Thank you for watching. I didn't catch your name."

"RaeLynn Horton."

The guy in the Uncle Sam hat dancing with the spotlight on him called out, "Someone bring me a beer."

Mary tilted her head in his direction. "What's his story?" She turned toward Brady, but he and the Villanova T-Shirt Guy were both gone. Thankfully.

"Marcus? Bless his heart," RaeLynn said. "Rookie at the fire station. They're hazing him, but they won't ever call it that. Making him dance all night. I told him he didn't have to, but he wouldn't listen." RaeLynn moved to the side to let someone by. The guy bumped Mary's cup, and beer spilled over her shirt.

"Whoops," he said without stopping.

Was "whoops" the new "sorry"? Mary had a good mind to chase the guy down and teach him how to apologize.

The music abruptly ended, and all the lights went out. Brady emerged from the kitchen carrying a long sheet cake with one fish-shaped candle. "Time to sing to Belli," he called. Everyone crammed under the bowl. The girl in front of Mary stepped on her foot. The man to her left accidentally jabbed his elbow into her ribs. Villanova T-Shirt Guy rested his hand on her shoulder. "Happy birthday to you . . . ," Brady started. The entire group joined in. The girl next to Mary sang the loudest, her hot breath tickling Mary's ear, making it itch.

Mary's wet, sticky shirt clung to her stomach. Her heart pounded and her breathing became shallow. She wanted to get out of there, get some air, but she was pinned in place. Long ago at a party in this same apartment, she'd had a panic attack under similar conditions where a crowd had boxed her in. Dean had sensed her discomfort and wrapped a protective arm around her shoulders, pushing people out of the way to get her to the door. He hadn't even thought her reaction was weird. He'd understood these attacks were something that happened to her every so often, and he read up on them so he could help her through them. She wished he were here now.

To calm herself, she looked around the room, silently naming things she saw: a girl with platinum blond hair, a guy wearing a Celtics T-shirt, a fish hanging from the ceiling. Her breathing started to slow, and she silently thanked Dean, who had taught her that trick long ago.

The singing stopped. Everyone high-fived one another. Brady cut the cake. RaeLynn handed Mary a slice. "You okay, sweetie? You look a little green around the gills." She laughed and looked up at the fish.

Mary placed her hand on her wet shirt. "I'm really uncomfortable. I'm going to go upstairs and change." She pointed at the aquarium. "Would you mind taking that down?"

"Belli?" RaeLynn reached up to unfasten the cords. "Yeah, he doesn't need to be up here anymore."

With the fishbowl tucked under her arm, Mary left the party. Back in her apartment, she placed Belli on the coffee table. Instead of changing into another shirt, she slipped into her pajamas and settled on the sofa with a book. Laughter from the party below drifted up through the floorboards. Mary exhaled loudly, grateful to be by herself in her apartment with the fish.

Chapter 14

On Monday, when Mary left for work, a black pickup was parked between her car and Brady's Jeep. The truck had been there since the party on Saturday night. She feared it belonged to Marcus, the kid in the Uncle Sam hat. She imagined he'd had to go to the hospital after his endless dancing. When she'd escaped the party with Belli, he looked like a marathoner who'd collapsed before reaching the finish line and was getting assistance from other runners and spectators while insisting he could finish the race. She would have even sworn she'd seen strobing red lights from an emergency vehicle reflected in her bedroom window a few minutes after she'd gone to bed that night.

As she unlocked her car, Brady's apartment door swung open. Giggling, Brady and RaeLynn stepped out with their arms wrapped around each other's waists. Frank Sinatra stood with his face pressed against the screen door, barking. Mary felt an emptiness in her stomach that it took her a minute to recognize as loneliness. Except for Darbi's visit and the hour or so she'd been at Brady's party, she'd spent the entire weekend by herself. On Sunday, she'd gone to the Natick Mall and had a blast trying on clothes in her new young body and charging a new wardrobe to a credit card she wouldn't be here long enough to have to pay off, but she would have had more fun if a friend had been with her. She'd forgotten how Sundays could be painful for single people. The first time she was in her twenties, she'd spent Friday and Saturday nights partying with her friends, but until she met Dean, she'd woken up alone every Sunday while her friends spent cozy mornings and afternoons cuddling with their significant others. No one had even texted or called her yesterday. Even when Dean golfed all weekend, he checked in with her throughout the day: You'll never believe who's in the foursome in front of me—Kendra's old boyfriend Max. Remember him?

Want to meet at the rail trail for a quick bite? I should be done by five.

Do you need anything?

Kendra, too, would send quick messages: Did I leave my sunglasses there?

Can you send me the recipe for that soup we had last time I was there?

When's the last time I had a tetanus shot?

Thinking about those messages that she'd taken for granted now made her feel needed, connected to something bigger than she was.

RaeLynn smiled at her. "You look pretty as a peach."

"Thank you." If only she—or some version of herself—hadn't slept with Brady, she could be good friends with RaeLynn. The girl was so stinking nice. She was even dressed in scrubs. Clearly, she spent her day helping people or animals, a job that mattered.

"Did you have a good time at the party?" Brady asked.

How could he act so normal toward her when RaeLynn was standing mere inches away? Was he that sure Mary wouldn't tell her that he'd cheated?

"More fun than I ever thought I'd have at a fish's birthday party." She stared at the ground, afraid that looking at him would trigger memories of their night together.

Brady let out a throaty laugh. "Speaking of which, someone fish-napped him. Would you know anything about that?"

"I prefer to think of it as a rescue mission."

Brady glanced behind him at his door, where Frank Sinatra still stood watching them. "You can have the fish for a few days, but don't get any ideas about my dog."

"Did Marcus survive?" Mary addressed RaeLynn.

"They couldn't break him," she said.

"I could have sworn I saw a fire truck in the driveway."

"That was just the guys from the firehouse stopping by on the way back from a call," Brady said.

"I need to get to work." RaeLynn leaned closer to Brady. He cupped her face, and their lips met.

Dean used to always kiss Mary goodbye before he left the house. He'd stopped after she'd snapped at him when he woke her up at five thirty to say goodbye before he left for an early-morning tee time. A wave of sorrow washed over her. When she got back, she'd apologize and tell him she wanted him to wake her up again with goodbye kisses.

"Have a good day, Mary. I'll be sure to tune in tonight." RaeLynn waved as she climbed into her truck.

Brady flashed his grin at Mary. "Should we get together tonight? Finish watching *Ozark*?"

Her cheeks flushed. Had they been watching that show when they slept together? Was he talking in code? Did he think she would sleep with him again? RaeLynn deserved so much better. She glared at Brady while thanking her lucky stars she'd never worried about Dean cheating. "We definitely should not."

~

After the morning meeting with the assignment editor, Mitchell summoned Mary and Kimberly Nash, one of the other reporters, to his office. As the two women walked down the hall together, memories of their interactions before Mary had arrived in this alternate universe flooded her mind. They'd spent a weekend at Kimberly's family beach house in Eastham on the Cape. They'd attended a Zac Brown concert at Fenway Park. They'd toasted each other with cosmopolitans at a popular bistro on Newbury Street.

"What do you think Mitchell wants?" Kimberly asked. She pushed a dark curl off her face, and the sparkling diamond on the fourth finger of her left hand caught Mary's attention. Another memory—or whatever these flashbacks that she hadn't lived through were—came to mind. She and Kimberly sat in a Chinese restaurant after work. Mary could even see the outfit she'd worn that night, a blue and tan dress that hung just below her knees, with tall tan boots. At the end of the meal, Kimberly had giggled as Mary cracked open a fortune cookie. Instead of a string of lucky numbers or a cryptic message, the piece of paper inside asked a question: *Will you be my bridesmaid?*

In the hallway, Mary blinked. Did that really happen? Customized fortune cookies seemed like an elaborate way to ask someone to be in your wedding party. Dean's proposal hadn't even been as creative. On his birthday, he'd dropped to his knee as they left Mother Anna's, his favorite restaurant in the North End. She thought he'd tripped and hadn't realized he was proposing until she noticed his eyes glistening. "Give me the greatest gift ever. Be my wife," he'd said. A warmth spread through Mary as she remembered how loved she'd felt at that moment.

"You're still coming with me tomorrow night?" Kimberly asked.

Mary nodded, glad to know she had a good friend in this version of her life. At the same time, she felt sad, thinking about the bridesmaids who had stood beside her when she'd married Dean. Other than Darbi, she'd lost touch with all of them. They had been closer than sisters and had sworn they always would be. Over the years, they had babies, and their priorities shifted. Daily phone calls turned into weekly chats and sporadic texts. Soon they spoke only a few times a year. Before Mary knew what had happened, a decade had passed without them seeing each other. When she got back to her life in Hudson, she'd arrange a reunion, a barbecue at her house. Dean would be happy to have another reason to fire up Gus.

In Mitchell's office, Mary and Kimberly sat side by side, looking at him across the desk. A framed picture of Mitchell with his two small girls and his wife faced out from the windowsill. Mary's stomach tightened when she remembered the picture in Darbi's sunroom of her on the rock without Dean and Kendra. She twisted in her seat so the photograph of Mitchell's family was no longer in her line of vision. Sunrays streaked through the open blinds, hitting her in the face. Still, having the sun in her eyes was more comfortable than thinking about the implication of that solo shot of her hanging on Darbi's wall. She was living in a world without Kendra, or Dean for that matter.

"We have a busy day, so I'll get right to it," Mitchell said. He rubbed his palms together. "There's an opening at ICNN's national *Morning Show* out of Chicago. Corporate wants me to recommend someone for the position. I've narrowed down my choice to the two of you."

Mary tightened her grip on the armrest to prevent herself from leaping out of her chair. This was it. Her chance to set her old life right. Finally.

"I'm thrilled to be considered," Kimberly said. "Tyler has offers at firms in Chicago and here in Boston. He wasn't even going to consider Chicago because my job's here, but it's great to know it might be an option."

Mary swallowed hard, feeling sorry for her friend. Kimberly had no shot. There was no way Mary would miss out on this magical second chance she'd been given. She would do whatever it took to get that promotion and return home as America's most trusted broadcaster.

~

On her way to the vending machine for a Diet Coke, Mary paused in front of the studio. As she stared through the sliding glass door at the empty room, her body buzzed with anticipation. As soon as she whipped

Kimberly's butt and earned that promotion, she would be sitting behind the anchor desk for a national network as her fifty-four-year-old self. She imagined Dean and Kendra stopping whatever they were doing every night to watch her, even if Kendra was watching over the internet from England.

Glancing over her shoulder to make sure no one could see her, she slid the door to the studio open and slipped inside. Her heart skipped as she looked at the anchor desk with the Channel 77 logo fastened to its front side and a mural of Boston's skyline on the wall behind it. She tiptoed across the floor toward the desk as if she were approaching a deity she was in awe of. She sneaked a look behind her. Certain no one was watching, she climbed into the anchor chair, brimming with excitement. Straightening her posture, she looked directly into the camera lens and whispered, "I'm Mary Mulligan, and this is Channel 77 N . . ." She giggled and started again. She was on her way to being the anchor for a major network, not just this cable station. "Good evening. I'm Mary Mulligan, and this is the *CBS Evening News.*"

The words felt like the truest statement she had spoken in years. She squealed and repeated the sentences louder, emphasizing her name and the station number. "I'm Mary Mulligan, and this is the *CBS Evening News.*"

Across the room, a man cleared his throat. Mary's face reddened. She wasn't alone. Carl leaned against the door to the control room, watching her. "Glad to hear you get your name right." He smirked. "When you're done playing anchorwoman, we have a story to cover. Train derailment on the Green Line."

Chapter 15

Kimberly let herself into Mary's apartment without knocking. She looked absolutely stylish in light-blue pants with a navy stripe and a white midriff shirt. Her hair curled all the way down to her chest. Mary had thrown on jeans with the left knee torn out. Size four! Her fifty-four-year-old self had worn a sixteen. She also wouldn't have been caught dead wearing jeans with a big ole hole in the leg, but people her new age found them stylish, so she'd bought them on Sunday. Her black tunic had peekaboo holes revealing her shoulders, which thankfully didn't have brown spots from too much sun exposure. If she were staying in this world, she'd be sure to always sit under an umbrella at the beach or pool. "Hey, make sure you always wear lots of sunscreen," she said.

Kimberly raised an eyebrow. "What are you even talking about?"

"Never mind."

Kimberly made her way to the living room and stared down into Belli's bowl on the coffee table. "When did you get a fish?"

"I had to save him before Brady killed him. He hung him from the ceiling at a party the other night."

"Is everything back to normal with Brady after last weekend?" Kimberly asked.

Mary's stomach dropped. "What happened last weekend?" She tried to make the question sound matter of fact and not as if she was desperate for information.

"Sorry. I know you made me promise to never bring it up again." Kimberly mimicked zippering her lips.

Oh boy, if she'd told Kimberly about it and promised her to secrecy, she must have slept with him. Ugh, she wanted to kick her own butt for being so stupid.

Kimberly's phone beeped. "Our Uber's here," she said.

"An Uber. All the way to Boston. That has to be close to a hundred dollars." Mary winced because she realized she sounded like her fifty-four-year-old self rather than the twenty-four-year-old she now was.

Kimberly made a face. "Still cheaper than a DUI."

Down on the driveway, Kimberly slid into the back seat of the Uber while Mary walked around to the passenger side, opening the front door. The driver, a woman who looked the age Mary used to be, startled.

"Why are you sitting in the front?" Kimberly asked.

Mary didn't know where she was supposed to sit, but it seemed rude to have this woman drive them around like a chauffeur. She'd ridden in an Uber only one other time, when the flight she and Dean had taken on the way home from the Turks and Caicos got delayed and they'd arrived back at the airport after two in the morning, well after the Logan Express bus had stopped running. The ride had cost them $160.

"I get carsick," she said. She didn't, but she wanted to save face.

"It's fine." The driver snatched an envelope off the seat and tossed it into the glove box.

"Whatever," Kimberly said. "You've never been carsick before."

"Would you like music?" the driver asked.

Mary answered without thinking. "103.3."

"We are not listening to the oldies station," Kimberly grumbled. "What is with you tonight?"

The driver tuned the radio to Kiss 108. "It's what my daughter likes when she's forced to listen to the radio and not Spotify."

Mary swallowed hard. "How old's your daughter?"

"Twenty-six. She's getting married. That's why I picked up this extra job. To help pay for the wedding."

"I'm getting married too," Kimberly said. "When's your daughter's wedding?"

The two of them talked about venues, florists, photographers, gowns, and bridesmaid dresses while Mary stared out the window with a pit in her stomach, wondering if Nate would propose to Kendra and where the wedding would be. She hoped it would be back in the States so she could help Kendra plan it.

The car jerked to a stop. They'd reached the Seaport. "Have fun tonight, girls," the driver said. "Look out for each other, and watch your drinks. Don't leave them unattended."

Mary had given Kendra the same warning too many times to count.

"I have it on a recording, Mom," Kendra had once joked. "I play it right before I leave my apartment."

A tear rolled down Mary's cheek. She wished that before having her wisdom teeth removed, she'd smoothed things over with her daughter. As soon as Mary returned, the two of them would have a long talk.

"What's wrong?" Kimberly asked. They were out on the sidewalk, the foul smell of the hot city in the air.

Mary wiped away a tear. *I miss my daughter.* Oh, how she wanted to talk about Kendra, but of course she couldn't. "All the talk about weddings, I guess."

Kimberly wrapped her arm around Mary's shoulders. "Don't worry. You'll meet someone. Maybe even tonight."

"I don't want to meet anyone. I came back to focus on my job, not date." A car honked, and Mary looked toward the street.

"Came back?"

Ugh. She really needed to stop slipping up with veiled references to her old life before people thought she was crazy. "I just want to focus on the opportunity we've been given. May the best journalist win." She'd said the last part to be gracious. She didn't mean it, because she had to win.

~

Sipping a dirty martini with blue cheese–stuffed olives, Mary stood next to Kimberly at the bar in the Adult Arcade, a new club in Boston's Seaport. Kimberly had ordered the drinks, and Mary was surprised how good hers was. The sounds of video games—buzzing, ringing, and electronic voices—echoed through the room. Groups of twenty- and thirty-somethings crowded pinball, *Galaga*, *Donkey Kong*, and other similar machines. In the back, lines waited outside rooms for axe throwing, laser tag, bowling, and go-karts. The place reminded her of Chuck E. Cheese, but instead of juice boxes and sippy cups, the clientele here clutched beer cans and cocktail glasses. Once at Chuck E. Cheese, Mary had lost sight of Kendra. Heart pounding, she'd frantically raced around the arcade shouting her daughter's name, grabbing strangers by the arm to ask if they'd seen a little girl with pigtails wearing a red shirt. She'd eventually found Kendra in a ball pit, but those five minutes her daughter had been missing were among the scariest moments of her motherhood. Standing in this adult club, Mary's heart pounded the same way it had that day at the children's arcade. Until she returned to her real life, Kendra truly was lost to her. Using her hand, Mary fanned her red-hot face. Mitchell would make his decision about the promotion soon. She could hang on for a little while longer.

Kimberly grabbed Mary's arm, pointing to three people leaving. They raced across the room, swooping in to claim the now-empty spot. When Mary sat, she saw the table was a sit-down *Ms. Pac-Man* machine. She'd loved *Pac-Man* as a teenager and challenged Kimberly to a game. Kimberly went first, losing her turn in a matter of seconds.

"Ha! I'm going to schmuck you," Mary said. She reached the next level without losing a life and smirked at Kimberly, who rolled her eyes.

"You're sure taking this seriously," Kimberly asked. "It's just a silly game."

Silly game or not, there was no way Mary would let Kimberly beat her. She didn't like losing, never had. People didn't take losers seriously.

She hadn't even let little-girl Kendra beat her at board games, something that had infuriated Dean. She'd explained to him that most people didn't get things handed to them in life; they had to work for them. Kendra needed to learn that. Looking back now, Mary thought maybe she should have let Kendra win a few games of Chutes and Ladders and Candyland after all.

Their game of *Ms. Pac-Man* ended with Kimberly still in "Act 1: They Meet," and Mary in "Act 3: Junior." Mary threw her arms up in triumph. "Woohoo!" she shouted.

A man standing nearby pointed at them. Mary wondered if he'd seen her celebration and felt a little ridiculous about it now. "Hey, I know you two," he said.

He didn't look familiar, and she waited for a memory dump. It didn't come.

"I catch you on the news every now and then. You're both good."

Mary grinned. People recognized her. First the guy at Brady's party, then RaeLynn, and now this guy.

Kimberly smiled up at him. "Thank you."

"Who's better?" Mary asked.

"Don't answer that," Kimberly said.

The horrified look on her friend's face shamed Mary, but she was curious about this man's opinion. Knowing what viewers thought could help her get the promotion. She might learn she was the underdog and would have to work extra hard. The thought frightened her. What if Mitchell chose Kimberly? No, she couldn't let that happen. No matter what.

After the man left, Kimberly stared at Mary across the table. "So, this is how it's going to be?" The hurt in Kimberly's voice reminded Mary of when her and Liz's friendship had started to splinter.

"I don't know what you mean."

"You're turning this opportunity for the promotion into a huge competition."

"We both can't get promoted, so it is a competition." *One that I'm going to win.*

"Just so you know, I'll be happy for you if you win," Kimberly said. "And I hope you'll be happy for me if I win."

"Of course." Under the table, Mary crossed her fingers. She'd be devastated if she didn't fix her mistake and return to her old life a success.

~

Mary arrived at work early the next morning, determined to get the juiciest story. Overhead, the fluorescent lights buzzed; to her left, someone furiously tapped away at a keyboard; and behind her, the police scanner squawked.

She sipped her coffee and leaned closer to her screen to read an email.

From: MrsTomKinney@Yahoo.com
To: Mary.Mulligan@ICNNBoston77.com
Subject: Your Wardrobe

Dear Ms. Mulligan,

I saw your story on the Scooper Bowl. I think someone needs to tell you, yellow is not your color. You look more washed out than usual when you wear it. Do yourself and your viewers a favor and stick to darker colors like navy and red. As I've said before, the station should really think about hiring a wardrobe consultant. I'd be glad to lend my expertise.

Sincerely,
Barbara M. Kinney

Mary fought the urge to smash her mug into her monitor. She'd forgotten all about the criticism she'd received the first time around, the letters and phone calls from viewers offering unsolicited advice about her outfits, haircut, and makeup. Even though most of the feedback she received was nice, the nasty ones like this one left a scar.

She jabbed at the delete key until the message disappeared.

"You should see your face right now." Kimberly strode into Mary's cube with a box of doughnuts. "What's the matter?"

Mary reached for a honey-dipped doughnut. "An email from a viewer telling me yellow is not my color."

Kimberly waved her hand in a dismissive motion. "That's nothing. Last week someone wrote in to tell me I'd gained weight and was becoming unsightly to watch. Don't let it get to you." She laughed and tapped the Dunkin' box. "You can see I don't."

The assignment editor raced into Mary's office. "Massive pileup near the Route 128 / Route 3 interchange—we need someone to get over there. Now."

"I'll go," Kimberly said.

Mary leaped to her feet. "I've got it."

As she walked away, she could feel Kimberly's eyes burning holes into the back of her head.

Chapter 16

Over a week had passed since Mary had her wisdom teeth removed. Each day when she woke up, she expected to be in her bed in Hudson, in the dentist's chair, or maybe in a hospital, waking up from a coma. She spent the first few minutes of every morning wondering how it was possible that she was twenty-four again and thanking her lucky stars that she had the opportunity to undo the greatest mistake of her life.

When she stepped outside onto the landing to leave for work, Brady was walking up the driveway with Frank Sinatra. She spun around and went back inside, shutting the door behind her. If she avoided him, then maybe she'd never remember what had happened between them, because she definitely didn't want to bring those memories home to her marriage.

When she finally arrived at work, there was a message from Mitchell, summoning her to his office. As she walked down the hallway, she wondered if he'd already decided about the promotion and picked up her pace. Kimberly and Harvey, the chief meteorologist, were there standing in front of Mitchell's desk. Mary squeezed in between them, hoping she hadn't missed out on a good assignment by being late.

"It's a rare summer nor'easter," Harvey said. "Damaging winds, dangerous tides, and soaking rain."

Mary knew what was coming—an assignment outside in driving rain and fierce winds, reporting on the storm. Mary version 1 had gotten stuck reporting in the thick of several storms. She and Carl had almost been killed during Hurricane Bob when a telephone pole came crashing down, just missing the news van. She glanced at Kimberly and stood a little taller. Her experience doing these types of stories would give her an edge over Kimberly.

"The coastal towns will get hammered. Hingham, Cohasset, Scituate, Gloucester, Marblehead," Harvey said. His eyes were bloodshot, and a tuft of his silver hair stood at attention in the center of his head. He'd unbuttoned the sleeves of his dress shirt and pushed them back to his elbows. A red tie hung out of his left pocket and streamed down his wrinkled pant leg. One of his shoes was even untied.

He must have been up all night tracking the storm. Still, Mary didn't feel sorry for him. At least he got to work inside the comfort of his warm, dry office. Mary and Kimberly didn't have that luxury. From the looks of things, they'd be outside all day tomorrow in the elements.

"Thanks, Harvey." Mitchell rubbed his hands together. "Ladies, looks like we're in for a doozy."

Harvey smiled at Kimberly and Mary on his way out of the room. "Don't either of you pull a Liz Collins," he said.

Mitchell laughed.

Kimberly scrunched her nose. "Never."

"Did he say Liz Collins?" Mary asked, her tone uncertain.

Mitchell's eyes widened. "Don't tell me you don't know who Liz Collins is?"

America's most trusted broadcaster. The words were on the tip of her tongue, but she knew they weren't true in this version of her life, so she swallowed them. Mitchell stared at her with his lips pressed tightly together. She had to say something. "Of course I do."

Mitchell raised an eyebrow. "Who is she?"

Mary's underarms felt sticky. Clearly everyone knew who Liz was. She shouldn't have listened to Darbi. She should have googled Liz. Hoping for help, she turned to Kimberly, but she should have known better. They were on opposite teams now. Kimberly picked a piece of lint off her sleeve.

Mary fiddled with the charm on her necklace. "She used to work here?" Her voice was barely a whisper. She wasn't even sure if that was true.

"Come on, Mitchell," Kimberly cut in. "Everyone knows she walked off camera straight into retirement in the middle of covering a raging storm."

Mary's hand shot up to cover her gaping mouth. The Liz she'd known had been a strong, determined woman. She never would have let a storm wash away her career.

"Watch video of her and learn," Mitchell said. "Until that infamous day, she was the best in the business at covering inclement weather. Tomorrow you both get your chance. Mary, you'll go with Carl to the South Shore, and Kimberly, you're with Matt up north." He rubbed his hands together. "Since you're both covering the same story, I'll have the perfect opportunity to compare your skills. So, up your game, ladies."

～

After work, Kimberly asked Mary to go to dinner. "I don't want this competition to ruin our friendship. We need to keep things normal," she said.

Mary felt a surge of affection for the girl. Certainly Liz had never said anything like that to her, nor had she said anything similar to Liz. Perhaps she and Kimberly could remain friends despite the competition.

At five thirty, they headed across the street to the Press Box, a restaurant that most of the news crew ate at from time to time. Fluffy white clouds floated in a blue sky, making it hard to believe a storm was blowing in. They sat at a high-top table outside on a deck that overlooked a highway. Cars were stacked up one behind another, trying to get home but not moving. The first time Mary had worked for Channel 77, Boston's rush hour really had been only an hour. Over the years, though, traffic in the area had become so bad that there was only a small window of time when there wasn't a backup on the highways.

As Mary read the menu, Kimberly fiddled with her phone. "I can't believe you don't know who Liz Collins is. Anyone who grew up around here remembers her dressed like the Gorton's Fisherman, standing by the seawall in Scituate, looking like she was about to be swept out to sea."

Under the table, Mary's knee bounced up and down as she waited for the dizzy spell that usually came before a brain dump. It didn't come. She needed to make up some type of excuse for not knowing who Liz was, but she couldn't think clearly. The sounds of horns blowing and motors idling from the traffic jam below them distracted her. She could even hear a radio, a booming bass, and then she could have sworn she heard Liz's voice, albeit a less refined version of the voice Liz used on the nightly news.

"High tide is still an hour away!" the voice that sounded like Liz's screamed, presumably trying to be heard over what sounded like gusting wind. "The people who live here have dealt with this before." The reporter's enunciation wasn't as pronounced, but it was definitely Liz.

Kimberly angled the phone so Mary could see it. Liz's image filled the small screen. She wore black rubber boots, bright-yellow snow pants, and a matching yellow bubble coat. The tip of her runny nose glowed bright red, her lips were chapped, and her windblown hair dripped water down her forehead. She held tight to a flagpole with the hand that wasn't holding the microphone. Behind her, the ocean raged, waves swelling higher than her head and crashing violently just before the seawall.

"The worst of the storm is still to come," Liz said.

Off camera, someone yelled, "Watch out!"

Liz turned toward the stormy Atlantic. A wave breached the wall, swallowing her whole. For a tense few seconds, there was no sign of her on-screen. The water retreated. Liz was on her knees, the water up to her chest, seaweed hanging from her hair. As she struggled to stand, another wave rolled over her.

Mary watched, horrified. Even though fifty-four-year-old Mary was jealous of her old nemesis's success, seeing Liz risk her life and be humiliated in the process brought Mary version 2 no joy.

Liz finally made it to her feet. The camera zoomed in on her face. Mascara streamed down her cheeks. She didn't have a microphone, and her voice was barely audible over the wind and crashing waves. But Mary could read her lips. The entire world could have read Liz's lips. The wind stopped, or Liz's voice had overpowered it. "I'm done. I"—here, there was a loud bleep—"quit." The camera followed her sopping-wet backside as she stormed away from the violent sea and toward the parking lot.

The server arrived at their table and looked down over Mary's shoulder at Kimberly's screen. "Whenever I think I'm having a bad day at work," she said, "I think of that poor woman."

The screen went black, and the anchors were back on camera, insincere looks of concern on their faces. "That's our Liz Collins braving the elements in Scituate to report the news to you," the male anchor said.

"Stay safe, Liz," the female anchor said.

Kimberly reached for her phone. "There are so many great memes from that day."

"Oh, I know," the server said. "Some of my favorites."

Kimberly tapped at her phone and turned the screen toward Mary and the server again. There was Liz halfway to her feet as the giant wave rolled over her, playing on an endless loop.

Mary thought of the version of Liz she had known, dignified and poised behind the CBS anchor desk, smiling and proud on the cover of *People*. She stared at this humiliated version of Liz on Kimberly's phone getting ragdolled by the waves, the worst moment of her career frozen on-screen, a joke for all eternity. Mary felt as if she herself had been pummeled by the waves and was now underwater, fighting to get to the surface but not knowing which direction was up.

Why was Liz's life so different just because she hadn't met Mary? It made no sense.

Mary tried to remember what she knew about the butterfly effect. Something about a butterfly flapping its wings in one part of the world causing a tornado someplace else several weeks later. The point was that a small change somewhere could result in enormous differences in something seemingly unrelated someplace else. She'd never thought much about it before, but thinking about it right now—with America's most trusted broadcaster frozen on a tiny screen, looking like a drowned rat for all the world to see—sent chills down Mary's spine. She swallowed hard as she looked away from the phone and out at the brake lights below her, and she wondered what other unintended damage she'd caused by having her wisdom teeth removed and if any of the changes would carry over to her real life.

Chapter 17

Mary and Carl stumbled into the Hungry Shark Tavern. As the door slammed behind them, loud voices and deep-throated laughter replaced the sound of the howling wind and angry surf. Although Mary had toweled herself off in the news van, water dripped off her pants, jacket, and hair, leaving a puddle by her feet. All morning, she'd been reporting in a torrential downpour and seventy-five-mile-per-hour wind gusts from the same seawall where Liz had stood in that awful video. Being there made Mary wonder what Liz was doing today. She couldn't help but think that wherever she was, Liz was miserable and drinking too much, obsessing over giving up her career in news.

The worst part of Mary's assignment was still to come. She had to file a report by the ocean at high tide, which was two hours away. Carl had suggested ducking into the pub to kill time.

"There are two seats at the bar," he said, pointing.

The overhead lights did little to illuminate the pub, and Mary had a hard time seeing across the room to the empty stools. Carl strode off, pushing his way through the crowd. She trailed behind, trying to keep up with his long strides. As they approached the bar, the smell of fried clams and onion rings wafted through the air. Mary's mouth watered. She hadn't had anything to eat since wolfing down a granola bar on the way to work.

"Two Sam Summers," Carl said to the bartender as he climbed onto a stool.

Mary shook her head. "We can't drink. We're working."

Carl rolled his eyes. "Two Sam Summers," he repeated.

"Actually, I'll have lemonade." She couldn't risk getting buzzed. She needed her wits about her because her story had to be better than Kimberly's.

"You're such a fuddy-duddy," Carl said. "You sure you're Gen Z and not a boomer?"

"I'm Gen X," Mary said. "The forgotten generation."

"Really? You're the same generation as me?"

Mary nodded, and it was if the movement of her head jarred her memory. In this do-over version of life, she was born in the late 1990s, not 1960s. She smiled at Carl. "Just seeing if you're paying attention."

The bartender returned with their drinks. Mary banged her glass against Carl's bottle. "Cheers."

"What's your story, Mary Mulligan—or is it Mary Amato?"

Hearing Carl say her real last name, Mary sat up straighter. She didn't want to think about the world she'd left behind and who she had been. As she pictured Dean and Kendra, her throat tightened. She missed them. When Kendra was younger, the three of them used to go to the beach in this town. She could almost feel the weight of four-year-old Kendra's hand in hers as they stood in ankle-deep water, almost hear her squeal as Dean lifted her to his shoulders and walked out deeper.

"Seriously, how did you get your name wrong? Who does that?" Carl stared at her as if he knew her secret. "And why would you claim to be part of Generation X?"

He'd never let her forget that she'd gotten her name wrong. Why would he? The mistake was impossible to explain. "I was kidding." Cool air from the air-conditioning blew down on Mary. She shivered, wishing she had dry clothes to change into.

"You weren't kidding. Something's off with you." He took a pull of his beer.

She wanted to tell him what had happened when she'd had her wisdom teeth removed. She needed to talk to someone about it other than Darbi, who'd already advised her not to think about what had happened and just live. In the last version of Mary's life, she and Carl had been friendly. Maybe they could be friends in this life too. Next to her, Carl peeled the label off his bottle. Mary tried to imagine him reacting to her confession. *What kind of drugs are you on?* That was exactly what he'd say, and he'd tease her about it, tell everyone at the station too. *She claimed to have aged backward thirty years when she got her wisdom teeth out.* If Mitchell found out, he'd never consider her for the promotion. No, she couldn't tell Carl. He wasn't the free-spirited young man she'd remembered. He'd aged into a curmudgeon. She sipped through the straw the bartender had placed in her drink. The feel of the soggy paper on her lips gave her the heebie-jeebies. "This is disgusting."

"Should have had a beer," Carl said.

"Not the drink, the straw." Mary pulled it from her glass. "Whatever happened to good ole plastic straws?"

"That's what I'm talking about," Carl said. "No one your age thinks that way. They're all too busy trying to save the environment, prevent global warming."

Mary shifted on her stool. She had to get back to her old life before she gave herself away.

The bartender approached. "You good here?"

"Can we see a menu?" Carl asked.

"We're supposed to be working." Kimberly probably hadn't stopped for lunch. No doubt she was working on a great story right now.

Carl looked at his watch. "We have plenty of time to eat."

Mary glanced around the room. The crowd stood shoulder to shoulder, laughing and guzzling down alcohol, apparently unbothered by the nor'easter barreling down on them. "We need to interview some of these people. Get their thoughts on the storm," she said.

"We will. After we eat."

She ordered a lobster roll and sweet potato fries, something Dean would have ordered if he'd been here. Carl watched her gobble them down, not touching his fish and chips.

"What are you staring at?" she asked.

"At the Scooper Bowl, you barely had a spoonful of ice cream. I thought you were one of those women in our industry who doesn't eat because you don't want to ruin your figure. But watching you inhale your lunch, I see I was wrong."

Mary took another bite into the toasted buttery roll. It was true. She didn't worry about her weight. Not in this version of her life. She knew from the last time she was in her twenties that she could eat whatever she wanted without packing on pounds, at least until she turned thirty. Besides, she didn't plan to be here much longer, so these were all free calories. Still, Carl's words offended her. The television station would never allow an overweight woman to appear on camera but had no issue giving airtime to portly men. Aaron, the sports anchor, had to be creeping up on three hundred pounds.

"I'm eating because I'm hungry," she said. "But for your information, women in my line of work lose their jobs if they 'ruin their figures.'" She used air quotes around the last three words.

Carl smirked and cut off a large piece of his fish. He lifted his fork to his lips. "I'm not getting into this with you." He slid the fork in his mouth and turned his head to chew.

They ate in silence. When they finished, Carl ran out to the news van for his camera. When he returned, he and Mary wandered around the bar looking for someone to interview. A man with a deeply wrinkled, sunburned face approached Mary. "You're that reporter from Channel 77," he said. "Mary Mulligan."

She nodded, unfazed by the recognition now. "I am."

"Eric O'Brien. I watch you all the time. You're good. My favorite."

Well, being someone's favorite was something new. Mary elbowed Carl, who rolled his eyes. "We're looking for people to go on camera and talk about the storm," he said.

"I'm a fisherman. Couldn't go out today."

"Can I interview you?" Mary asked.

"Sure," Eric said.

Carl pointed the camera at Mary. "On three," he said. "One, two, three."

"We're at the Hungry Shark Tavern in Scituate, talking to Eric O'Brien, a deep-sea fisherman who's forced to stay on land today because of the weather." Mary shouted over the noise in the bar. "Are you enjoying the unexpected day off?"

"Not really," Eric said. "I'd rather be out on my boat making money, but me and the guys are making the most of it." He jerked his beer mug in the direction of a group of men in the corner laughing.

A man in a postal uniform sat alone at a table a few feet from them. His back was toward her, so Mary couldn't see his face, but something about the way his right shoulder rested slightly higher than his left seemed familiar. She couldn't pull her eyes away from him.

"Mulligan," Carl said.

Mary swung her head back toward Eric. "How much do you think the storm is costing you?"

Eric frowned. "A couple of grand for sure."

From the corner of her eye, Mary saw the mailman stand. He turned and stepped in her direction. She blinked hard, not believing what she saw. The man looked like a down-on-his-luck version of James, at least in the dim light. Her eyes locked on the US postal logo on his shirt. A shiver ran down her spine. Years ago in her other life, James had worn a shirt just like that one as they sat at the top of the steps at the Framingham apartment, drinking Captain and Cokes at the end of the workday. *No, no, no, James can't still be a mailman. He's a famous musician.*

The man who looked like James had almost reached the door. Mary had to talk to him. Make sure he wasn't James. She raced after him.

"Mulligan!" Carl shouted. "Where are you going? You're in the middle of an interview."

She continued to rush across the room, pushing through groups of people. Just before the James look-alike pushed the door open, Mary reached out and grabbed his arm.

He whirled around toward her. "Do you need something?" he asked, impatient.

His skin didn't glow the way her James's did. His eyes didn't sparkle, and his voice had no hint of amusement, but this man had to be James, a version of him that had never been bedazzled, as her James claimed to be.

"What are you doing here? Why aren't you in LA?"

The man tilted his head. "Never once been to LA. You're confusing me with someone else."

She wasn't, though. She knew exactly who he was. The bar suddenly seemed too loud, the room too cold, the smell of fried seafood nauseating. "You look like an old friend of mine." She waited for him to say her friend must be a good-looking son of a gun because that's what her James would say.

This James folded his arms across his chest. "Poor guy."

There was no amusement in his voice. He meant it. Mary swallowed the lump in her throat, wondering what had happened to him in this version of his life to take away his sparkle. She thought of Liz getting pummeled by waves. *What have I done?*

With the camera still on his shoulder, Carl bulldozed his way between Mary and James. "You can't just walk away in the middle of an interview."

People standing by stopped to look at them. The last thing Mary needed right now was to be scolded by her cameraman. James was standing in front of her, his life nothing like it was in the real world, and she had a sick feeling she was to blame.

James stared at the logo on Carl's camera. "You're with Channel 77?"

Mary nodded. "Mary Mulligan." She paused, waiting for him to give a sign that he recognized her name. He didn't. "I'm covering the storm. Can I ask you a few questions for my story?"

"I don't know." He stepped away from the door toward her. "I have to get back to work, and I really don't have anything interesting to say."

"I'll be the judge of that. Let's start with your name?" She crossed her fingers. *Say Mike, Tom, or Bill, anything but James.* Please, let her James still be singing his heart out to sold-out electrified crowds.

"James Morisette."

She had known this man was her James, but hearing him confirm it deflated her the same way she'd been deflated in her early twenties when her James had informed her that the girl who danced with Bruce Springsteen in the "Dancing in the Dark" video was Courteney Cox, an actress planted in the audience, not a random fan he'd pulled up onstage. It was one of the reasons she'd never warmed to Monica on *Friends.*

"Mulligan," Carl said. "Do you have a question for the mailman?"

"Did the storm interfere with your job today?" she asked.

"The rain and wind made it challenging, but I got it done," James said. "You know what they say about the US Postal Service delivering mail in rain, sleet, or snow."

"Can you tell me about any specific challenges?"

"There was a tree down on Hibiscus Lane blocking the road. I parked the mail truck and walked the rest of the way with my mailbag."

"Nicely done." Mary smiled, happy he was committed to his job but wondering where his commitment to music had gone. She had to find out if he still sang.

By now, aware of the camera, a large crowd had gathered around them.

"What do you do when you're not delivering mail?"

James scratched his head. "What do you mean?"

"Do you have any hobbies?"

Behind her, Carl sighed.

"I read a lot. Mysteries and thrillers," James said.

"You read books?" Her James wouldn't be able to sit still long enough to finish a novel.

This James shifted his weight from one leg to the other. His ears turned red. "I listen to them on my route, but maybe you shouldn't put that on the news."

"I can edit it out," Mary said.

Carl stepped forward. "We have enough."

Mary waved him off. "Do you sing? Play the guitar?"

James crossed his arms. "Why would you ask that?"

She glanced up at the lobster traps and buoys hanging from the ceiling, hoping for inspiration. "My friend who you look like does."

"I used to in another life, but not anymore."

In another life. He didn't mean the phrase literally, but still it hit so close to home that it knocked the wind out of Mary. Her eyes fell to the floor as she tried to collect herself. *Please let him still be a singer in his other life.* "I bet you were good."

James shrugged.

"Let me hear you sing something." There had to be some showboating left in this version of him.

Carl cleared his throat. "What are you doing? We're supposed to be covering the storm, not filming *America's Got Talent*."

Mary addressed the crowd watching the interview. "Do you want to hear him sing?"

"Sing, sing, sing," they all chanted, except for one guy who slurred, "Hell no."

The first time she'd ever heard him, James was singing Rod Stewart's "Maggie May." His voice had drifted out his open window to the patio in the backyard, where she sat reading *The Firm.*

She'd clapped when James finished, and he'd stuck his head out the window. "I didn't know you were out there."

"You were wonderful," she'd said. "You should go to open mic at the Skunk."

James had scrunched his nose. "I'm much too good for that dump."

"Well, no one's going to hear you singing in your apartment," she'd said.

Two weeks later, he agreed to go with her to the Skunk, and he took down the place.

Now in this pub, she said, "I bet you do a mean Rod Stewart."

His cheek twitched. "I'm not sure about this."

Mary could tell by the way he threw back his shoulders and stood a little bit taller that he wanted to sing. She belted out the first line of "Maggie May."

James winced just like her James did whenever Mary version 1 sang. "Girl, you know nothing about carrying a tune."

Finally, he sounded like the man she knew and loved. She beamed at him. "Show me how it's done."

Carl mumbled under his breath.

James broke out into song. At first, his voice was soft, but as all the other sounds in the pub faded and more people crowded around him, his confidence increased and his voice grew stronger. When he finished, the entire place was on their feet clapping. Even Carl and the man who had screamed "Hell no" nodded in approval.

James high-fived Mary.

"That's definitely going on air," she said, thinking she could get him a little recognition for his velvet voice in this weird world.

Chapter 18

Mary stood in the shower, letting the hot water stream down her back. She moved in slow motion, trying to wash her melancholy away. Usually the scent of her coconut lime soap made her happy, but tonight even that couldn't cheer her up. Kimberly's story had been much better than hers. Somehow, Kimberly had managed to cover the rescue of a surfer who had foolishly tried to ride the waves at the height of the storm. Matt, her cameraman, had filmed the entire incident, from the moment the surfer went under to when he'd been pulled safely out of the raging ocean. Incredibly, after being rescued once, the surfer went right back out in the stormy sea. He rode a wave to the shore and then agreed to an interview. He was surprisingly well spoken, too, for someone who'd done something so foolish not once, but twice, talking about the importance of riding the waves that come at you in life and being resilient.

The highlight of Mary's story had been James's singing. She couldn't shake the image of him wearing that tight-fitting postal uniform. He had seemed so downtrodden, and somehow she was responsible for everything that had gone wrong in this version of his life. He was so happy when he sang for the crowd in that bar, and they'd loved him. Why hadn't he been able to pursue a career in music without her?

She turned the knob to shut off the faucet and stepped out of the shower into the steamy bathroom. The foggy mirror showed a cloudy image of herself, reflective of her internal confusion. How had erasing

thirty years from her life had such a devastating impact on Liz's and James's lives?

She settled on the sofa with soup and a box of crackers. "Hey, little guy," she said to Belli. Brady hadn't asked for the fish back, and she had no intention of returning him. Her apartment was lonely without anyone else puttering around. Belli was the best company she had in her new life. Watching the fish swim in circles, she wondered who took care of it in her real life. If she hadn't been in this alternate universe the night of Brady's party, the poor little thing might not have survived. Oh no. Back in her real life, Belli was probably dead. If her being here had changed Belli's life, it must have also caused changes to other people's besides hers. The soup she'd just swallowed came back up to her mouth, and she raced to the bathroom to spit it out. Was James a postman in her real life too? Would she turn on the nightly news and see that Nora O'Donnell person behind the anchor desk instead of Liz? And what about Dean? What if, when she got back to her real life, he was married to someone else? Kendra wouldn't . . . no. No. No.

She raced back to the living room and called Darbi. Darbi didn't pick up, so Mary left a desperate message: "I need to talk to you. Call me right away."

Outside, the storm raged on, with rain battering the roof and wind rattling the shutters. She turned on the six o'clock news, hoping the sound of voices would stop her mind from spiraling deeper down the black hole. The television and lights flickered. Great. The last thing she needed was for the electricity to go out. In case it did, she searched the apartment for a flashlight. She couldn't find one, but she did find candles and matches in the kitchen drawers. She lit the candles and placed them in the living room on the coffee table next to Belli.

The doorbell rang, startling her. Maybe it was Darbi. She rushed to the door and pulled it open. Of course it wasn't Darbi. She wouldn't venture out on such a stormy evening. It was Brady. He stood on the landing holding a dish, the hood of his gray sweatshirt pulled over his head. He stepped inside, bringing the delicious smell of barbecue sauce with him. "I came here for two things," he said.

She backed away from him, not wanting to think about what he might want, and then she froze. The most unsettling question popped into her head. Had she and Brady used protection? Her face heated up. She hadn't seen any birth control pills in the apartment. What if . . . no, no. No.

"The first thing is I made you dinner." He thrust the dish at her. "Ribs."

She hadn't had her period since waking up young.

"Nice pajamas." He placed his hand on her sleeve, rubbing the fabric. "Soft."

She jerked her arm away. How long had she been here? It seemed like a lifetime, but little more than a week had passed. No need to worry, yet.

Brady stepped out of his shoes and pulled off his wet sweatshirt, then hung it on the doorknob.

Why was he undressing? Oh boy, he'd said he'd come up for two things. If he removed his T-shirt, she'd ask him to leave.

"Everything okay?" he asked. "You seem wound up. Must have been a tough day." He pointed to the television, where on-screen Mary stood outside the pub in Scituate in the driving rain and howling wind.

"With the weather outside nasty . . . ," the TV version of herself began. The camera zoomed in on the hood of her bright-blue raincoat flapping over her shoulder and her soaking-wet hair blowing across her face. "Many in the town of Scituate spent the day eating, drinking, and laughing with friends inside one of the town's oldest taverns, the Hungry Shark. Hidden among the crowd was James Morisette, the Singing Mailman, who filled the place with a whole lot of sunshine on this stormy day."

The image on the television changed to the warm, dry inside of the pub, where James did his best Rod Stewart impersonation and the crowd gave him a raucous ovation.

"The 'Singing Mailman' has a nice ring to it." Brady had wandered into the living room and made himself at home. He reclined on the sofa with his feet up on the coffee table, precariously close to Belli's bowl.

Mary stayed where she was, by the door. "Where's RaeLynn tonight?" she blurted out, feeling the need to remind him about his girlfriend.

"She'll be here any second."

Mary blew out a long breath and sat down on the opposite end of the couch.

"Why didn't you film your part inside?" Brady asked.

"My cameraman insisted that viewers love to see reporters getting smacked down by the weather."

"Want me to give him a smackdown?" Brady flexed his arm, showing off his biceps.

She knew he was kidding, but the thought of him wanting to protect her warmed her insides. If she didn't feel so uncomfortable around him, he could have been a good friend to her while she was here. If she hadn't known he'd cheated on his girlfriend, she would have thought he was a good guy.

Brady picked up her bowl of soup and made a face. "You're lucky I brought you a real dinner."

Yes, he definitely would be a good friend to have.

His phone buzzed. He looked down at it and smiled. "RaeLynn's here." He jumped up from the sofa. "See you soon."

"What was the second thing you were here for?" He had just pulled the door open when Mary worked up the nerve to ask.

He turned and pointed toward the coffee table, where the candles were glowing. "Wanted to make sure you were prepared if the lights went out. Should have known you would be."

She watched him descend the stairway, reassured by his words. Surely no version of herself would sleep with him without protection, and he seemed responsible too.

Just in case, she'd pick up a pregnancy test in the morning.

Chapter 19

Before Mary left for work the next morning, she ran to the drugstore across the street for a pregnancy test. To try to detract attention from it, she threw a bunch of items she didn't need into her basket. Still, the cashier, a woman she figured to be in her seventies, rang up the test while making eye contact with her. "Are you hoping for positive or negative?" she asked.

"Definitely negative." Mary returned home to pee on the stick, thinking that moment in Walgreens was the most humiliating in either of her lives. The three minutes she waited for the results were also the longest of either life, but her entire body relaxed when the results came back negative.

On her drive into work, she called Darbi again and left a second voicemail. "Call me back. I'm freaking out about the changes I might be causing in my real life."

By the time she arrived at the office, she'd worked herself into a tizzy again, wondering what James's and Liz's lives would look like when she got back. At the worst, James would be a mailman like he was here, but what about Liz? What did her life look like? Mary had to know what Liz was doing in this life. She started to type her name in the search bar but then stopped, thinking about Darbi's warning. Kimberly had already shown her videos of Liz, so what would looking her up now hurt? Nothing.

She finished typing Liz's name and hit the return key. Pages of results came back about women named Liz Collins from all over the country. Mary narrowed the search by adding "ICNN reporter." She leaned back in her chair and scrolled through the findings. Most were related to stories Liz had reported on for Channel 77 and of course the infamous day she'd walked away from her career.

Mary skimmed through the articles, going down several rabbit holes. Eventually she discovered that Liz had married a veterinarian, and they lived in Bolton, Massachusetts, which, oddly enough, was a neighboring town to Hudson, where Mary version 1 lived with Dean and Kendra. Mary closed her eyes, trying to imagine Liz living in a small town, doing ordinary things like grocery shopping. All she could picture was a camera crew following Liz through the aisles of Hannaford.

With a few more clicks of her mouse, she found a telephone number for Liz. She stared at it, hearing Darbi's ominous words: *Bad things will happen.* On the other hand, she had interacted with James, and nothing bad had happened. She took a deep breath and picked up the receiver of her desk phone. Her finger trembled as she punched in Liz's number.

"Hello," a woman said.

The person had spoken only one word, but the singsong way she said it let Mary know her Liz Collins was on the other end of the line. The receiver felt slick in her sweaty hand. She had to remind herself she wasn't talking to a celebrity. In this life, Liz had thrown away her career.

She cleared her throat. "My name is Mary Mulligan." She paused, expecting Liz to recognize her name, but of course they had never met. "I'm a reporter at the Independent Cable News Network in Boston. Is this Liz Collins?"

"Every year, just like the groundhog coming out of his hole, someone from a local media outlet calls me. My answer is always the same: no." Liz didn't say it unkindly. In fact, she sounded as if she was on the verge of laughter. "Sorry to disappoint."

Mary glanced out her door to the office diagonal from hers, where Liz used to sit. She could almost see young Liz, her hair tied in a ponytail, sitting at her desk typing a story. The vision made her nostalgic for the old days when the two worked side by side, and Mary ended long workdays by meeting Dean for dinner. "I don't want to interview you. I just want to know what you're doing today."

"Now, why would you want to know that?" The tone and inflection matched that of Liz, America's most trusted newscaster.

"I'm wondering if there's life after the news." Mary hadn't planned to say that. The words had just spilled out, but that's what she wanted to know, because she couldn't imagine Liz being happy away from the anchor desk. Mary certainly hadn't been.

Liz clicked her tongue. "Oh, honey. Mary, is it? Of course there is."

"What do you do all day?"

Liz didn't speak for a few seconds, but Mary heard the whirling of a fan in the background. "My husband and I live a quiet life with our horses. I make lopsided mugs, pitchers, and vases in a small pottery studio in the backyard, and I do a lot of jigsaw puzzles."

"Do you have children?"

"No, it's just us and the animals."

Mary chewed on her lip. She'd had more than Liz. She'd had Kendra to look after, a daughter's love, and that hadn't been enough. What was wrong with her? "You must miss the news."

"Not at all. I don't even watch it. Working in the media and reporting on all the horrible things that happen, I'd started seeing only the bad in people. I'm much happier without it."

Liz's words triggered a memory of something Mary had said to Dean twenty-four years earlier, something she'd pushed from her thoughts and reshaped because it was easier to blame Dean for leaving her career than admitting that quitting was her decision: "Why do I want to spend the day reporting on tragedies when I can stay home with this little cherub." She'd kissed Kendra's cheek.

Mary closed her eyes. Even now in this second-chance career, she preferred covering stories like the Scooper Bowl, one-hundred-year-olds' birthday parties, and hot dog–eating contests that represented American goodness.

In the hallway outside her office, the police scanner squawked.

"Are you still there?" Liz asked.

"You're really happy?"

"Happy as a lark," Liz said.

In the hallway, Carl called Mary's name. "Hit-and-run in Wellesley. A girl on a bike. Let's roll."

Mary said goodbye to Liz and went to meet Carl, knowing she'd be depressed the rest of the day after covering a story about some heartless jerk who'd hit a little girl on a bike and driven off, leaving the poor kid injured or worse on the side of the road. Maybe Liz had a point, one that Mary had realized on her own long ago but then forgotten.

Chapter 20

The next morning, Saturday, Mary burst into Darbi's backyard. Darbi sat alone at the patio table eating her breakfast. Mary had waited to come over until after nine, knowing Jacqui would be at the store.

"Why haven't you returned my calls?"

"Well, good morning to you too." Darbi pointed to a bowl with scrambled eggs. "Run inside and get a plate."

"Not hungry." Mary pulled out the chair across from Darbi and perched on its edge. "Did you see my story on James?"

"Who's James?"

"James, the singer. My friend. I saw him and he's a mailman." She brought up the video on her phone.

Darbi's face tightened as she watched, and Mary's feeling of dread intensified.

"Have I ruined his real life by being here? Maybe I should go back now before I cause other changes. To Dean and Kendra."

Darbi's cheek twitched. She looked at Mary for a long time without saying anything, her eyes glistening. "I really wish you had let me explain things to you before getting your wisdom teeth out."

"What does that mean?" Mary's entire body heated up, fearing Darbi was about to tell her she had permanently ruined the lives of the people she loved. Sweat pooled above her lips. She cranked the handle of the umbrella until it blocked the sun and the table was cast in shade.

Darbi sat without saying anything, chewing on her lip.

Mary's phone rang. She saw the call was from the news station.

Darbi stood. "Answer that, and I'll get you a plate."

"No, I don't want . . ."

She trailed off as Darbi disappeared through the sliding glass doors.

Mary pushed the green icon button on her phone. "We need all hands on deck," Mitchell said. "There's a big fire in the Back Bay. How soon can you be here?"

She didn't want to leave. She needed to keep talking to Darbi, but she also knew she had to go, or she could kiss that promotion goodbye. "A half hour."

Mary went inside to say goodbye. The house reeked of patchouli, and Darbi sat at the kitchen table, a bag of gummy bears in front of her.

"Are those—"

"Yes, they're my magical chews."

"Why are you having them now?"

Darbi sighed. "I told you. I don't like talking about all this." She gestured to Mary's new young body.

"I have to go to work, but I'll be back in the morning. In the meantime, can you look for Uncle Cillian's letters again? Maybe he mentioned something about how being here changes things."

"Jacqui will be home."

"You come to my apartment then. Ten?"

Darbi nodded, but Mary had the feeling her cousin had no intention of showing up tomorrow.

~

When Mary got off work on Saturday night, she walked across the street with Kimberly to the Press Box, where Kimberly's fiancé, Tyler, waited with his friend Reiss. At the entrance, Kimberly scanned the restaurant. At nine thirty, the place was mostly empty, with just a few customers sitting at the bar watching the Red Sox play the Yankees. In a booth by the windows, two men sat clutching their phones in a way that reminded Mary of toddlers clinging to their blankies. Kimberly set off toward them, and Mary followed.

A dark-haired man stood and kissed Kimberly hello. He waved at Mary. Images of other times some version of herself had hung out with Tyler and Kimberly flooded Mary's mind: watching a Celtics game at the Garden, water-skiing on Sebago Lake in Maine, playing pool at a bar in Cambridge. Somehow she knew he was a good person.

"This is my buddy Reiss," Tyler said, pointing to the redhead across from him. As Mary slid in next to him, Reiss nodded while he typed into his phone. She thought about ripping it from his hands or telling him he was being rude. The server came over with an appetizer sampler and Kentucky mules for Mary and Kimberly. "I figured you guys must be starving," Tyler said. "Long day."

"You've got that right," Kimberly said. "How did studying go?"

"Great," Tyler said.

Reiss glanced up from his screen. "Remind me why I want to be a lawyer again."

"Why do you?" Kimberly asked.

"I don't. I want to be a photographer, but there's not a lot of money in that." He looked down at his phone again. "Have you always wanted to be a reporter?"

"My parents say I came out of the womb holding a microphone," Kimberly said.

"She was the anchor of our middle school and high school news," Tyler said. "'Good morning, Northgate students, I'm Kimberly Nash, and this is what you need to know today.'" He made his voice sound high.

Kimberly fake swatted him. "I didn't sound like that."

Mary reached for a mozzarella stick, trying to picture Kimberly as a little girl reporting the news to her classmates. The image made her uncomfortable. When she was in school, she'd had no idea what she wanted to be. That Kimberly always knew she wanted to be a newscaster made Mary feel like if she got the promotion, she'd be stealing it from her friend.

"Must be cool to be living your dream," Reiss said.

"Not there quite yet." Kimberly cut a potato skin into small bites. "Need to work for a major network first."

Mary turned away from Kimberly and trained her eyes on the baseball game. She'd never thought about how much Kimberly loved their job. All she'd thought about was how much she wanted and deserved that promotion, but Kimberly wanted and deserved it just as much as she did. By being here, she was ruining everything for everybody.

The Yankees scored a run, and the few people watching at the bar booed. Mary took a long sip from her pewter mug. Maybe she should go back now, not wait for the promotion. On the other hand, she was so close, and once she returned to her real life, Kimberly would get promoted. She had to talk to Darbi tomorrow. Make sure the changes she was causing weren't permanent.

Chapter 21

Mary turned into the driveway, her headlights illuminating the dark night. Brady was carrying RaeLynn from his Jeep toward his front door the same way a groom would carry his bride over the threshold. She hit her brakes, feeling as if she was interrupting. Brady and RaeLynn disappeared into his apartment. Every time Mary had seen Brady with RaeLynn, he'd acted as if he was in love with her. She'd never understand why he'd cheated. Was his relationship another thing she'd wrecked by being here?

She turned on the television and lay down on the couch, thinking again of how Kimberly had glowed as she talked about her love of broadcast journalism. Mary had never been as excited about reporting as her friend was. The sad stories affected her too much. Thank goodness no one had been hurt in the fire today. She yawned. Her eyes felt heavy. She couldn't keep them open, but she didn't have the energy to go to her bedroom.

She awoke to the sound of Dean's familiar voice.

Dean!

Her eyes flew open, and she shot up to a sitting position. Dean's bronzed face filled her television screen. "The best drive I ever had wasn't with my Callaway; it was on Dunlop tires," he said.

What in the world? That couldn't really be Dean, could it? It had to be someone who sounded like him. She rubbed her eyes and leaned forward on the sofa. The man on the television had deep crow's-feet that her Dean didn't have; instead of a buzz cut, his hair was long enough to curl; and he was more muscular than the Dean she knew. Still, she was sure it was Dean. She'd recognize him anywhere. She blinked hard, trying to make sense of it. Why was he doing tire commercials? From the screen, he pointed at her. "Tell them Dean Amato sent you." Then he vanished. Mary stared at the television as if she were waiting for Dean to walk through the screen into her apartment. She wished he would.

He'd kissed her for the first time in this very room. It was their first official date. He was early, and she wasn't dressed. He waited on the couch, flipping through the latest issue of *People*. "This is the sexiest man alive? Please." He'd held up the cover with Patrick Swayze on it. "I have it all over this guy." He dropped the magazine on the coffee table and stood to help Mary with her jacket. After she'd slipped her arms through the sleeves, he pulled her toward him. His eyes met hers before slowly dropping to her lips. He leaned closer and kissed her. Mary's knees gave out and she stumbled, falling into him. "What did I tell you?"

"I wasn't expecting you to kiss me." She could barely hear herself speak over her pounding heart. It was the best kiss of her life. As they drove to the restaurant and shared a meal, she couldn't concentrate on a thing he said. She couldn't wait for his mouth to be on hers again. At the end of the night, when he walked her back up the stairs, their second kiss outdid the first.

She knew then she wanted a lifetime of kisses just like it.

Frank Sinatra's barking interrupted her memory. A few minutes later, she heard music and laughter coming from downstairs. At that moment, Mary missed Dean more than she had at any moment in either of her lives. When she got back, she would work hard to recapture that magic they'd once shared, starting by telling him how abandoned she felt when he left her to play golf every weekend. She'd come up with a list of activities they could enjoy together. She touched her lips, imagining him kissing her like he had on their first date.

~

After Mary saw Dean on television, she couldn't stop thinking about him. Why was he doing tire commercials? What did his life look like without her? Did he have a wife and children? If he did, would he have them when she returned to her real life? There was a pit in her stomach. She had to learn more. She had so many questions. Sitting on the sofa, she opened her laptop. Her hands hovered over the keyboard. The cursor blinked in the empty search bar as Darbi's warning came back to her. *Bad things will happen.* Maybe she shouldn't enter Dean's name. She clenched and unclenched her fist.

She'd seen James in person and spoken to Liz on the phone, and nothing bad had happened. She worked with Carl. Darbi didn't know what she was talking about. She'd admitted herself that she didn't have all the answers. Mary paced her apartment. Downstairs, Brady's door squeaked open and slammed shut. She peeked out the window into the darkness and saw him walking the dog down the driveway, a flashlight illuminating his path. She sat back down and began typing. Her trembling fingers tapped the wrong letters. She started over but unknowingly hit the *S* key instead of the *D*. Turned out there were plenty of Sean Amatos. On the third try, she correctly typed *Dean Amato*.

Her mouth went dry and her chest tightened as the screen filled with pages of pictures and articles. She clicked on the Images tab to ensure the results were for her Dean. She enlarged a photograph and leaned closer to her monitor. Her heart cracked open. There stood the man who had been her husband, his puckered lips grazing his putter. She'd seen him kiss his club just like that several times when he and Kendra had faced off on the green in their backyard.

"Hey, Mary, what chore do you want Kendra to do for the week when I win?" Dean would ask.

"Hey, Mom, where should Dad take us for dinner tomorrow if I win?" Kendra always responded.

She'd usually win, because unlike Mary, Dean let her.

The memory was bittersweet. Her eyes filled with tears as she felt an acute sense of homesickness. All she wanted to do was hug Kendra, but Kendra didn't exist in this world, and somewhere in another universe they were bickering. Wait, was there another version of her, and was she making things worse with her family? Mary had to get back and make things right.

Outside, Frank Sinatra barked, and Brady hushed him.

Mary scrolled to a photo of Dean hitting out of a sand trap at Augusta with large crowds looking on. She clicked on another picture. In this one, Dean looked right at her with a smug expression. *I did it,* he seemed to be saying.

Caressing the image on her screen with her index finger, she smiled and spoke aloud. "Yes, you did." He'd made his dream come true. He was a professional golfer. Her smile faded. The spaces in her mouth where her wisdom teeth used to be throbbed. A wave of guilt rushed over her. *Why couldn't you do it when you were with me? Did I hold you back?*

She continued scrolling through the images. In all of them, Dean's thick brown hair covered the top of his ears, showing off his luscious curls. He'd worn it that way when they were dating. After they got married and he'd been promoted a few times, he started to get buzz cuts. She'd always thought the longer hair suited him better, and the crew cuts were necessitated by a corporate role he was forced to play. Did he do that for her? To provide for their family?

He'd never complained about his corporate job, and through the years she'd forgotten that, until he'd met her, he'd planned to make his living on the golf course. Maybe "forgot" wasn't the right word. She'd chosen not to think about the sacrifices he'd made for their family. Dean's voice popped into her head, a memory from long ago. *This sales associate job is just a way to make ends meet until I turn pro.* It was their first date. They sat at a picnic table in Ipswich eating lobster rolls, and he told her about his dream of becoming a professional golfer. *I know the odds are against me, but I'm going to make it.*

She'd believed him. He'd already made a name for himself on the amateur circuit. Now she felt a lump in her throat, and her face burned with shame. When did Dean give up his dream of playing in the PGA? Why hadn't she encouraged him to keep trying? She'd always thought she was the one who'd given up her dream for their family, but Dean, too, had made sacrifices. Unlike her, he'd never complained. She wanted to hug him. Thank him.

Her foot fell asleep from sitting on the sofa with her leg folded under her for too long. She stood, trying to stop the feeling of being pricked by pins and needles. By now, it was after two in the morning. There was no noise coming from downstairs or out on the street. She strolled to her refrigerator and pulled a Milky Way from the crisper, savoring each bite of the sweet chocolate and gooey caramel, a treat she'd rarely allowed her fifty-something self. Her eyelids felt heavy and her mind cloudy. She hoped the rush of sugar would jolt her awake.

Returning to the couch, she began reading articles.

OFFICIALS STRIP AMATO OF US OPEN VICTORY IN DUBIOUS GROUNDING CALL

Sheboygan, WI—For a brief moment, Dean Amato believed he'd accomplished something he never had before in his 22-year pro golfing career: won a major, specifically the US Open. He finished five under, one stroke ahead of Jordy Maverick. Before Amato even had a chance to pump his fist in celebration, however, officials notified him that he was being penalized two strokes for grounding his club in the most contentious ruling ever at the US Open.

The controversy centered around Amato's second shot on the 495-yard par 4 hole from a sandy stick-laden patch of dirt far left of the fairway and inconsistent with the typical positioning of bunkers. Nevertheless, the area was considered a bunker, and the rules prohibit players from grounding their clubs in bunkers, clearly stating that if they do, they will be penalized two strokes.

A stunned Amato argued with officials before storming off the green. He left the course without speaking to the media and has yet to comment.

Maverick, who was awarded the victory, said Amato's penalty surprised him. "I had no idea the area was a bunker. I thought the crowd had battered down the ground. It's not how I wanted to win."

Mary didn't know enough about golf to understand the controversy. She did know winning the US Open was a big deal, and her heart broke for Dean. The next articles were op-eds from sports columnists, some defending Dean and others claiming he'd cheated. The Dean she knew would never cheat. That she was sure of. Next there was an article announcing Dean's retirement and that he refused to talk to the press, stating that he'd turned down interview requests from ESPN, *Sports Illustrated*, Jimmy Kimmel, and Jimmy Fallon. That certainly didn't sound like the Dean she knew. He was almost always accommodating, hating to disappoint anyone—especially her. As soon as the thought popped into her head, she knew it was true, and her stomach twisted with guilt. She'd never sat him down to talk about how unhappy she was. She'd never told him what she'd needed from him. Instead, she'd mentioned it at inopportune times, when he was just leaving or getting back from golf. She hadn't been fair, blaming him for her unhappiness, when he would have tried to help her if he'd known. She glanced at her phone. She wanted to pick it up and call Dean, have the conversation they should have had before she had her wisdom teeth out, but of course she couldn't. *I'll make things right as soon as I get back.*

She continued reading about Dean's life in this alternate world.

AMATO'S POOR PUTTING ON THE 18TH HOLE COSTS
HIM THE GREEN JACKET

AMATO FORCES SUDDEN DEATH AT THE PGA
CHAMPIONSHIP BUT CHOKES AWAY THE
OPPORTUNITY

TENDINITIS OF THE SHOULDER KEEPS AMATO OUT
OF THE RYDER CUP

DEAN AMATO GETS COZY WITH JULIA ROBERTS

Mary's hand froze on the mouse. She enlarged the photo. Sure enough, a thirtyish Dean sat next to the famous actress at an outdoor table. He sipped a beer, gazing at his date with a devilish grin. With her hand resting on his arm, Julia was turned sideways, beaming at him. Mary clenched her teeth as she glared at the beautiful actress. Dean had always put up a stink when Mary asked him to go to the movies, unless Julia Roberts starred in it. Then he'd even been willing to watch the movie again and again once it became available on streaming services.

From a story written in 2009, she learned Dean lived in Ponte Vedra Beach, Florida. She frowned. Her Dean hated Florida, referred to it as a cultural wasteland. Why would this Dean choose to live there? What if he lived there without her when she got back?

Mary kept reading about Dean. Nothing she read referenced a wife or family. In 2010, *People* magazine named the then forty-four-year-old one of the ten most eligible bachelors in the world. She watched a clip of an interview of him on the *Today* show. "I have to ask you, Dean," Savannah Guthrie said with a smile, "women all over the world swoon over you, so why is it you've never married?"

"Swoon?" Dean laughed and looked directly in the camera. "I'm married to the game, Savannah. Married. To. The. Game."

A ray of sun streaked through the blinds. How could it be morning already? Mary had never left the sofa or slept. Her brain was shutting down, making her mind foggy. Reading all these articles about Dean made her long for news about her daughter. Recognizing on some level that what she was doing didn't make sense, she typed Kendra's name into the Google search bar. Four different women with the name Kendra Amato came up in the results, and for a few seconds Mary was hopeful. One of the Kendras lived in Texas and appeared to be in her late forties or early fifties. Another, about Kendra's age, lived in New Jersey and was Black. The third was a wiry White woman who'd run for mayor of Saint Louis. There was no image for the fourth, but the article indicated that this Kendra lived in Alaska and was training for the Iditarod, a dogsled race.

Every year, Hudson High posted a picture of the graduating class on Facebook. Mary's leg bounced as she navigated to the school's page and clicked on a photograph from the year her daughter graduated high school. She knew exactly where her Kendra stood in the picture, between Quinlan Adams and Josslyn Bartolini, but in the photo she looked at now, Quinlan and Josslyn stood next to each other, without Kendra between them. The hairs on the back of Mary's neck stood. Her entire body shook. She'd known from the moment she'd seen that picture on Darbi's wall that she was living in a world without Kendra, but being directly confronted with evidence of that gutted her. What if something happened to Mary in this alternate world and she couldn't get back to her other life? Would that mean Kendra had never existed? Or would it mean Mary would spend all eternity knowing she and her daughter were on the outs? She'd been so foolish, so selfish to stay here. She had to go back. Right now.

She reached for her phone and scrolled to her cousin's name. The call went straight to voicemail. She tried Jacqui next, but Jacqui didn't answer either. They were probably still sleeping. It wasn't quite six yet. Mary stood and stretched. She would go to Darbi's house and wake her. Pound on the door until she answered. She had to. This was too important.

Chapter 22

Fifteen minutes later, Mary stood on Darbi's stoop, ringing the doorbell over and over again and shouting her cousin's name. A jogger running by the house gave her the side-eye but said nothing. Mary banged on the door. The curtains in the living room shifted. Jacqui yawned as she peered out the narrow opening, looking toward the steps. "Let me in!" Mary yelled.

Jacqui's face disappeared from the window. A minute later, the door opened. Dressed in a red bathrobe, Jacqui blinked several times, staring at Mary. "Are you okay?" she asked, her voice hoarse.

"No! I need to get back to Kendra and Dean. Right now."

Jacqui tilted her head and narrowed her eyes. "Who?"

"My husband and daughter." Mary pushed her way inside and stormed through the living room.

Jacqui trailed behind. "Husband and daughter?"

Mary froze, realizing what she'd said. Darbi was going to kill her, but she couldn't backtrack now. There was no way she could explain being here so early in the morning, acting like a raving lunatic. Maybe Jacqui could help her get the truth out of Darbi, because Mary was sick of her cousin's evasiveness. Darbi knew much more than she was saying.

Jacqui stared at her wide eyed, waiting for a response.

"I need to talk to Darbi." Mary continued her beeline down the hall. Loud snoring came from the bedroom on the right. Mary burst into the room. "Darbi."

Sprawled out on her back, Darbi flipped to her stomach.

Mary stomped across the rug and leaned over the bed, shaking her cousin's shoulder. Darbi scooched toward the center of the king, away from Mary's reach.

Mary grabbed her arm and yanked her toward the side of the bed.

Pulling a sleep mask from her face, Darbi snapped awake. "What's happening?"

"That's what I came to find out. I googled my family. Dean's a professional golfer, and Kendra, well, she doesn't even exist here. What if that's the way it is in my real life too?" The horrifying thought caused Mary's entire body to convulse.

Darbi shot up to a sitting position.

"She's ranting about a daughter. Must have had a bad dream."

At the sound of Jacqui's voice, Darbi's eyes snapped to her. "Could you make coffee while I talk to Mary?"

Jacqui folded her arms across her chest. "I'm not going anywhere." She pointed to Mary, who was pacing by the bed. "Poor girl's having a breakdown. I'm about to call 911."

"I just need to get back to my real life." Mary bent down toward her cousin so they were nose to nose. "How do I get back?"

Darbi fell back against the headboard. "I've been dreading this." Her voice was barely a whisper, and sorrow filled her eyes.

Mary's body went rigid. Her breath caught in her throat. "Dreading what?"

"There is no going back." Tears streamed down Darbi's face. "You're here for good."

A wave of nausea hit Mary. Her stomach cramped, and she doubled over in pain. Her knees gave out, and she crumpled to the ground. Everything in the room went gray.

She felt the weight of the key in her hand on the day she and Dean had bought the house in Hudson, saw the tears in his eyes the night she'd told him she was pregnant, pictured the bright-red leaves on the maple tree he'd planted the day Kendra was born. None of it had happened in this world she was stuck in.

Kendra didn't exist. Impossible. Her body contracted as if she were in labor. She breathed in the intoxicating scent of newborn Kendra's head, and heard the soft *kkk* sound the baby made while eating. She saw Kendra's toothless grin on Mother's Day, when Mary had opened the gift her daughter had made, a ceramic smiley face that Kendra had painted purple instead of yellow because purple was Mary's favorite color. She brought her hand to her cheek, feeling Kendra's kiss goodbye at the airport. Mary never would have imagined that would be the last time she'd see or speak to her daughter again. All because she'd wanted to be a famous broadcaster. How shallow. How selfish. She had wanted more from her old life, but she'd ended with so much less. She'd ended up with nothing.

The bed squeaked as Darbi stood. She leaned over Mary, putting a hand on her shoulder. "I'm sorry. I tried to stop you from getting your wisdom teeth out."

"I asked you about going back, and you said we'd talk later."

"Because I dreaded this conversation."

Jacqui cleared her throat. "Someone better tell me what's going on."

~

"What have I done?" Mary asked. How could she have wanted to live in a world without her daughter even for a minute? She was a horrible mother. So selfish.

She sat on the couch in Jacqui and Darbi's living room with her elbows resting on her knees and her face buried in her hands. Her stomach spasmed and bile rose in her throat. She'd been awake for over twenty-four hours straight, and her head pounded from lack of sleep. She'd downed two ibuprofen, but they weren't helping. She realized she would feel this awful, or worse, for the rest of her life.

Outside, the neighborhood started to come to life, with cars driving by and people out walking. Every now and then snippets of conversations drifted in through the open windows.

Darbi paced the living room, holding a cup of coffee. "It's why I said the memories could make it a curse."

Mary's head snapped up. She glared at her cousin. This was all her fault. Instead of saying "Don't get your wisdom teeth removed," Darbi should have told her she'd be stuck in a world without Dean and where Kendra didn't exist. Mary glanced at a glass vase on the table and imagined hurling it across the room at Darbi. "You should have told me I couldn't go back!" she screamed.

Darbi recoiled, spilling coffee from her mug. "I pleaded with you not to have your wisdom teeth out. You didn't listen."

Mary's thoughts were like a pinball machine, ricocheting around her mind. Darbi had tried to warn her, but Mary hadn't believed her. No sane person would have believed that story. Mary didn't want to accept all the blame. Darbi was at fault too. Did it matter who was at fault? Mary was stuck here. There had to be a way back.

Jacqui rocked back and forth in the chair across from Mary. She'd sat trancelike, not saying a word since Darbi had told her about the Mulligan gene that had allowed her and Mary to erase years off their lives. "Any minute now, I'm going to wake up and realize this crazy story has been the weirdest, most lifelike dream I have ever had. Either that, or you two are pulling some kind of wild elaborate joke over on me."

Darbi stopped pacing and stood still, huddled behind a potted plant, addressing Jacqui. "I started to tell you so many times. Honestly, I'm relieved you know."

Jacqui blinked but said nothing. In one of the bedrooms, an alarm clock blared. She headed down the hallway. A moment later the beeping stopped.

"I miss them, too, you know." Darbi's face contorted with pain, and her voice broke.

After Dean and Mary, Darbi had been the first one to hold Kendra, and from that moment on, she'd spoiled the girl rotten, bestowing gifts on birthdays, half birthdays, and just because. Growing up, Kendra had often spent hot summer days with Darbi by the pool and cold winter afternoons playing board games by the woodstove. Sometimes Kendra even referred to Darbi as her much cooler second mother. Darbi loved Dean, too, calling him her favorite man on the planet.

Mary's voice softened. "You need to find Uncle Cillian's letters. Maybe he mentioned something about how to get back."

"I've looked. I'm afraid they're long gone."

Jacqui returned and sat down on the sofa, angling her body so her back was to Darbi. She wrapped her arm around Mary's shoulders. "Tell me about Kendra."

As she pictured her daughter's face, the deep dimples and enormous smile, Mary's eyes filled with tears. How was it possible that Kendra didn't exist when Mary had twenty-four years of memories of the two of them together? She thought about the day Kendra was born, January 2, at exactly one minute and nine seconds after midnight, two weeks earlier than expected. She'd launched herself into the world with a content smile. That's how Dean had described their daughter's expression. She hadn't immediately cried, and the silence had worried Mary until she saw the ear-to-ear grin on Dean's face. The doctor handed him the scissors, and he cut the umbilical cord with tears streaming down his cheeks. Mary's heart had overflowed with joy. She and the man she loved more than anything had created a person, a blend of both of them.

"She's a daddy's girl," Mary said. Shame washed over her as she thought about the sting of jealousy she'd felt because Kendra had always seemed closer to Dean. What she would do for even a fraction of her daughter's attention now.

"She never misses an opportunity to tell us she loves us," Mary said.

Dean had claimed their daughter's first word had been "Dad," spoken at four months. Mary had let him believe it, but she knew Kendra had only been babbling "Dadada." Her first words came five months later at nine months, when she mimicked Mary saying, "I love you." After she'd grown and moved away to college, Kendra ended every phone conversation with those same three words, and Mary always thought of toddler Kendra lying on the changing table in the nursery wearing nothing but a diaper, saying that phrase for the very first time. She'd never hear those words from her daughter again, never be able to say them to her, either, all because she'd thought she'd missed out on a meaningless career.

"Anyone want an english muffin?" Darbi called from the kitchen, where she'd gone to make breakfast. The smell of bread toasting floated into the living room, making Mary's stomach turn.

"With strawberry jam," Jacqui said.

Darbi returned to the living room with two plates. "Kendra was innately kind," she said. Her use of the past tense caused a new wave of tears to run down Mary's face. She wiped them away and told Jacqui some of her favorite stories about Kendra.

When Kendra was five or six, Mary and Dean had taken her to Ben & Jerry's for ice cream. There was a long line at the entrance, where a greeter gave every child a balloon. As they sat in a booth eating their ice cream—Phish Food for Kendra because she always ordered the same exact thing as Dean—a little boy by the door started crying because they'd run out of balloons. Fifteen minutes later, the kid sat in a booth across from theirs, still crying and refusing to eat his ice cream. Unprompted by Mary or Dean, Kendra marched over to the crying boy. "You can have mine," she said, handing him her balloon.

Mary and Dean had smiled at each other across their table. "We created that kind, bighearted girl," Dean had said.

At the end of the summer before sixth grade, when Mary had taken Kendra back-to-school shopping, Kendra had refused to hold her hand. They were walking by the cosmetics counter at Macy's, the overbearing scent of a flowery perfume assaulting them. Mary reached for Kendra's hand, but Kendra pulled it away, stuffing it in her pocket. "I'm sorry,

Mom," she said. "I'm too old for that now." A tiny piece of Mary's heart had broken off that day and never grown back.

"She stopped holding my hand when she went to middle school," Mary said now. "But we celebrated her transition to womanhood."

When Kendra was thirteen, she'd woken Mary in the middle of the night and whispered that she'd gotten her period. Mary took her to Bickford's the next morning to celebrate. Kendra ordered chocolate chip pancakes and hot chocolate with whipped cream, proving she was still Mary's little girl and always would be—except now she wasn't, because she no longer existed. Telling Jacqui all the stories about Kendra had made Kendra seem like a real live person, and now the awful truth sucker punched Mary again: she'd wiped Kendra off the planet by being so self-centered. All the fame and fortune in the world couldn't make up for the hole she felt in her soul.

Jacqui had listened to one story after the other without interrupting, occasionally rubbing Mary's back. Now that Mary had finished speaking, Jacqui pulled her into a tight embrace. "I'm not saying I believe all this, but if it's true, one thing I've learned is that love always leads you back. We'll figure it out."

Mary needed to believe that. If she didn't, she wouldn't be able to go on.

Chapter 23

Darbi and Jacqui didn't want Mary to leave, but she insisted she needed to be alone. How would she ever live with herself knowing that, because of her jealousy of Liz and a prolonged bad mood with her husband, Kendra didn't exist? As she sat at a red light in bumper-to-bumper traffic on Route 9 while making her way home, she wished she could drive right back into her old life. At the exit for Shoppers World, she banged a U-ey and headed west toward Hudson. Dean and Kendra wouldn't be there, but she thought being near her old home would make her feel closer to them. Then maybe she could figure out a way to return to her old life as Kendra's mom and Dean's wife.

As she turned onto the street where she used to live, nostalgia overwhelmed her. Hot, gummy tears clouded her vision. How many times had she driven around that corner with Kendra, first in a car seat behind her, an infant sleeping or a toddler clutching Yogi, her stuffed bear, then as a school-age child or tween riding beside her in the passenger seat, fiddling with the stereo, and finally as a teenager and young adult behind the steering wheel, talking about her future.

Mary had read once that criminals often returned to the scene of the crime. She didn't know why that popped into her head. She hadn't committed a crime, after all. Though she imagined what she'd done was much worse.

The houses on the road looked exactly as she remembered. Split levels, colonials, and raised ranches. Finally, she saw her and Dean's colonial. She stopped her car in the middle of the road, wanting to run inside, right back to her old life. She shifted the car into park and placed a hand on the driver's side door handle. The house was the same brown it had been the day she and Dean had moved in. Poop brown, Dean had called it. They'd had it painted a beautiful blue gray within the first few weeks of living there, and oh how the neighbors had complimented her for that choice. The landscaping was as unappealing as the house color. Crabgrass and dandelions had replaced her lush green lawn. Weeds dominated the flower beds, and of course Kendra's tree, the maple Dean had planted the day she was born, didn't exist. Mary stared at the barren spot in the yard, devastated. Her chest tightened as she started a new round of ugly crying. She'd been holding out hope that somehow Kendra and Dean still lived there. Instead, she'd gotten a visible heartbreaking reminder that her daughter no longer existed.

A horn beeped. She looked in the rearview mirror. Jenni's ex-husband, Scott, gestured from the driver's seat of the car behind her. He was probably there to pick up his and Jenni's son, Scotty. The passenger, a woman, grimaced as if embarrassed by his impatience. Mary was about to give them an apologetic wave when Scott beeped again. He motioned with his hand for her to move and then leaned on the horn. Mary inched forward, giving him enough room to turn into Jenni's driveway. He glared as he passed her. Still the same old jerk he was in the last version of her life.

She idled in front of her old house, desperately needing to see Jenni. The two of them could sit at Jenni's kitchen table like they had so many times, and Mary could confide in her old friend about the blasted Mulligan gene that had gotten her in this predicament. There was no one more understanding than Jenni. The right-front door of Scott's car opened, and the passenger stepped out. Mary's back tightened as the woman made her way down the driveway toward the spot where Mary was parked. Jenni? When the woman reached Mary's car, she knocked on the passenger window. Mary scrambled to push the button to lower the glass. The back window on the driver's side zipped down. She tried again. This time her window came down. On the third try, she got it right.

Jenni leaned into the car. At least Mary thought it was Jenni. This woman looked a decade older than Mary's friend. Her hair was almost all gray. She had put on thirty pounds, and the lines around her eyes and mouth seemed an inch deep.

"Jenni?" Seeing her vibrant, funny friend so worn down caused fresh tears to well up in Mary's eyes. She blinked them away.

Jenni tilted her head. "Do I know you?"

The question was like a slap to the face. Other than Dean, Jenni knew her better than anyone. The day Mary and Dean had moved in to their Hudson home, Jenni had knocked on their door to introduce herself. Mary had made a joke about needing a margarita to get through the unpacking. A half hour later, Jenni returned with a pitcher of margaritas, and Mary put her to work emptying the kitchen boxes. Ever since then, the two had supported each other through life's ups and downs—the birth of their children, the death of their parents, and Jenni's divorce. Even Jenni's support wouldn't be able to get her through this, though. She'd lost her entire life.

"I used to work at Holy Grounds," Mary lied, referring to a coffee shop she and Jenni used to go to together all the time.

Jenni narrowed her eyes. "I don't remember you."

"House light with skim milk and two Sweet'n Lows."

Jenni nodded. "Good memory." Her hand rested on the frame of the window, giving Mary a clear view of her gold wedding band. Her heart sank. By having her wisdom teeth removed and turning twenty-four again, she'd ruined Jenni's life too. Kendra, Liz, James, and now Jenni. Her selfish decision was claiming more casualties. The only person whose life seemed better without her was Dean's. On the other hand, he'd lost out on his cherished daughter, so maybe she should count him as a victim too.

"Jenni," Scott growled, staring at Mary's car with his hands on his hips.

"You look upset," Jenni said. "Do you need help?"

Mary needed to find a way to keep Jenni there. Sitting in front of her house talking to her old friend, even this sad, dejected version of Jenni, was the closest she would ever get to her old life again. "I'm thinking of moving here someday, so I'm checking out the area."

Jenni scraped her teeth over her bottom lip. Her eyes roamed around Mary's car as if she was looking for something suspicious. "Really?"

"Do you know anyone who's thinking of selling?"

"Actually, the Millers are." She pointed to Mary's house. "They're moving to Connecticut to be closer to their grandchildren."

Grandchildren. The word triggered a fresh onslaught of emotion. Mary would never be a grandmother to Kendra's kids, the ones with the posh British accents.

"Are you sure you're okay?" Jenni stared at Mary with a compassionate look.

Mary was far from okay, but she nodded. She wanted to scream, *It's me. Mary Amato. Your best friend for the past two decades.* She missed her old friend so much. Even though she was close enough to touch Jenni, she felt far away and lonely, and she would feel that way for the rest of her life.

Jenni backed out of the window, but Mary wasn't ready for her to leave. "Do you like living here?"

Jenni leaned back in the car. "It's a nice neighborhood."

Mary looked over her shoulder at Scott, who was taking groceries out of the trunk. "And you're happy?"

Jenni turned to see what Mary was looking at. "Am I happy?"

Somehow, having Mary as a friend had given Jenni the strength she'd needed to leave Scott. Without Mary, she'd stayed and seemed miserable. Mary couldn't help but feel responsible. She hoped against hope that she was misreading the situation, that Jenni was the same happy-go-lucky woman she was in Mary's real life, and today was just a bad day. The way Jenni stared at her now with her mouth twisted and eyes narrow told Mary she'd asked an inappropriate question. After all,

Jenni didn't know her from Adam in this alternate life. "I mean living here. Are you happy living in this town? The neighborhood?"

Jenni squinted. "Hudson's going through a resurrection. It's one of the most desired places to live in Massachusetts right now."

Mary's mouth tingled. Jenni wasn't happy, and Mary was to blame. She'd left when she herself had been happy—or at the very least could have been. If she'd only told Dean about the things that had upset her, if she'd only understood the positive impact she'd had on other people's lives, she would have seen that her life mattered, that she had contributed. Why was she so convinced that she'd done nothing with her life when she'd brought Kendra into the world and raised her to be a strong, kind adult?

"Jenni, what are you doing?" Scott yelled. "These groceries aren't going to put themselves away."

"Maybe I'll see you again sometime," Mary said.

Jenni hung her head, and Mary eyed her empty passenger seat. She wanted to tell her old friend to climb in so she could drive her far away from Scott. Pulling herself from the window again, Jenni took a deep breath and crossed the street with her neck bent down. Scott thrust grocery bags into her hands. "Who were you talking to for so long? I pay for all this food and help you shop for it, now you expect me to put it all away?"

Mary stepped on the gas. *I've ruined everything for everyone,* she thought, hating herself a little bit more. She'd had a husband who loved her, a kind, smart, healthy daughter, and friends who'd treated her like family. Why had she thought life owed her anything else?

Chapter 24

At seven o'clock on Wednesday night, Mary was slumped on her sofa still wearing the pajamas she'd worn to bed the night before. She hadn't left the apartment since returning from her old neighborhood and had called in sick to work for three consecutive days. Her despondency about living a life without Kendra and Dean was taking up too much space inside her. She could feel it overflowing from her pores.

All the curtains in her apartment were drawn, and the only light in the place came from the television screen. She'd been watching a marathon of the program *House* all day. She and Dean used to watch the medical drama together. He'd always made a bowl of popcorn before it started. She pictured the two of them curled up on the couch, their popcorn long gone and him rubbing her feet, which rested in his lap. Tears streaked down her face. Dean had loved her and treated her well. Yes, they'd started to drift away from each other recently, but every couple went through rough patches. They would have worked it out. She would have sorted things out with Kendra too. Probably Kendra would have called, asking for a recipe, and Mary would have been so happy to hear from her that she wouldn't even have mentioned how hurt she'd been.

In the *House* episode Mary watched now, the doctor and his team tried to figure out why their patient couldn't walk. They were experts at diagnosing mystery illnesses. She wished the characters were real so they could help her return to her old life. She should call the doctor fifty-something Mary used, Dr. Kreiger. She imagined walking into his office and describing her condition. *Ever since I had my wisdom teeth removed, I've been living in another reality where I'm thirty years younger.*

He would look at her over the top of his glasses. *Have you ever experienced issues with your mental health?*

A commercial came on the television for a psoriasis medication. Mary hit the mute button on the remote control so she wouldn't have to listen to the long list of potential side effects. Sounds from outside filtered into her apartment, footsteps climbing the stairs. She hoped it wasn't Brady. Then again, it didn't matter now if she remembered sleeping with him because she wouldn't be bringing those memories home.

There was banging on the door and then Darbi's voice. "I know you're in there." The doorknob jingled. "I have your emergency key down in the car. Don't make me go all the way back there to get it. I might die if I have to climb these stairs again." As if to make her point, she gasped for air.

Mary sighed and dragged herself across the room to open the door.

Darbi stiffened when she saw Mary. "When's the last time you showered or ate? You need to take care of yourself."

"Why are you here?" Mary glared at her cousin, thinking she'd never forgive her.

Darbi pushed her way past Mary into the kitchen. "I've been calling you for the past few days."

Jacqui's voice floated up from the middle of the staircase. "You haven't been on the news all week." When she reached the landing, she thrust a paper bag at Mary. "Dinner, steak and cheese subs."

Steak and cheese subs made Mary miss Dean and Kendra even more. They'd always ordered those from a local sub shop on Main Street. Mary refused to go there because the owner had been rude to her once. She pictured her daughter and husband sitting at their breakfast bar devouring their sandwiches. "Mmmm, so good," they would say in unison.

Would she spend her entire new life mourning them and hating herself for losing them because of her misplaced longing for a career she'd left behind, a career she realized now wasn't as glamorous as she'd remembered? Yes, she most certainly would.

Jacqui wrapped her arm around Mary's shoulder as she entered the house. "As much as I'm having a hard time believing this crazy story, we're worried about you and wanted to be sure you're okay."

"I won't ever be okay again." Mary collapsed into a kitchen chair. The smell of the greasy meat turned her stomach. She couldn't think about eating at a time like this. "I drove through my old neighborhood. Saw my friend Jenni. I wanted to tell her who I was."

"You'd better not have." Darbi's tone warned of dire consequences, but the worst had already happened. Kendra no longer existed, and Mary was no longer Dean's wife.

Mary didn't answer. The only sound in the kitchen was the butcher paper crinkling as Darbi and Jacqui unwrapped their sandwiches.

"We do have news," Jacqui said. "I'd even say it's good news."

"What?" Mary asked.

Darbi wrung her hands. "I don't want you to get too excited." She kept her eyes trained on a spot above Mary's head as she spoke. "I found a letter Uncle Cillian sent me after I had my wisdom teeth out and moved here. I don't know what I did with the others, but this one was tucked in—"

"What did it say?"

Darbi took a bite of her sandwich while Mary resisted the urge to reach down her cousin's throat and pull the words out. Finally, Darbi swallowed. She wiped her mouth with a napkin and fished around inside her purse, then pulled out a folded piece of white lined paper with ragged edges as if it had been torn out of a notebook. Her hands trembled, and the paper fell to the ground.

Mary bent to retrieve it.

Dear Darbi,

I'm delighted to hear you found your happiness in America. We Mulligans are given these do-overs for the opportunity to pursue happiness so it appears you are taking advantage of yours.

I have wanted to visit you in America, but I'm afraid I've waited too long. My health has taken a turn for the worse, and I can't get around like I used to.

I do hope you continue to enjoy your new life, but I would be remiss if I didn't warn you that sometimes these do-overs don't stick. At some point, you may be tested by being presented with a decision similar to the one you regretted making the first time around. If you make the same decision you made in the past, you will find yourself right back in Ireland in your old life.

Fondly,
Uncle Cillian

Mary read the last paragraph again to herself and then again out loud. She threw the letter down on the table. "I don't understand. I want to go back—isn't that enough?"

Darbi slid the letter to her side of the table and stared down at it without speaking.

"What is the decision you regret?" Jacqui asked.

"I turned down a promotion because I didn't want to leave Dean. I wanted to see what my life would have been like if I accepted it."

Jacqui read out loud. "'If you make the same decision you made in the past, you will find yourself right back in Ireland in your old life.'" She ran her index finger over the words.

"For you, that means working hard enough to get the promotion," Darbi said.

Mary's entire body hummed. "And then turning it down."

A flush crept up Darbi's neck. "Just focus on working hard enough to get the promotion."

Chapter 25

Mary returned to work the next day, a woman on a mission her life depended on, because it did. She would never be happy in this alternate world knowing she'd sacrificed her family to be here. Her assignment today was to interview a navy combat veteran, Todd Bacco, who ran the Baystate Veterans Foundation, a nonprofit to help prevent suicides among veterans. He was planning a July Fourth 5K fundraiser, and Mary was determined to make it the best story she'd ever done.

She and Carl stood with Todd on a quiet street in Worcester in front of a yellow two-story house. "Suicide is the second-leading cause of death for post-911 veterans," Todd said. Behind him, Old Glory fluttered high on a tall pole. "More than four times as many Global War on Terrorism veterans have died by their own hand than in combat. We need to get them the help they deserve."

"What kind of resources does Baystate Veterans Foundation provide?" Mary asked.

"Our mission is to create a sense of community, connect veterans to others with similar experiences, but we're here to give help wherever they need it. Building ramps or doing other home renovations, raising money for food or heat, providing access to mental health. Whatever we can do." Todd gave examples of veterans his organization had helped, and his stories both warmed and broke Mary's heart. *Our veterans deserve so much more from us,* she thought.

They wrapped up the interview with talk about the race route, which would start and end in Green Hill Park. She hoped her viewers would be as moved as she was by the interview and donate to his cause. It was the kind of story she enjoyed most, examples of people helping others.

"How do you think that went?" she asked Carl as they drove back to the station. She sat ramrod straight in the passenger seat, all her muscles tight, wanting him to say it was her best work yet. It had to be.

Carl snapped the piece of peppermint gum he was chewing. "Fine for what it was, I guess."

Mary felt herself deflating. That wasn't nearly good enough. "What do you mean 'for what it was'?"

He lowered the radio. "If you want to be taken seriously as a journalist, you need to cover bigger stories. Most of the stories you cover end up as kickers because they're all fluff pieces."

"That story on Todd was not fluff. We're bringing attention to a serious problem."

"Yeah, well, it's not the kind of story that's going to get you a promotion."

Mary felt her entire body go still as Carl's words registered. Even her blood seemed to stop flowing. Viewers liked sensational stories, people hurting others or doing them wrong in another way. They didn't want to hear about people helping each other. In a way, she understood that. People helping people should be the default, the ordinary. There should be no need to report on it because kindness shouldn't be news. The problem was that the news reported on so many horrible crimes and dirty politicians that those stories seemed to be the norm, making viewers forget that man was kind. She didn't like reporting on all the bad in the world. She wanted to help people see the good in life, but because she hadn't been able to see the good in her own life, she was going to be forced to report on horrific things to get back to Dean and Kendra.

Maybe Carl could help her think of another type of story to cover. "What kind of story will?"

"The one Nash is doing on the Harrison murder."

Mary winced. While she'd been home miserable about Dean and Kendra for the past three days, Kimberly had been covering the most talked-about trial in New England. "I don't like covering stuff like that."

Carl glanced over at her. "Stuff like what? News?"

"I like human interest stories. Help me think of one that's compelling. In your experience, what do viewers get excited about?"

He drummed his fingers on the steering wheel. "Interview someone people want to hear from who doesn't ordinarily talk to the press."

"Like Liz Collins."

Carl shook his head. "She only has local appeal. Think bigger. Beyoncé or Taylor Swift."

Mary made a face. "They won't talk to me."

"Probably not," Carl agreed.

~

Back at the station, Mary sat at her desk with her head in her hands, trying to come up with a story that would help her get the promotion. She came up with nothing and considered explaining to Kimberly that getting the promotion meant life or death to her. Still, Mary wasn't guaranteed to get the promotion even if Kimberly bowed out of their competition. She had to earn it.

Mary put her head down on her desk, Carl's advice replaying through her mind: interview someone people want to hear from who doesn't ordinarily talk to the press. She jerked upright. Dean! In all the articles she'd read since the controversial call at the US Open, he'd refused to talk to the press.

She ran through the newsroom to find Carl. "Dean!" she shouted.

Carl looked at her blankly.

"What if I interview Dean Amato? Would that get me the promotion?"

Mitchell's voice came from behind her. "Assuming you do everything else right, it would certainly help, but I wouldn't count on getting one."

"Yeah, good luck with that," Carl said. "Rumor has it he said no to Oprah."

Dean wouldn't say no to her. Somehow he'd feel their connection. She was sure of it and couldn't stop smiling. Dean was her ticket back to her other life. It was too perfect. Early in their marriage, she and Dean had gone to a Halloween party dressed as Wonder Woman and Superman. Now she imagined Dean in that costume, red cape flapping in the wind as he swooped in to save her and carry her back to their family.

Back at her computer, she typed *Addison Heights Golf Club* in the search bar, hoping his brother worked there in this version of her life because he would know how to get in touch with Dean. She didn't have to call Anthony, though, because there was a post on the home page telling her exactly where Dean was:

DEAN AMATO TEACHING AT ADDISON HEIGHTS GOLF CLUB

(Boylston, MA)—Addison Heights Golf Club is pleased to announce that former PGA golfer and all-around good guy Dean Amato will be working at the Club this summer as a visiting pro. He'll be giving lessons from June 15 through Labor Day weekend. On Saturday, July 1, Amato will host the Club's fifth annual *American Idol* show in the Ballroom, and we'll celebrate his career to kick off the festivities. The cost of a single lesson is $175, with sessions of four available for $625. Tickets for the show are $150 per person. Half of all proceeds from the lessons and banquet will be donated to the Jimmy Fund. Anyone who would like to compete in the event should complete this form and send it and a short video to Stephanie.Pauler@AddisonHeightsGC.com.

Amato, who grew up in Boylston, holds the record for winning the Club's junior championship for eight consecutive years.

"Addison Heights is where I spent most of my childhood. I learned how to play here and have so many fond memories on this course. My dad, brother, and I often played 36 holes over a weekend," Amato said. "I'm excited to be working here this summer, teaching the world's greatest game to a new generation. It's good to be home."

Amato retired three years ago after a controversial call stripped him of a first-place finish at the US Open. His older brother, Anthony, has been the head pro at Addison Heights for nine years.

Mary had met Dean at Addison Heights all those years ago. She was attending a bridal shower in the function room, and Dean was there playing in a charity tournament for Ken, his friend who had died of cancer at the young age of seventeen. Trying to find the banquet after his round, Dean mistakenly walked into the room where the shower was being held. Instead of leaving, he dashed to the table with the decadent-looking cake, chocolate with raspberry filling. Standing there to get her own slice, Mary watched him help himself to a piece and assumed he was the groom-to-be, who was supposed to stop by to open gifts with his fiancée, Melissa.

"Hello," Mary said, surprised by how good looking he was. Melissa had described him as a tall Dustin Hoffman, but to Mary, with his wavy dark hair and chiseled cheekbones, he more closely resembled Richard

Gere. And what was with his eyelashes? She used several coats of mascara and a curling wand, and hers still didn't look as good as his. She extended her hand, thinking Melissa was a lucky girl. "Mary Mulligan."

"Mulligan." Dean seemed to consider the word. "Meeting a girl with the name Mulligan at a golf course. That has to be some kind of sign." He held on to her hand for a beat too long.

"What kind of sign?" She shifted her weight from one leg to the other, uncomfortable with the way her friend's fiancé was looking at her.

"That I shouldn't give up dating."

Mary's face flushed. Could he tell she was attracted to him? Was that why he was flirting? She glanced around the room, hoping no one was in earshot. "So inappropriate."

Dean's smile slipped off his face. "What did I do?"

"You're coming on to me at Melissa's bridal shower."

She'd expected him to be embarrassed or ashamed, but her words seemed to embolden him. He leaned in so their shoulders touched. "Right, not the best place to get to know each other. We should grab a drink sometime."

She shoved her hand in her pocket to stop herself from slapping him and stepped backward to create more space between them. "You're a jerk." The words came out louder than she'd intended. Across the room, Melissa and her mother stared at her with twisted mouths.

"Sorry if I've somehow offended you. It's just, you have the greenest eyes I've ever seen. They remind me of a fairway."

"A fairway?"

Dean stepped toward her. "A fairway as in a golf course," he said. "My favorite place to be."

For a split second, she reveled in his attention. Her cheeks flushed and her heart fluttered. After all, it wasn't every day an extremely handsome man found her attractive, but then the grim reality struck. This man was off limits. Way off limits. Guilt washed over her. She wished the floor would open up and swallow her whole as Melissa crossed the room.

"What's going on over here?" Melissa asked.

Mary wrung her hands. She couldn't tell her friend that her fiancé was hitting on her during the bridal shower, could she? Yes, she could. Melissa had to know.

One of the bridesmaids clanked a fork against a glass. "Time to open the gifts."

Nope. This was definitely not the time or place to tell Melissa. She would talk to her later.

"Who's your friend, Mary?" Melissa asked.

Mary's eyes widened. "My friend?"

Dean cleared his throat. "Dean Amato." He flashed a smile so beautiful that Mary's knees buckled. "I stumbled into the wrong room looking for the tournament banquet and couldn't resist the cake." She could have sworn he batted those fabulous eyelashes of his.

Melissa laughed. "It's amazing, isn't it?"

"Delicious." Dean stuffed the last bite on his plate into his mouth.

"You're welcome to sit down and have another piece," Melissa said.

And he did. He sat down next to Mary and watched the bride-to-be and her soon-to-be-groom open gifts, oohing and aahing at all the appropriate times. When Dean finished his second slice of cake, he quietly excused himself, but he left with Mary's phone number scribbled on a napkin that he'd folded into fours and slipped into his back pocket. He called her that night, and the following afternoon they drove to Woodman's on the North Shore for lobster rolls and clam chowder.

Remembering their first meeting now, the tension headache that Mary had had ever since she'd learned she might be stuck in this world vanished, and the muscles in her back relaxed. Dean would agree to an interview with her. She was sure of it. She grabbed her keys and ran out the door, headed for the golf club.

Chapter 26

Mary pressed the gas pedal to the floor. Her car lurched forward. According to Google Maps, she would arrive at the golf course for her reunion with Dean in thirty-seven minutes. Her whole body felt jittery. Mitchell had said this would give her a good chance of getting the promotion. If Uncle Cillian was right, all she had to do was crush the interview with Dean, and she'd be back in her old life soon. The first thing she planned to do was call Kendra. In fact, she'd jump on a plane and visit her daughter in London. *Stop it! You're getting ahead of yourself. Dean needs to agree to the interview,* a cautious voice in her head shouted, and she could have sworn the warning was from her wiser fifty-four-year-old self.

The highway curved left, and Mary found herself staring into the setting sun. She slipped on her sunglasses and lowered the visor. Still, the sun shone directly in her eyes. Ahead of her, brake lights glowed red. Mary eased up on the gas. She let out a startled gasp as Google's computerized voice spoke through her car speakers: "A crash up ahead has added nine minutes to your trip. You're still on the fastest route."

The left lane came to a stop. "Move, move, move!" Mary yelled out in the quiet of her Corolla. Vehicles in the center lane zoomed past her. She checked her rearview mirror for a chance to dash over. There was a small gap between a minivan and an Audi A4. She jerked the steering wheel right and stepped on the gas. The driver in the Audi leaned on the horn and gave her the finger.

A few yards up the road, the center lane came to a halt. Mary sighed and turned on the radio. Elton John sang the song from *The Lion King*, "Can You Feel the Love Tonight?" Mary and Dean once took a nine-year-old Kendra to see the musical. Kendra had sat between the two of them on the edge of her seat with her eyes wide and her mouth hanging open. Mary and Dean spent more time smiling at each other over Kendra's head than looking at the stage. They'd had so many happy times together. Why had Mary believed the career she'd given up would bring her more joy than her family had? She had to get to Dean and convince him to do the interview.

I promise I'll appreciate my family more if I can just get back.

The traffic inched forward. A police car pulled out of the median. A minute later, a siren blared. Mary checked her rearview mirror and saw blue flashing lights in the distance. The cars behind her all moved right. The cruiser got closer. Soon the trooper was riding her bumper. She moved right, allowing him to pass. Instead, he followed her. Her stomach sank. She steered into the breakdown lane and stopped. The police car pulled in several feet behind her.

She watched the state trooper through her rear window. He sat behind his steering wheel, staring down toward his lap. Her muscles tightened. She had no idea why he'd pulled her over. An eighteen-wheeler rumbled by, shaking her car. She checked on the police officer again. He remained sitting in the same position. Her phone rang. Darbi's face flashed across the screen, and Mary sighed. She'd forgotten she was supposed to have dinner with Darbi and Jacqui. Her cousin had insisted to make sure Mary wasn't still mad at her. While she hadn't completely forgiven Darbi, she was less angry. She swiped to take the call.

"Where are you?" Darbi asked. "The food's getting cold."

"Dean's at the golf course. I'm on my way to see him."

The line went silent. "Not a good idea," Darbi finally said. "You haven't prepared."

"What's to prepare? I'm going to ask for an interview."

"He won't agree. Come over, and let's come up with the best plan for you to approach him."

A bang on the driver's side window made Mary jump. The trooper stood beside the door with his hands on his hips.

"I have to go." She disconnected and lowered the window.

The trooper bent a long way down to look at her. "License and registration."

"What did I do? I couldn't have been speeding." She tilted her head toward the three lanes of slow-moving traffic.

"License and registration." He said it louder and slower this time.

She fumbled through her glove box, removing a pile of napkins from Dunkin', old sunglasses, packets of ketchup, a pair of mittens, plastic cutlery, a notepad, and the owner's manual.

"I'm having trouble finding the registration."

The police officer rapped on the roof of her car with his knuckles, his stern expression unnerving Mary.

She turned the owner's manual upside down and fanned through the pages. The registration fluttered to the floor, landing between the gas pedal and brake. She bent to retrieve it and handed it to the officer, along with her license.

He studied the documents. "Ms. Mulligan, are you aware that your registration has expired?"

Expired? Mary's mouth dropped open. "I, no. My husband usually takes care of that." She pictured Dean bending at the back of her car, placing the new sticker on her license plate. He usually ended up taking her Lexus to the car wash and filling her tank as well. She moved her thumb to twist her wedding ring, but of course her finger was bare. Her face flushed. "I'll take care of it. Today." Could she do it online, or did she have to go to the registry? She had no idea because Dean had handled this task for her for the past twenty-six years. She felt a tender ache in her chest. He'd looked after her in all these little ways that she'd never noticed or appreciated.

She flashed her best smile at the trooper. "I really need to get going."

The state trooper widened his stance. "I can't let you drive an unregistered vehicle. Tow truck is on the way."

~

Tom Petty singing "Even the Losers" blasted through the parking lot seconds before the yellow punch buggy turned into the tow yard. Darbi's voice singing off key drifted out the car's open roof. Mary closed her eyes. Darbi had pulled up to meet her so many times in Mary's real life with the roof down singing at the top of her lungs that she could almost pretend she was home in Hudson sitting on her stoop. If everything went right, she could be back there soon.

She crossed her fingers and leaped off the metal folding chair, rushing to the VW's passenger side. "You have to take me to Addison Heights Golf Club."

Darbi removed her pink sunglasses and switched off the stereo. "Don't you want to take care of this situation?" She waved her hand in the direction of Mary's car. Even with its faded blue paint and many scratches, the Corolla looked pristine in this lot filled with totaled wrecks.

"They're holding it hostage until I get it registered and pay them $250. Cash."

"Damn crooks." Darbi eyed the trailer that the tow yard used as an office as if she was considering busting in and giving them a piece of her mind.

"I'll deal with it tomorrow. I want to see Dean."

The muscles in Darbi's cheeks twitched. "What are you going to say to him?"

The smell of a cigar drifted through the air. The tow truck driver stood by the trailer, smoking.

"I'm going to introduce myself, ask for an interview."

"You think he's going to know who you are, don't you?"

"I'm leaving in twenty minutes," the tow truck driver hollered. "If you don't get me the cash by then, the car stays here until tomorrow, and it will cost another hundred for being here overnight."

"You should be ashamed of yourself!" Darbi yelled, but the driver had his back to them, climbing the stairs to go inside.

"Let's get out of here," Mary said.

Darbi shifted the Volkswagen into drive and steered toward the exit while Mary pulled up directions to Addison Heights on her phone. "Golf course is twenty-six minutes away. We should be able to get there before it gets dark."

Darbi said nothing, rubbing the back of her neck. The punch buggy bounced up and down as they drove over the bumpy dirt parking lot. At the exit, Darbi turned left. They traveled three miles down a country road with fields of cornstalks on one side and apple trees on the other until they reached an intersection.

"Take a left," Mary said.

Darbi turned right. "I'm bringing you to the bank. I'll even lend you the money."

Mary twisted in her seat toward her cousin. "I appreciate that, but we don't have time. I need to get to Dean before it gets dark and he leaves."

"What are you going to do when you see him?"

"I'll figure it out when I get there."

"I knew it. You have no plan. You can't just approach him." Darbi spoke much faster than she usually did and drove much slower. "He won't know who you are."

Mary rolled her head from shoulder to shoulder, trying to release the tension in her neck, her anger at Darbi for getting her in this situation bubbling up. "Why are you trying to talk me out of going to see Dean?"

"You never think about consequences. That's why you're in this mess."

"You didn't explain things to me." Mary spoke through gritted teeth. "That's how I got in this mess."

"I tried, but you wouldn't listen." Darbi turned onto a road lined with strip malls, restaurants, and gas stations. In the distance, a sign for MetroWest Bank stood taller than all the others. The electronic message under the bank's name showed the temperature as eighty-one degrees and the time as 7:37. The sun would set soon.

The traffic light in front of them turned yellow. Darbi slammed on the brakes. As the VW came to a sudden stop, she threw her arm across Mary's body.

Mary had done the same thing so many times in the car with Kendra that Kendra referred to Mary's right arm as the "magical safety bar." Mary's eyes brimmed with tears. She needed to convince Dean to agree to the interview so she could get back to Kendra. "You should have driven through the light."

"Says the woman who just had her car impounded."

"We need to get to the golf course."

"We're not going there." Darbi pulled at her seat belt as if it was suddenly too tight.

Mary jabbed at her phone's keyboard, searching for the Massachusetts Registry of Motor Vehicles, and then hit the link for the website. "I won't blow this. Is that what you're worried about?"

The light turned green, and Darbi continued toward the bank. Finally, she pulled into the parking lot and steered toward the ATM. After throwing the car into park, she turned toward Mary, rocking back and forth. For a few seconds she stared without saying anything. "I need to . . ." She buried her head in her hands.

"What?" Mary asked. She was so close to getting back that she couldn't understand why Darbi wasn't as excited as she was. "I'm so close to getting that promotion."

Darbi looked up, the rims of her eyes bright red. "I need to." She swallowed hard. "To prepare you for seeing Dean again. Let's strategize tomorrow."

"No, I'm going to see him as soon as I get my car." Mary stared down at her phone. The website still hadn't come up. "Load, already," she pleaded. An error message popped up: *The Massachusetts Registry of Motor Vehicles website is unavailable while we conduct emergency maintenance.* "I feel like the universe is conspiring against me today."

Chapter 27

Mary tossed and turned. The clock on the nightstand glowed 1:09 a.m., three minutes later than the last time she'd looked. The money Darbi had withdrawn for her sat in an envelope on the dresser. While Mary was grateful her cousin had helped her, she wondered if Darbi was trying to buy a clean conscience. Her behavior had been so weird.

A breeze blew through the open windows, rattling the hanger with Mary's green sundress on the back of the closet door. She planned to wear the dress when she saw Dean because green was his favorite color. Despite Darbi's warning that he wouldn't know her, Mary felt that on some level he would, that the love they'd shared in the other version of her life was tattooed on his soul as it was on hers. At the very least, he would immediately feel comfortable with her, and they would strike up an easy conversation.

She drifted off to a fitful sleep and woke at six thirty. An hour later, she called into work sick again and jumped in an Uber for a ride to the RMV. Once her car was registered, she took another Uber to retrieve her car. At ten, she sat behind the steering wheel of her Corolla as she drove out of the tow yard. When she reached the highway, she kept a watchful eye on her speedometer, making sure she was driving under the speed limit. Finally, she came to her exit. Google Maps told her she was only six minutes from her destination. She had never been more excited to see Dean.

On the back streets of Boylston, she had to stop for a flock of wild turkeys blocking the road. As she waited for them to move, she heard a rooster crowing in the backyard of one of the neighboring houses. Over the years, she'd attended several dinners with Dean and his golf friends at Addison Heights, and once he and Kendra had brought her there for a Mother's Day brunch. Still, she didn't remember the town being so rural. The turkeys finally made it across the street, and Mary continued down the winding street for several miles. A large black pickup truck drove toward her. Mary steered to the side of the road and pumped the brakes, fearing the narrow street wasn't wide enough for two vehicles. The other driver waved a thank-you as he passed. A sign for the golf course indicating she was a mile away came into view. She clenched and unclenched her fist. What if Darbi was right, and Dean didn't recognize her? What would she say to him? She would figure it out. After all, it was just Dean she was going to see. She'd had thousands of conversations with him through the years and hadn't planned out a single one.

At a four-way intersection, she brought the car to a stop to let a man on a bicycle pass. The cyclist smiled and raised his hand to thank her. For a fleeting second as he rode by, she'd caught a glimpse of his dark eyes. Brown eyes that she'd know anywhere. Eyes that she'd looked into for over half of her other life. It made no sense because her Dean didn't like bike riding, but she was certain the man on the bike wearing tight spandex bike shorts, a green shirt, and a matching green helmet was Dean.

Her legs shook so violently that she feared moving her foot off the brake to the gas pedal. She waited for a car to pass and turned behind it in the same direction that Dean had been traveling. She could no longer see him because he had disappeared around a curve in the road. The car in front of her puttered along as if it were in bumper-to-bumper traffic. She thought about blowing by it but instead beeped, hoping the driver would speed up. The beep backfired. The driver hit his brakes and moved even slower. Finally, though, she wound around a bend in the road, and the bike came into view. As she drove closer, she studied

Dean's broad shoulders rounded over the handlebars and watched his powerful legs turn the pedals. A warmth spread through her. For the first time since she'd entered this do-over life of hers, she felt a sense of peace.

When she was a few feet behind him, she lowered the passenger window and leaned across the front seat toward it. "Dean."

He kept pedaling as if he hadn't heard her. She tapped her horn and inched her car toward him. Still, he didn't react. She blew the horn and steered closer to him. He glanced over his shoulder and pedaled faster.

She turned toward him so that her front bumper was mere inches from his back tire.

He glowered at her over his shoulder and motioned with his arm for her to pass. His mouth moved. Although Mary had a hard time hearing his words, she was almost certain he'd screamed, "Lunatic!"

In front of him, a large tree limb had fallen across the road, most likely from the storm the other day, but Dean wasn't looking at the road. He was looking at Mary's car.

"Dean! Dean!" Mary blew her horn, trying to warn him. She hit her brakes, giving him room to maneuver around the branch.

He continued staring at her until his front wheel hit the limb. The back of his bike tilted upward as if he were popping a wheelie in reverse. He somersaulted over the handlebars and tumbled down the embankment as his bike crashed to the ground. Mary felt as if she were watching the accident in slow motion, powerless to stop it. Her stomach twisted and turned. *No, no, no. Don't let anything happen to him. Let him be okay. Please. Don't be hurt. Don't be hurt.*

She stopped her car and sat frozen behind the steering wheel, afraid to turn her head and see what had happened to Dean. On shaky legs, she exited the car. There at the bottom of the hill lay Dean's motionless body. She'd not only wiped Kendra off the face of the planet. She'd killed Dean too.

$\sim$

Mary sprinted down the embankment, jumping over boulders and ducking under tree limbs. Her open-toed sandals provided no traction on the steep incline, and she slipped, almost losing her balance several times on her way to Dean's side.

He lay on his back, twisted like a pretzel. His helmet hung at an awkward angle on his head, the clasp somehow in his mouth. Blood ran down his left leg, and his right arm covered his eyes. Mary's life with him flashed before her eyes, from the moment she'd spotted him eating cake at the bridal shower to the day he'd dropped her off to get her wisdom teeth removed. She saw the good days. There were many. She saw the bumpy moments. They really weren't that bad. This couldn't be the end, because the one thing she knew was that she wanted more time with him and Kendra.

His chest rose and fell in a slow, steady rhythm. Mary gasped in relief. *Oh, thank goodness.* She knelt beside him, the rocky ground scraping her bare knees. "Dean. Dean. Are you okay?"

He moved his arm away from his face and blinked. "You."

There was a softness in his voice that made Mary certain he recognized her. Her eyes welled up. "Yes, it's me, Mary." She pointed to herself. "I knew you'd remember me."

Groaning, he propped himself up to a sitting position. A nasty red scrape zigzagged across his cheek. A red welt swelled under his right eye. Blood oozed out of a deep gash on his knee, and a bruise tattooed his forearm. "You almost killed me." His words were measured, as if stating a fact that he expected her to disagree with.

"I-I," she stammered. "I was excited to see you."

"I don't know who you are, but I want you to stay away from me." He spoke through gritted teeth.

She leaned away from him, realizing his voice was soft and his words were measured because he was trying to control his temper. He had no idea who she was. All the love they shared in their other life didn't matter here. It wasn't powerful enough to break through to this alternate universe. Yet, for her, being here had taught her that their love was stronger than she had thought. She had to find a way to reach him, to make him understand how much they meant to one another.

Kendra had fallen off her bike when she was eleven and needed fourteen stitches: six in her elbow and eight above her ankle. If only Mary could remind Dean of how they had taken her to the ER together and then taken her to the pancake house after because she loved having breakfast food for dinner. The memory was so vivid that Mary could feel her daughter's hand, sticky with syrup, in hers as they left the restaurant. How could Kendra not exist? How could Dean not feel Mary's love for him?

He reached toward a tree behind him and used it for leverage to lift himself off the ground. A look of pain streaked across his face as he stood.

Mary stepped toward him. "Let me help."

He raised his hand so that his palm faced her. It, too, was scraped and dotted with tiny pieces of gravel. "I'm all set."

She sucked on her lower lip, trying to think of something to say. On the road above them, cars made whooshing sounds as they drove by.

Dean grimaced as he put his weight on his left leg and limped toward the hill.

"Please, let me help you," Mary repeated.

Dean pointed above them to the street. "Just go."

Ominous low dark clouds hung over them. "I can't leave you in a ditch on the side of the road." Thunder boomed. "Let me help you up the hill." She slid an arm around his waist. Her touch caused an electric shock, and a spark lit up the air. He flinched but didn't push her away like she'd expected. Instead, he leaned his shoulder into her, sighing as he rested some of his weight on her. He smelled like the same mixture of fresh-cut grass and suntan lotion that her Dean always smelled like. The familiar scent gave her hope that things would be all right.

Together, they climbed the steep incline, navigating around sticks, roots, and rocks. At the top of the hill, Dean pushed her away and limped toward his bike. The front wheel was folded in on itself.

"I can give you a ride."

He shook his head. "You've done enough. I'll call someone."

Mary pointed to his phone at the side of the road, its screen shattered. She picked it up and handed it to him. "Let me take you someplace."

"My bike won't fit in your car. I can't leave it here." Rain spit down on them.

She reached into the passenger window of her Corolla, pulled out her phone, and extended it to him.

He stared at it for a few seconds as if he might get cooties by touching it. Finally, he took it from her and tapped on the screen. "Hey. Had an accident with the bike. The wheel's tacoed. Can you come get me?" Thunder rumbled in the distance. Dean looked up at the sky. "Yeah, on Rocky Pond Road, about a half mile from the turnoff to the course."

He handed the phone back to Mary. "I'm all set." He shooed her away as if she were an annoying fly. "You can be on your way."

The rain came down faster, soon turning into a soaking downpour. Mary pulled the passenger door open for him. "Wait in my car."

He sighed as he removed his helmet before climbing in.

She raced around to the driver's side and slid behind the steering wheel. For just a second, she considered driving off, holding him captive until he let her interview him. No, that definitely wouldn't work. She glanced at his knee, saw the blood running down his shin. "You might need stitches." She handed him a wad of tissues that were in the center console.

He took them without saying anything and used one to mop up the blood oozing from the cut. She closed her eyes and was back at the barbecue for Kendra, the day she'd decided to have her wisdom teeth removed. He'd tenderly held a facecloth wrapped in ice against her knee. He was being kind, taking care of her, as he always had. Why hadn't she seen that?

They sat in silence, listening to the rain beat against the roof of the car. This was definitely not the time to ask him for an interview or even identify herself as a reporter. Her underarms felt damp with sweat. This was the worst introduction to Dean possible.

"It's not my fault you ran into a tree limb," she said.

He glanced at her without moving his head. "What were you doing driving on the side of the road like that?"

"Trying to warn you about debris in the road."

"Bullshit."

"Since when do you swear?"

He moved his hand to the door handle. "You watched me play golf on television, and you think you know me?"

She'd been wrong. There was no connection between them. The realization made her feel as if she had been rejected, as if the Mary she'd been in her other life wasn't good enough for him here in this life. He'd achieved more without her than he had with her. A streak of lightning lit up the sky, and thunder boomed.

Dean filled his cheeks with air and slowly blew it out. "You're much younger and a lot more aggressive than the usual deranged fans who chase after me."

Fans chased after him? She laughed, picturing a mob of middle-aged women running behind him. "What do you think would happen if they caught you?"

Maybe they would smother him with kisses, leaving bright-pink lipstick smears all over his face. The image made her take a closer look at him, beyond the scrapes and bruises. He had sturdy shoulders, probably from hauling around his heavy golf bag. His biceps screamed that he lifted weights, and his thick thighs let her know biking was a regular occurrence in his life without her. He had the same strong chin and thick full lips she knew so well. His dimples were just as deep, but his dark hair was long enough to curl. Wide horizontal lines cut across his forehead, and his crow's-feet were more pronounced than she remembered. Somehow, the wrinkles made him distinguished. She'd forgotten how handsome he was. Seeing him day after day for twenty-six years had made her not see him at all.

He rubbed his face, and she noticed a faint red line that zigzagged across his jawline. The scar hadn't been there when he was her husband. She was about to ask him how he got it when an SUV pulled up behind them. Dean flung the door open and hobbled out of Mary's car.

She reached for him, tugging at the back of his shirt, wanting to pull him back into the passenger seat. She wanted him—no, she needed him—to see her, the woman he had loved. After abandoning her other life for a career, she was finding it hard to love—or even like—herself.

He spun to look at her, his eyes blazing and his expression stern. His anger surprised her. She jerked away from him and slumped against the driver's side door. She swallowed hard, trying not to be intimidated by the way he glared at her. "I'm so sorry about what happened. Let me pay for your bike repairs."

"That's not necessary." He slammed the car door before she could say anything else.

His friend stepped out of the SUV and examined the bent bicycle on the side of the road. "What happened? Are you hurt?"

"I'll survive." Dean pointed a thumb at Mary. The man glanced in her direction, and they made eye contact. Anthony. It was Anthony. Of course he'd called his brother. Anthony waved. Mary's eyes grew wide. Did he recognize her? No, he was just waving to be friendly. Of course he would be friendly. She was young and pretty, just his type.

"That lunatic ran me off the road," Dean said.

That lunatic. Never mind not loving her; he didn't even like her. She didn't blame him. No matter which life she was living, she was a selfish person.

Chapter 28

After Dean's angry departure, Mary drove straight to Darbi and Jacqui's. She let herself in and found the two women playing backgammon in the sunroom. On a television in the corner, Judge Judy lectured a plaintiff, her grating voice competing with the rain pounding on the metal roof.

Darbi startled when Mary burst through the door. "Scared the bejesus out of me."

Jacqui moved her red disk, bumping one of Darbi's black ones, before looking up from the board. She narrowed her eyes. "Have you been crying?"

Mary paced in front of the table they sat behind. "I almost killed Dean today, and now I think he hates me. He'll never agree to an interview." She launched into the story of her encounter with Dean on that narrow winding road near the golf course. As she spoke, Darbi pressed her fist to her mouth, and Jacqui's hand flew to her chest.

When Mary finished, Darbi stood. "You've made a mess of things." She stalked out of the room.

"Not the first impression you wanted to make," Jacqui said.

Even Judge Judy seemed to weigh in. "It was a stupid thing to do," she admonished the defendant.

In another part of the house, cabinets banged shut. Darbi returned with a small plastic bag filled with gummy bears.

"How can I fix this?" Mary asked.

Darbi pointed a finger at her. "I told you to have a plan before you went to see him. We were supposed to come up with one together today." She picked through the gummy bears and popped a red one in her mouth.

Outside, lightning streaked across the sky, followed by the loud boom of thunder. *God's bowling again.* As a little girl, Kendra had said those words every time she heard thunder. *He got a strike.*

Gutter ball, Dean would tease.

Mary sank into a beanbag chair by the window and watched raindrops ripple through the pool, thinking the water pouring from the sky might be the old version of herself crying for this young version. "How can I make it right?"

Darbi extended the bag of gummies toward her. Mary hesitated, knowing the candy was laced, but decided there was no better time in her life to get high than now to help her forget what had happened with Dean. She picked out two orange ones.

"You'll want to be careful with those," Jacqui warned.

"Did you ask Dean if you could interview him?" Darbi asked.

Mary shook her head. "The timing didn't seem ideal." What an understatement. She reached for another gummy, yellow this time. "You should have seen the way he looked at me. I've never seen him so mad."

Jacqui patted Mary's shoulder. "It will be all right."

"Maybe not," Darbi said. "You need to forget about getting back to your old life and focus on being happy in this one."

"Why in the world would you say that? Instead of helping me get back, I feel like you're fighting it every step of the way. Like you want me to stay this way."

Darbi's face turned bright red. "I pleaded with you not to get your wisdom teeth out. All I want is for you to be happy."

Mary covered her face with her hands. "I can't be happy without my family." She was so excited when she'd first seen Dean pedaling by her on that narrow road. Thinking about her husband now, a feeling of warmth spread through her. "I love them so much." Her vision blurred and the walls seemed to spin. Outside, raindrops danced in the pool. "Dean was wearing those biking shorts today. Left little to the imagination." She laughed. The laugh started soft but grew to a roar. Tears streaked down her face. She slapped her knee. She bent her head and gasped for air. "He called me a . . ." What was the word Dean had used? "Moron"? No, definitely not that. Her mind was so fuzzy she couldn't think clearly. The room was definitely spinning. No doubt about it. "Lunatic!" she hollered. "He called me it twice."

Jacqui pointed to the gummies and looked at Darbi. "Don't let her have any more of those."

Mary closed her eyes. She thought of the time she and Dean had taken Kendra to an escape room and couldn't solve the puzzle. Kendra had started to cry, thinking they would be stuck in the small dark room forever. Being stuck in a world without Kendra and Dean would be worse than being trapped in that tiny, dark space. She would be living in a world where none of her senses worked. She'd only see their faces, hear their voices, smell their skin, feel their hugs, and taste Dean's kisses. Nothing else would compare. She wouldn't be able to function in that world. She'd stay in her apartment, sitting on the couch catatonic.

Somehow, she fell asleep in the beanbag chair, her head resting at an awkward angle on the wall beside her. She woke alone in the sunroom with a crick in her neck. The television was off, and outside, the rain had stopped. A sliver of the moon shone in the approaching night sky. She gasped when she saw it. She had slept the day away. The house smelled like browned beef. Darbi and Jacqui relaxed at the kitchen table with empty dishes in front of them. A red ceramic taco stand holding two hard shells rested on a third plate. Small colorful bowls filled with cheese, peppers, and onions sat beside it.

"Sleeping Beauty awakes." Darbi motioned to the dish with the food. "Rice is on the stove."

Mary assembled her dinner, melancholy replacing the giddiness she'd felt before she fell asleep. "What am I going to do?"

Darbi plucked a red pepper from Mary's plate. "You're going to be honest with Dean."

Mary's bite of taco got caught in her throat. She broke out in a coughing fit and chugged water until the food became dislodged. "You want me to tell him what happened when I had my wisdom teeth removed? That in another life, we're married and have a kind, beautiful daughter, and he needs to do the interview so I can get back to the other world where she exists?"

"Don't be ridiculous," Darbi said. "Tell him you were excited to see him because your promotion depends on him giving you an interview."

Chapter 29

Mary peered in the window outside the pro shop, watching Dean. Yellow and gray bruises and angry red scratches marked his handsome face. Still, he laughed as he leaned against the counter, talking to two men in their thirties wearing Titleist hats. Using his index finger, he drew a cross over his heart. Mary's chest squeezed at the familiar gesture, and she mouthed the words she knew he had just said: *Swear to God.* Her Dean.

Three days had passed since he'd tumbled off his bicycle. She'd waited to come to the golf course to give him time to cool off and hoped he wasn't still angry at her. During that time, she'd thrown herself into her job, even working over the weekend with Carl, doing everything she could do to earn that promotion in case her interview with Dean didn't pan out. Keeping busy was also the only way to prevent herself from slipping down a black hole of despair. Doing her job didn't make her forget her situation. If anything, reporting on stories that pointed out the evil in the world reminded her of all the love she'd lost. She also knew that to earn the promotion and reclaim her old life, she had to be at her best, so she put on a brave face and did the work. Even Carl had commented on the improvement in her reporting, telling her she was finally covering stories with substance.

As a way to apologize to Dean, she'd baked chocolate chip butterscotch cookies for him. The version of him whom she had known loved them.

She took a deep breath, squared her shoulders, and pushed the door open. A bell chimed, announcing her presence. Dean and the two men looked toward her. One of the men smiled; the other nodded. Dean bit down on his lip and shook his head. "What are you doing here?" Contempt dripped off each word. Mary imagined it spilling onto the floor in front of him, creating a dangerous, slick path that she had to cross to reach him.

She slunk toward the counter, stopping next to the register beside a display of decals, Sasquatch with a golf bag slung over his shoulder. "I came to apologize and brought homemade cookies as a peace offering."

Dean's hostile expression didn't change. The two men he'd been talking to shook his hand.

"Looking forward to celebrating your career at the fundraiser next week," the taller of the men said.

"I'd rather think of it as a celebration of the game," Dean said.

The two men made their way outside toward a parked golf cart.

Mary inched toward Dean and placed the dish down in front of him. "Chocolate chip, butterscotch, your favorite." She winced, realizing she wasn't supposed to know that.

He cocked his head. "I've never had a chocolate chip cookie with butterscotch in it."

Of course he hadn't. Mary's grandmother had given her the recipe. Dean had never tried them until he met Mary. "I meant your soon-to-be favorite." She lifted the tinfoil off the plate.

"I don't like butterscotch."

He'd said the same exact thing the first time she'd made them for him. "You do."

He folded his arms across his chest. "I don't."

"Try one." She pushed the plate closer to him.

The rich scent of caramelized brown sugar filled the air between them. Dean took a deep breath in. He licked the corner of his mouth.

Mary smiled, knowing he was about to give in. "I guess I'll bring them to work with me then." She pulled the dish toward her.

Dean's hand shot through the air toward the plate. He snatched a cookie and lifted it to his mouth. Mary watched his face as he bit into it. He swallowed, and his dark eyes lightened. She'd always been able to read his mood by their color, almost black when he was angry and a warm brown, like coffee with lots of cream, when he was happy.

He reached for another. For a split second, they were standing in the kitchen in their Hudson home, Dean snatching up cookies as fast as they came out of the oven. Mary sighed, savoring the moment.

"Not bad," Dean said.

"Not bad? Really? That's all I get?" Teasing him made her feel like her old self.

Dean slid the dish toward him. "They're good."

"Good enough to accept my apology?" She gave him a sheepish grin.

"For almost killing me."

Her knees weakened. He could have died in that accident. If he had, she would not only have lost the love of her life, but her daughter too. "You have no idea how happy I am that you weren't badly hurt. I'm truly sorry for causing you to crash."

"Apology accepted." He re-covered the cookies with the tinfoil and moved the plate to a shelf behind the counter. "Now, if you'll excuse me, I have a lesson to teach." He stepped toward a side door behind the counter.

"Before you go . . . ," she called to his retreating back. "I need to ask you something."

He spun to face her.

"I'm a reporter for the Independent Cable News Network, Channel 77. Mary Mulligan." She extended her hand.

He folded his arms across his chest. "I should have known you were with the press. Only a reporter or the paparazzi would be crazy enough to follow me like that."

"It's a local cable station. I'm just starting out. Hardly a threat," she said.

His arms remained pinned to his chest.

She slid the charm on her necklace back and forth across the chain. The rhythmic motion calmed her nerves. This wasn't going to be easy. She took a deep breath in and slowly released it, remembering Darbi's advice to be honest—well, as honest as she could be, given the circumstances. "My lifelong dream is to be an anchor for a national newscast. If I can convince you to grant me an interview, I'll get a big promotion, leading me one step closer to my dream." Saying those words now made her shudder the same way she did when she saw a creepy-looking bug. Being a news anchor, even the world's most trusted broadcaster, didn't hold one iota of the appeal as being Dean's wife and Kendra's mom. If only she'd realized she had been living her dream, she wouldn't be in this mess.

"I don't talk to the press." He said it slowly, as if talking to a small child.

Undeterred, she pasted on her biggest smile. "Please. Just this one time."

He smiled back at her. His dimples even made an appearance. Ha! She felt the same joy she had on her wedding day when he'd smiled at her as she made her way down the aisle toward him. She knew he wouldn't let her down. Tension seeped out of her shoulders.

"Not going to happen." He turned on his heel and stepped toward the side door.

She'd been so certain he was going to say yes that she didn't immediately understand that he had not only turned her down but he was also leaving. When the door shut behind him, adrenaline surged through her veins. She had to stop him. She lunged toward the door, intending to follow Dean, but it suddenly swung toward her. Anthony waltzed into the room, whistling and unwrapping a Snickers bar. "You're not supposed to be behind the counter," he said.

"I need to talk to Dean."

He squinted and tilted his head as if something had dawned on him. "You're that girl on the news." He waved the candy bar in her direction. "Channel 77, right? Thought you looked familiar the other day."

Like an unattended pot of water on a hot burner, Mary's anxiety threatened to boil over. She needed Dean's help. "He just went back there." She pointed behind Anthony to the door.

"I can't let you back there. Staff only. Besides, once Dean finds out you're with the press, he's not going to want anything to do with you."

"I need to talk to him." She lost the battle to control her despair. Her voice cracked and her eyes welled up.

Anthony looked at her with such empathy that Mary feared he somehow knew she would never make it back to her old life. No! That couldn't be true. There was a buzzing in her head. She *had* to get back.

"Why do you need to talk to him?" he asked. "What's so important?"

"My promotion depends on getting an interview with him."

"Well then, you'd better kiss that promotion goodbye." He kissed his hand and made a throwing motion.

Mary eyed the bag of golf clubs in the sale section and fantasized about beating him over the head with one. She needed him to help her, not tell her how impossible the task was. "If I can just get some time alone with him to talk, I can convince him." She had to reach deep within herself to put conviction in her voice because she had an overwhelming fear that Anthony was right. There was no way Dean would do an interview with her, an unknown reporter just starting her career at a cable news station who'd almost killed him. After all, he'd already refused the most notable names with the biggest platforms in the industry.

Anthony tapped one of the decals in the display. "Honey, you have a better chance of interviewing Bigfoot than my brother." He leaned toward the computer on the counter, one hand on the mouse, scrolling. "But if you think you can convince him, I can give you an opportunity to talk to him. Your timing is perfect. His lesson on Thursday night just canceled. He has an opening at six. That's the only one for the rest of the summer."

"I'll take it."

"It's $175. Paid in advance. Half goes to charity."

Mary fished her credit card out of her wristlet and slid it into the machine. The screen lit up with the message *Transaction processing.* She swayed from side to side, waiting. Anthony bit into his candy bar. A piece of chocolate smeared the corner of his mouth.

The machine beeped, and the message on the screen changed: *Declined.*

"No, no, no."

"Try again," Anthony offered.

Mary's throat burned, and her eyes filled with tears. There was no point in trying again. She'd been charging almost everything.

"I'll hold the spot for you until tomorrow at six," he said in a gentle voice. "After that, I have to release it."

Chapter 30

Mary lay down on top of her comforter, trying to fall asleep, her mind racing. After leaving the golf course that afternoon, she'd driven to the office to ask Mitchell if the station would pay for her lesson.

"If you get the interview, we'll reimburse you," he'd said.

When she'd tried to explain that she didn't have the money to pay for the lesson up front, he'd acted as if he hadn't heard her. "Kimberly is anchoring next Thursday. You can do Friday." He looked at her as if waiting for her to react, so she gave him a halfhearted thumbs-up. Before she'd found out she was stuck here, her celebration would have been real, but now she thought of the opportunity as a task she had to accomplish to get home.

From the station, she had driven straight to Darbi's, certain her cousin would help, but Darbi had snapped at Mary. "What am I, the Bank of Mulligan? I just gave you money to get your car out of the tow yard."

Mouth gaping, Mary had stared at Darbi. Surely her cousin knew how important this was to her, more important than getting her car from the tow yard. She couldn't believe she had to explain it. "It's to help me return to my old life."

Darbi's entire body buzzed with a nervous energy. Her hands fluttered, and she tapped her toes on her chair. "Return to your old life, humph." She'd made fleeting eye contact with Mary while repeatedly tugging at the strap of her wet bathing suit. Each time, it made a thwacking sound as it pulled away from her skin. "I'm not giving you money for a golf lesson." She'd risen from her chaise longue like a rocket launching and stalked into the house to take a shower, leaving Mary bewildered by the pool, her anger with her cousin growing by the second.

Now, Mary tossed and turned. She flipped her pillow, hoping the other side would be cool. It wasn't. The fans in her windows whirled at full speed, doing absolutely nothing to counter the oppressive heat. She'd forgotten how the attic apartment turned into the world's hottest sauna during the dog days of summer. The first time she'd lived here, Dean had surprised her during a prolonged heat wave by buying and installing portable air conditioner units in her bedroom and living room. Thinking about all the little ways he'd looked out for her through the years that she didn't appreciate made her heart ache. He'd always come through for her. He would come through for her this time too. He had to. For their family.

There had to be a way for her to get the money for the lesson. Jacqui would help, but she was in New York at a trade show, and Mary hadn't been able to get a hold of her. There was no one else she could ask. She felt that familiar tightness in her chest that preceded a panic attack. No, no, no. She couldn't afford to have a full-blown panic attack. Not now. She needed to figure this out. Fresh air usually calmed her. She raced out of her bedroom and across her apartment to the outdoor stairway. Leaning against the banister, she gulped in huge breaths of air.

Once the viselike grip on her chest had loosened, she sank to the top step, relishing the slight breeze that brought momentary relief from the stifling heat. She rested her head against the side of the house and closed her eyes. Headlights from Brady's Jeep illuminated the driveway. In the quiet of the night, she heard music from his car stereo, Brett Young begging someone to have mercy on him. She knew exactly how the singer felt. Brady backed into his spot like he always did, as if he needed to be ready to make a quick getaway at any time. The music petered out, and he jumped out of the vehicle, striding around to the passenger side to unfasten Frank Sinatra's seat belt. The dog leaped onto the driveway and trotted toward the staircase, his long tail slashing side to side through the thick night air.

"Frank," Brady called, charging across the lawn after the dog. Frank stopped on the step below Mary, nudging her with his nose, demanding to be patted. The feel of his silky hair helped slow her pounding heart.

Brady took the stairs two at a time, coming to an abrupt stop when he saw Mary sitting on the top step scratching the dog's neck. "Everything okay? Why are you out here in the middle of the night?"

Everything's fine. The words were on the tip of her tongue. It's what she always said when someone asked her how she was, not wanting to bother them with her troubles. She'd even used the line on Dean through the years. This time, she stopped herself. She was scared out of her mind. In all likelihood, she wouldn't be able to scrounge up the money for a lesson with Dean. She needed someone to talk to about it other than Belli.

She sucked in a big breath, ready to spill her guts. "Trying to figure out a work problem."

Brady slid down next to her on the stair. "Hit me up."

He seemed like he really wanted to help, and Mary felt a tad bad for always thinking the worst of him. After all, she'd definitely played a part in whatever had happened between them.

Frank Sinatra squeezed between them and made his way to the welcome mat for a nap, as if he knew they'd be talking for a long time.

"I'm up for a big promotion, but to get it, I have to interview someone who never talks to the press."

On the street in front of the house, a motorcycle raced by.

"What's the promotion?" Brady asked.

"Reporter for the *Morning Show* in Chicago."

His jaw tensed. "You're moving to Chicago?"

The disappointment in his voice and look of sorrow on his face triggered a memory, or whatever the uploads of past experiences that she sometimes received were. He'd been sitting next to her on the sofa in her apartment. *Ozark* was playing on the television, but neither of them was watching. Brady wore the same sorrowful expression he wore now.

His voice interrupted the memory. "I'd really miss you if you move to Chicago."

Again, he sounded like he meant it. Maybe she'd had it all wrong about him, and he was a good guy. She certainly hadn't gotten many things right, starting with when she'd dismissed Darbi's story out of hand at lunch that day. She pushed away the thought, uncomfortable with how it made her feel, as if she were at fault for getting herself into this predicament. "I only get to go if he agrees to the interview."

"Who?"

"Dean Amato." Thinking Brady wouldn't know who Dean was, she added, "The golfer."

Brady whistled. "America's lovable loser. That's going to be tough. Rumor has it that he said no to Oprah."

Realizing that Brady not only knew who Dean was but apparently was aware of his boycott of the press made her task seem insurmountable. She slumped over, her head curling toward her chest.

"Come on, now." Brady rubbed her back. "I said tough, not impossible."

She stiffened at his touch and slid away from him, feeling guilty because he was being so nice, but she definitely didn't want him to get the wrong idea.

They sat without speaking. Frank Sinatra's snoring provided the soundtrack for the moment. Mary turned to look at the dog. He was stretched out on the mat, his legs twitching as if he were dreaming about chasing a squirrel. She feared Frank had a better chance of catching the imaginary squirrel than she did of landing an interview with Dean.

"I was able to get on the schedule for a golf lesson with him. It's my last chance to try to convince him, but I don't have the money to pay for it. The station will only reimburse me if he agrees to the interview."

"How's a lesson going to help? You want to interview him, not challenge him to a round."

An ant crawled up Mary's leg, and she flicked it away. "While he's giving me the lesson, I can talk to him, try to change his mind."

"What are you going to say?"

She shrugged because she hadn't figured that part out yet.

"You need a plan," Brady said.

It was exactly what Darbi always said. They were right, yet somewhere inside her she believed Dean would agree to the interview. The connection they shared from their other lives would break through at some point, and he would want to help her. That was her plan.

"How much?"

She knew Brady had said something but, lost in thought, she hadn't been paying attention to the words. "Excuse me?"

"How much do you need for the lesson?"

"One hundred and seventy-five." Ordinarily, she'd never ask him for money, but these were no ordinary times. She studied the night sky so she wouldn't have to look at Brady, hoping the stars would give her the strength she needed to ask him.

As if he sensed she was about to hit him up for money, he stood.

Mary expected he'd grab Frank and race down the stairs. Instead, he reached into his back pocket and pulled out his wallet.

"You'll loan me the money?"

He handed her a wad of cash.

Tears clouded her eyes. "Thank you, thank you."

"That's what friends do, Mary. They help each other out."

Friends. He'd stressed that word. She knew he was trying to convey some kind of a message, and she suspected it had to do with whatever had happened between them. All she could think about now, though, was convincing Dean to do the interview and getting home.

Chapter 31

"Mary Mulligan, why are you here?" Dean asked. He'd been sitting on a stool behind the counter in the pro shop at Addison Heights, watching golf on a television mounted to the side wall, but he stood when Mary entered. Though his tone was friendly and he smiled, her presence there clearly annoyed him. Anyone else might have missed the signs, but after twenty-six years of marriage, Mary knew his tells: the slight twitch in his right cheek, the way his index finger slid under his watch band to pull it off his skin, and his use of her first and last name. Hope swelled inside her because in those few seconds, she was watching her Dean. Her husband was still there, living somewhere inside this man, and she could convince that version of Dean to do the interview.

She put on what she hoped was a sweet smile. "I'm here for my lesson."

His eyes widened. "A golf lesson? With who?"

Her neck prickled with irritation. Hadn't Anthony told him, or at least put her name on the schedule? "You."

He shook his head as his hand flew to the mouse, waking up his computer. "Says here my six o'clock is with Steve B."

The side door opened, and Anthony popped his head out. "Steve canceled. Last-minute business trip. I forgot to update the schedule."

Dean glowered at his brother. "You forgot?"

Anthony shrugged. "The young woman paid for a lesson with you. Teach her how to hit a golf ball."

"This is the young woman who ran me off the road." Dean gestured to his face. A few scratches and a yellowish bruise remained.

"So, after you teach her how to drive a golf ball, teach her how to drive a car." Anthony disappeared behind the door again, closing it tightly after himself.

Dean rubbed his temple. Something he always did at the onset of a headache, and again, the familiarity buoyed Mary. Still, she squared her shoulders, prepared for him to tell her he wouldn't give her a lesson and ready to argue with him.

"You don't want to learn how to play golf," he said. "You're here to interview me."

She made a show of looking behind her toward the entrance. "If that were the case, my cameraman would be here with me."

"Okay then, you're going to try to convince me to let you interview me, and I'm telling you now, it's a waste of your time and mine."

Mary sighed. He'd always been able to see through her. "I have an hour to try."

"Forty-five minutes," Dean said.

~

He strapped the golf bag to the back of the cart and slid in behind the steering wheel, next to Mary. Her leg bounced up and down, and her mind raced. She couldn't screw this up. Her life depended on it, and so did his and Kendra's. She took a deep breath, trying to calm herself.

His arm brushed against hers, and a small spark lit up the air. "Let's get this over with," he said.

This was the first time Mary had ever ridden in a golf cart with Dean. Her cheeks burned with shame. She should have shown more of an interest in this game that her husband had loved so much, or at least learned more about it before declaring she wanted nothing to do with it. When they were dating, she'd accompanied him to the driving range and even slapped out a bucket of balls, taking advice from him about her swing as she did so. After they married, she stopped going, just like he'd stopped spending afternoons on the beach with her. How had they become so comfortable with each other that they had stopped trying to please one another?

Dean fidgeted on the cart bench, getting comfortable, his familiar scent filling the small space between them. Oh, how she'd missed that smell. She inhaled deeply to breathe it in, realizing his scent relaxed her. "You smell like you've been on the course all day."

"Are you saying I stink?" He sniffed his underarm.

She laughed. "Not at all. The smell reminds me of fresh-cut grass and Coppertone."

He shivered, and his face paled. "Whoa. Hearing you say that"—he turned toward her, his eyes watering as he looked toward the bright sun—"gave me an intense case of déjà vu."

Mary's stomach fluttered, sure that somewhere inside him, memories of his life with her were trying to break through. She considered telling him about the other dimension—or whatever it was—where they were married and how she needed his help to get back to that world for their family. No, he would think she was crazy. A lighter touch would be better. "Maybe you knew me in another life."

Dean rolled his eyes. "You believe in reincarnation."

"I do." Fifty-something Mary had been skeptical of any fact she couldn't confirm, but after what had happened to her, she now believed anything was possible.

They crossed a road and drove through a parking lot. Golfers stood by their open car trunks, pulling out or packing up their bags of clubs and changing into or out of their golf shoes. Some shouted Dean's name. Others waved. Dean nodded or raised his hand in response.

This was what it felt like to ride with a celebrity. She flexed and unflexed her legs. The realization that Dean was a celebrity hit her hard. Somehow, she had held him back in their life together.

A ball came flying toward them from the left, bouncing off the cart's roof and landing in a flower bed with varying shades of pink daisies. Mary flinched, but Dean didn't react.

"So, what were you in your past life? A queen? A pop star? A famous actress?" he asked. They reached the practice area, and the cart squeaked to a stop.

A woman on the putting green hit a row of balls, striking one ball and then another. Instead of seeing her, Mary saw Kendra in their backyard in Hudson, practicing with Dean. She could hear their laughter and even feel the weight of the book in her lap as she watched them play. Her hand flew to her heart. "A mother and a wife." Her voice thickened. "I didn't realize it at the time, but it was incredibly special, having a family."

The corner of Dean's mouth tipped downward, his Adam's apple bobbed, and his shoulders drooped. His melancholy expression was one Mary had never seen on her husband. He looked in desperate need of a hug. Studying him, she wondered if this version of Dean regretted his choice not to marry and have children. She wanted to comfort him, but before she could think of anything to say, he shot out of the cart and busied himself with unstrapping the bag of clubs from the back.

Three teenage boys lugging bags over their shoulders walked by, their irons clanking together with each step they took. "Hey, Mr. Amato," one of them called. "I'm coming for you. Shot a seventy-four last round."

"Yeah, but you were playing from the ladies' tees," Dean teased.

The boy's friends burst out in laughter. "He roasted you, dude," one said.

"Let's do this," Dean called to Mary, walking off behind the boys toward the driving range. She couldn't keep up with his long strides, and by the time she'd made it to the bay, he had a ball set up on a tee. "Let's see what you got." He tilted his head in the direction of the tee.

"Aren't you supposed to give me instructions or show me what to do?" Mary asked.

"First, I want to see your swing." He handed her the seven iron.

The club felt awkward in her hands. She wasn't even sure how to hold it. The woman in the bay next to hers looked like she knew what she was doing, or maybe her adorable outfit—a pink-and-gray-plaid skort with a pink sleeveless polo shirt and a gray poufy baseball cap—made her look like a confident pro. Dang, Mary should have worn something cute instead of dressing for the upcoming July Fourth holiday in blue shorts and a red-and-white-striped shirt that made her look like a walking version of the American flag. Only the stars were missing. She could erase thirty years off her age, but at her core, she was still a dowdy, middle-aged woman.

Not only was the woman next to her dressed like a real golfer, but she knew how to play. With an effortless swing, she sent every ball soaring into the air. Kendra could give her a run for her money. The thought sparked Mary's determination. She was here to get back to her life with her family. She needed to convince Dean to do the interview.

He tapped the face of his watch with his index finger. "Anytime now. I've got another lesson in less than an hour."

"How do you go from being a media darling to refusing to talk to the press?"

"I'm a has-been. No one wants to hear from me."

"You know that's not true. People want to hear your version of what happened at the US Open."

"One more word about the Open or interviewing me, and this lesson is over."

He slid his sunglasses down off his baseball hat and over his eyes. He was so familiar, yet something was off. Unlike her Dean, he was lean and muscular, but the difference went beyond his appearance to the way he carried himself. He seemed unreachable, distant, sad even. This version of Dean lacked the warmth that made her Dean so lovable. Her Dean *was* lovable. They'd loved each other for more than a quarter century. Of course they'd experienced occasional hard times. Didn't all couples? They'd always worked out their issues because they loved each other. How hadn't she realized that?

"Let's go." Impatience tinged his voice.

If she could figure out how to play this game, she might be able to distract Dean into talking about himself, and he'd see that an interview wouldn't be so bad. She tried to remember what she knew about swinging a golf club from the times he'd taken her to the driving range while they were dating. Nothing came to her, but really how hard could it be to hit a stationary object with a big club? She stepped up to the tee and swung with all her might. The iron made a swishing sound as it cut through the air, missing the ball.

Dean offered no advice or explanation about what she'd done wrong. Instead, he twirled his finger in the air, indicating she should try again. Mary swung a second time, with the same results. She whiffed swing after swing, but Dean didn't say a word. After missing a dozen or so times, she turned to look at him again. He was watching the boy who had spoken to him earlier. "Garrett," he called out. "Belly button should be facing the flag at the end of your swing." The boy swung again, and Dean gave him a thumbs-up.

Mary jabbed him with the shaft of her club. "You're supposed to be teaching me, not him."

Dean reached into his pocket and pulled out a pack of gum. He unwrapped a piece and folded it into his mouth. The scent of spearmint floated in the air. "Before we work on your swing, we have to teach you how to hold the club." He took the seven iron from her. "There are three basic kinds of grips. The overlap, the interlock, and the baseball grip." He explained the differences and demonstrated each. "I recommend you start with the interlock. It locks the hands together and forces them to act as a unit. See how the fingers on my right hand wrap around my left thumb."

Mary focused on his hands, noticing the bare ring finger on his left hand. His lack of a wedding ring brightened her outlook, reassuring her that she hadn't lost him to someone else. He was still hers, and that made her almost certain he'd help her just like he always had.

"How come you never married?" The question spilled out before she could stop herself.

Dean snapped his gum. "Are you even listening?"

She pushed her hair away from her face. "Yes, and I'm watching your hands, and I noticed your ring finger is bare."

Dean bent to place a ball on the rubber tee. He swung at the ball, sending it soaring across the range. She didn't know much about golf swings, but she thought his was beautiful. His arms moved across his body with a liquid fluidity. His weight shifted from his back leg to his front leg with a loose ease. The heel of his right foot came off the ground as if it were on a spring. He set up another ball and pointed to his feet with the club. "Notice the ball is in the middle of my stance."

His left golf shoe was approximately two inches in front of the ball, and his right foot was an equal distance behind it.

Dean swung. There was a crisp, clean sound at contact. The ball soared into the air and landed mere inches from a flag marking 175 yards. "Your turn," he said, handing her the club.

"What if we do a story on you giving me a lesson?"

"How about you pay attention to what we're doing here?"

Once she had her hands in position, he reached toward her fingers to adjust them. The touch of his skin against hers gave them both an electrical shock. "Ouch." He pulled his hand away. "Why does that keep happening?"

The static electricity between them had to have something to do with their connection in their other life, didn't it? Maybe each shock was a spark of memory, and Dean was on the way to remembering exactly who Mary was. That would be amazing. It would mean she might make it home.

She swung at the ball. This time her club made contact. The ball traveled less than ten yards, but it was a start.

"Now we're getting somewhere," Dean said before giving her other instructions.

"How did you get into the game?" She knew the answer. It was his family's folklore, but she wanted to get him talking, to open up.

"My dad introduced me to it."

Disappointed he didn't say more, she filled in the rest of the story. "He played to get away from your mom for a good chunk of time on the weekend. Otherwise, she'd inundate him with a long list of annoying chores. You and Anthony went with him so you wouldn't be stuck doing them," Mary said, remembering the story Dean had told her long ago.

His O-shaped mouth conveyed his shock. "How do you know that?"

She twisted a strand of hair around her finger. "I-I read it. In an old interview."

Dean shook his head. "I never mentioned that to a reporter. My dad and mom both would have throttled me."

"You must have."

"Definitely not." He chewed on his inner cheek. "'Good chunk of time.' 'Long list of annoying chores.' Those are the exact words my father used."

She could see that her knowledge of what his father had told him had thrown him off balance. He stroked his chin as he watched her. Maybe now was the time to confess what had happened when she'd gotten her wisdom teeth removed.

"We used to . . ."

His phone rang, and he looked at the screen. "Sorry, I have to take this."

Mary watched him walk away. If she told him the truth, he would think she was crazy and never agree to the interview. Her desperation was affecting her decision-making. Thank goodness they'd been interrupted. She busied herself by practicing what he'd taught her, keeping her head still, shifting her weight from her back foot to her front, and following through on the swing. Each time she struck the ball, it traveled a little bit farther than the last time.

Dean returned to the bay, muttering under his breath.

"I thought I was doing better," she said.

"You are." He adjusted his baseball cap. Even with the adjustment, the hat looked all wrong on him because it wasn't the old tattered royal blue one Kendra had given him on Father's Day all those years ago. This one was black, with a red circle around a white tee logo in the center. She wanted to knock it off his head because now that she'd noticed it, she felt as if she were looking in a mirror and seeing her selfishness reflected back at her. Kendra didn't exist in this world, and Dean wasn't her husband, all because Mary had wanted another chance to anchor the news. Until she got back to her other life, she'd have to live with that gut-wrenching knowledge.

"I have to cut the lesson short," Dean said. "There's a problem at the house. A pipe burst."

An image of their home in Hudson popped into Mary's head, but then her stomach fell as she realized he was talking about another place where he lived without her. Meanwhile, after the lesson, she'd climb the thirty-eight steps to her attic apartment, and the only one there to greet her would be Belli. A wave of loneliness rolled over her. What had she done?

"Where do you live?" she asked, wondering what his home looked like without her around to decorate it.

He cocked his head in a way that let her know he wouldn't answer.

"I still have fifteen minutes left of my lesson." He couldn't leave. She hadn't convinced him to do the interview yet.

Dean was walking toward the parking lot. "You can reschedule with Anthony."

She chased after him. "He already told me you're booked for the summer."

"Well then, have him give you a ticket to the fundraiser they're doing this weekend instead."

Mary smiled all the way to the clubhouse, certain she was getting through to Dean. Why else would he suggest that she attend the fundraiser?

~

The first time Mary had read the press release about Dean teaching at Addison Heights, she'd skimmed right over the part about the *American Idol*–like talent show. Now, in the pro shop waiting for Anthony to finish with a customer, she read the same information again on a flyer posted to the bulletin board, and she immediately thought of James. After seeing that depressed version of him in Scituate, she'd promised herself she would help him. She owed him that much for ruining his life, even if he didn't know it.

"Is it too late for someone to register to participate?" she asked.

"Actually, someone just canceled. Steph's going through the videos right now, looking for another contestant," Anthony said. "Do you sing?"

Mary shook her head. "No, but I know someone who does."

Chapter 32

Two nights later, an hour before the fundraiser, Mary waited for James in the Addison Heights parking lot, where they'd agreed to meet. She'd had to spend more than an hour on the phone to convince him to participate. He'd kept insisting he wasn't good enough to play in front of a crowd, and he feared he would be booed off the stage. She'd repeatedly reminded him how the video of him singing during the storm had gone viral. Finally, he'd said, "I guess I should give the people what they want." He'd sounded so much like her James then that she was certain he would kill it.

Now, she looked at her phone. He was ten minutes late, and she feared he'd changed his mind. The entire flow of the night would be ruined if he didn't show up. He was one of four contestants, each allotted twenty minutes to sing. The winner would be awarded an extra twenty minutes at the end of the night. Another five minutes ticked by, and Mary wished she'd never asked James to participate. She was already nervous enough about whether she would be able to convince Dean to do the interview. She decided she'd wait until the end of the evening to talk to him about it. Her stomach dropped as she thought about the conversation.

Finally, a Prius turned into the parking lot and pulled into a spot. Mary let out a deep breath as James stepped out of the car.

"I almost chickened out." He bent his arms and tucked his hands under his armpits, flapping his elbows up and down and clucking like a chicken. Mary laughed, seeing and hearing her old friend. The resemblance gave her a good feeling about tonight. Maybe her husband would show up too. She looped her arm through James's and walked him toward the entrance.

~

While James met with the event coordinator and other contestants, Mary wandered around the empty banquet room. Photographs of Dean at various ages throughout his career hung on the walls: A twenty-five-year-old at the first tee of the Open Championship, his first major; a twenty-eight-year-old Dean posing with Tiger Woods and Phil Mickelson at the PGA Championship; a thirty-six-year-old competing with the team from the United States in the World Cup; a forty-four-year-old at the British Open. Mary paused in front of each image, searching for something that would give her insight into this man who was so similar to Dean her husband but somehow so different too.

He had changed as he aged. That she was sure of. He fake smiled in many of the photos taken in the second half of his career. She could tell by the way his top row of teeth overlapped the bottom row. When he was genuinely happy, like in the candid shots from earlier in his career, his mouth hung open, and his bottom row of teeth barely showed.

"You're walking around here like it's an art exhibit." Mary jumped at the sound of Dean's voice coming from behind her. "What's so fascinating about pictures of me?" He wore a sharp gray suit with a gray-and-white-checkered shirt and a navy tie dotted with golf balls. If he disliked dressing up as much as her Dean did, he'd loosen the tie's knot by the end of the night.

"At the start of your career, you look happy, but later you look miserable. Why?"

Dean studied the picture on the wall in front of them, taken at the Masters, two years before he retired. His three putt on the seventeenth hole had cost him the Green Jacket. "I do not look miserable."

"It's your fake smile."

His head jerked back as if he was surprised by the confidence with which she spoke. "How would you know?"

Because I was married to you for twenty-six years. Oh, how she wanted to tell him. "You're gritting your teeth."

He leaned closer to the picture and rubbed his jaw. "Guess I was just constantly disappointed that I never finished first."

She hadn't been expecting his raw honesty or the flash of disappointment that wrecked his face. The fifty-four-year-old woman who used to be his wife wanted to comfort him, to tell him that even though he'd never won a major, just by playing in PGA tournaments he'd accomplished something that most people only fantasized about. She had the urge to hug him and tell him he should be proud of his accomplishments.

The twenty-four-year-old reporter desperate to get back to her old life batted down the idea. She knew she should take advantage of his vulnerability by asking him more questions and videoing his responses, but Dean had made it clear she couldn't film him at the event, and she'd agreed. She didn't want to go back on her word, but if she did film him and ran the footage on the news, she'd have something no other journalist had been able to get in years, and that could help her get back to their family. Her hand slipped inside her wristlet, and she started to pull out her phone.

"Oh no, you don't." Dean grabbed her wrist. Like every other time they'd touched, an electrical shock jolted him. "Damn." He pulled away from her and shook out his hand. "Put that away."

"Please. Your fans, the entire golf world, wants to hear from you."

"What about what I want?" he asked.

The question hit her as if Dean her husband had asked it and not this Dean she hardly knew. On their first date, her Dean had told her he planned to be a professional golfer, and then they got married and she'd quit her job and they'd become completely dependent on his salary. He'd had to work more and ended up missing tournaments. Somehow over the years the story had changed in her memory, and she believed she'd given up her career for him, but she saw now that he had sacrificed his dream to support their family. The room became unbearably hot. Sweat dripped down her back, or maybe it was shame oozing from her body.

"I'm so sorry."

Dean gave a curt nod, but she wasn't talking to him. She was apologizing to her husband.

~

While the waiters and waitresses passed out dessert, a choice of key lime pie or chocolate mousse, James sat on a stool in the front-right corner of the dance floor, strumming his guitar and singing "Sweet Caroline," a favorite in the Boston area. Just as Mary had suspected, he'd crushed his performance and won the event. When they'd announced his name as the winner, the self-doubt choking the life out of him had seemed to unravel. He stood taller, pointing to the crowd and then tapping his heart. Now, he was playing the extra set, taking requests and showing a little of her James's pizzazz as he hammed it up for the crowd.

Everyone at Mary's table had left after the winner was announced, so she sat by herself, eating her chocolate mousse. As James played, she kept her eye on Dean. He sat at a table diagonal from hers with a blonde who appeared to be his age. The woman repeatedly touched him as she spoke. Each time she did, Mary felt a prick of jealousy, even though this version of herself had no right to feel that way.

Anthony noticed Mary sitting alone and moved to join her, bringing his date. The woman, close to Mary's new age, looked familiar. Mary wondered if she'd met her through Brady or Kimberly.

The woman waved. "I'm Jessica."

Jessica. The golfing goddess from Kendra's bon voyage party. Oh, what Mary would do to go back to that day and not have made the decision to get her wisdom teeth extracted.

"The Singing Mailman's good," Anthony said. James had chosen the moniker for tonight's contest. While the crowd tonight loved James and he appeared to be having a great time, Mary couldn't help but be a little sad for all the glory he'd never experience in this version of his life. All because of her.

At the other table, Dean and the blond woman stood. He walked her to the exit, and she leaned toward him to kiss him. The kiss would have landed on his mouth if he hadn't turned his head at the last moment. Anthony chuckled. He'd been watching the interaction too.

Dean walked back across the room toward Mary's table, undoing the knot in his tie. "Everyone having fun?"

"Hey, Singing Mailman," Anthony called out. "Can you play 'Still the One' for my brother here?" He winked at Dean as James played the opening notes of the Orleans song from the 1970s. "Can't believe Michelle still has a thing for you after all this time."

Mary's head whipped back toward the door, but the blonde was gone. "That was Michelle Anderson."

Dean narrowed his eyes. "What do you know about Michelle?"

"She was your high school sweetheart."

Mary version 1 had never met the woman, but she'd certainly heard all about her. Michelle had dated Dean from sophomore through senior year. She broke up with a devastated Dean the summer before they started college because she didn't want to be tied down with a home-town boyfriend. After Dean and Mary's engagement announcement appeared in the local paper, Michelle had sent a letter addressed to him to his parents' house, confessing that she'd made a horrible mistake by letting him go all those years ago and begging him to get back together. At times when Mary version 1 fought with Dean, she would mumble, "I should have encouraged you to respond to Michelle's letter."

"It's not too late," Dean would tease. "I can join Facebook and send her a friend request."

The memory broke Mary's heart. How could she have been so cavalier? She was lucky to have Dean, as he was lucky to have her. They'd been a good team. Kendra was proof of that.

Now Dean elbowed Anthony. "Did you tell her about Michelle or about the reason Dad encouraged us to take up golf?"

Sipping on his bottle of beer, Anthony shook his head. "Why would I do that?"

"My research is impeccable," Mary said, hoping he'd believe her.

"It must be."

James finished the song. "Any other requests?"

"'Thunder Road,'" Mary called.

"Never heard of it," Jessica said.

"Springsteen?"

Jessica shrugged.

Mary, Dean, Anthony, and everyone in the room over the age of forty sang along, vigorously applauding when James finished. Mary thought back to the songs he used to practice in the apartment below hers and later performed at the Skunk. "'Love Stinks,' by J. Geils!" she yelled.

He sang it, and the older folks in the crowd responded with the same enthusiasm they'd had for the Springsteen tune.

"'Best Friend's Girl,' by the Cars!" Mary called. Song after song, she shouted out other recommendations: "Jump," by Van Halen; "Sweet Emotion," by Aerosmith; "Burning Down the House," by the Talking Heads.

Nothing she suggested stumped James. He smiled and murmured something like, "Oh, I love that one," or he'd nod and say, "That one's from my prime time."

Seeing him enjoy himself gave Mary a rush. Finally, she'd done something good in this alternate world.

Jessica listened, playing with the silverware still on the table and sipping her dirty martini. "What are these songs? I've never heard any of them," she whined.

Dean's gaze shifted from Jessica to Mary. "How do you know all these songs, Mary?" There was an accusation in his question, or at least suspicion. Mary couldn't help but be hopeful that the version of him whom she had known had cracked open a door in this Dean's mind, and memories were starting to slip through. The Dean sitting with her continued to study her, waiting for an answer.

She dipped her spoon into her remaining dessert and slowly brought the spoonful of mousse to her lips, giving herself time to consider whether she should tell him the truth. If Anthony and Jessica weren't sitting with them, she would tell him, but she couldn't risk Anthony thinking she was crazy. She might need his help again.

"These are all from before you were born," Dean said.

"I used to listen to them with my parents. My dad even gave me an iPod loaded with songs from his teenage years." Of course that was a lie, but Mary had given Kendra a similar gift after George Michael's death.

Dean nodded. "That makes sense."

James played the opening chord for "Money for Nothing," by Dire Straits.

"Love this one," Mary and Dean both said at the same time. They sang along, smiling at each other. She felt the connection between them growing stronger, like a cell phone signal increasing from one to three bars. She needed it to amp up to five. When the song ended, Dean clinked his bottle of beer against her glass of wine. He seemed more like Dean her husband than the uptight retired PGA golfer she'd been trying to secure an interview with, and again she realized how often they'd had fun together. She shifted in her chair. It was almost time to talk to him about the interview.

~

At the end of the night, Dean, Mary, and James walked to the parking lot together. They reached James's car first. Dean pumped James's hand. "You were the star of the night. I hope you'll perform here again."

"Already arranged. Saturday night in the pub," James said. "Will you be there?"

"Wouldn't miss it," Dean said.

James kissed Mary's cheek. "Best night of my life, and I owe it all to you."

Mary floated on air. She'd been able to help James in this version of their lives. "You were brilliant."

She and Dean stood beneath an overhead light, watching James back out of his parking spot. He tapped his horn and waved before he drove off. Seeing him acting like the James she knew all night made her believe that Dean, too, would be the man she knew and help her by doing the interview. All she needed to do was gather the courage to ask him.

"That's me." Mary pointed to her Corolla two spots beyond where James had been parked. It was one of only a smattering of vehicles remaining in the lot.

Dean walked with her toward the Toyota, humming a song Mary recognized as the Cars' "Drive." In her real life, they'd been side by side like this countless times, but being with him now, when he seemed so much like her Dean, she had a new appreciation for how comfortable she'd always been around him. No matter what, she could be herself with him. She belted out a line to the chorus. Dean stopped short, looking at her and blocking his ears. "You really can't sing." He laughed.

"Sure I can." She sang the next line.

Dean tried to sing over her, so she sang louder. They ended up doing a duet, her singing one line and him the next.

"You're both awful," someone from the other side of the parking lot hollered.

Mary started to laugh, which made Dean laugh. She snorted, making Dean laugh harder. Soon she was hunched over, holding her stomach. Dean wiped tears from his face. "Good thing James wasn't around to hear that," he said, still fighting to control his laughter.

"That was fun," Mary said, smiling up at him. Oh, how she'd missed laughing with him like that, here and in her real life too.

"A great night," Dean agreed. They'd reached her car. "Drive safe. Make sure you buckle up."

It was exactly what he'd always said to her and Kendra when they left the house. Every single time, Kendra would correct him. The caring comments and good-natured ribbing happened all the time in their family, and Mary had taken all of it for granted. Would the three of them ever be together again? She took a deep breath in, working up the courage to ask about the interview. The words were on the tip of her tongue, but she swallowed them down, afraid of his answer, and instead said what Kendra always did: "Drive 'safely,' not 'safe.'"

Dean flinched. "Déjà vu."

"You get that a lot."

"Just around you. That and shocks." He smiled. His mouth hung open, and his bottom row of teeth was barely visible. Here in this parking lot, he was her Dean, and she was his Mary. The connection between them inched up to four bars. Now was as good a time as any to try her luck one more time. She straightened her spine and pushed back her shoulders. "So, about the interview. When can we schedule it?"

Dean kept smiling, giving Mary a spark of hope that he had warmed to the idea. Before the spark could ignite, his expression hardened. There was a stubborn set to his jaw that let her know he hadn't changed his mind, and he never would. "There's not going to be an interview." He pulled open the door of her car. "Sorry," he said, his voice gentle.

Her body started to shake. He wasn't going to change his mind. She was stuck here in a world without her family. Singing with him just then was the last moment of joy she would ever experience. She couldn't be happy in a world without him or Kendra. She didn't want to leave the parking lot. It was the last place her life would have any meaning, because until a second ago, she still had a chance to be Dean's wife and Kendra's mom. Now, she had nothing.

Chapter 33

The Friday after the banquet, Mary sulked into the news studio to coanchor the six o'clock news, her stomach dropping as if she were on a roller coaster. If she didn't do well, she'd destroy the small chance she had of returning to her real life. She paused just beyond the doorway, taking deep breaths to try to slow her pounding heart. Back in her real life, all she'd wanted was to be a newscaster. Now, she'd do anything to be Dean's wife and Kendra's mother again. She didn't even care that Kendra felt smothered or that Dean spent more time on the golf course than with her. She'd cherish whatever time they gave her.

"You okay?" Mitchell asked.

She walked across the room without answering. Behind the anchor desk, she lowered herself into the stool, half expecting it to buckle under the weight of her self-loathing. She'd thrown away her life and ruined the lives of the people she most cared about.

Next to her, the coanchor, William, stared into a handheld mirror and adjusted a strand of his spiky silver hair. Across the room, cameras pointed at them. They'd be bringing her image into homes all across Greater Boston. Would Dean be watching? She pictured the hard set of his jaw when he again refused to be interviewed. He meant it. Everything was riding on the next thirty minutes. Her hands shook as she clipped her microphone to her dress. "Testing. Testing." Her voice trembled.

After a few beats of silence, someone speaking in her earpiece shot back, "Levels are good."

William turned sideways to look at her, his lips curled down. "Nothing to be nervous about."

The voice in her ear spoke again: "We're on in thirty seconds."

Mary's throat went dry. If she didn't get the promotion, she would be stuck here. She couldn't let that happen. She reached for her glass, but her motion was so jerky and her hand so shaky that she knocked it over. Water spilled onto the anchor desk and dripped down on her leg.

"Oh shoot!" She jumped up from her seat.

The door to the production room opened. Someone threw her a cloth. She mopped up the spill.

"You've got this?" William said the last word higher than the others so the sentence came out as a question rather than as reassurance.

The earpiece crackled again. "We're on in three, two, one."

"Good evening, I'm William Casey."

Mary was supposed to talk now. Words on the teleprompter rolled by: *I'm Mary Mulligan, filling in for Alex Mason.* Seeing her name added anger to her mix of sadness and anxiety. She didn't want to be Mary Mulligan anymore. She wanted to be Mary Amato again. She opened her mouth to speak. Nothing came out. She couldn't make herself say the name. It hadn't been hers for twenty-six years.

"Say your name," the voice in her headset whispered.

She felt as if her vocal cords were paralyzed. Her heart pounded so loud she was certain her microphone would pick up the sound. Sweat beaded above her upper lip. She swiped it away with her tongue. Her knee bounced up and down under the anchor desk.

"Take a deep breath and say your name."

Mary looked up toward the ceiling as if the voice were coming from up there. Her chest tightened, and her hands tingled. *Get it together.*

"Will, introduce her."

William smiled at the camera. "Alex is enjoying a night off, and Mary Mulligan is filling in."

She would never be Mary Amato again. She'd never be Dean's wife or Kendra's mom. All because she wanted to be on television reporting the news. *News flash, Mary. It wasn't worth it.*

"Mary, say something, anything," the person on the other end of her headset commanded.

She cleared her throat. "Good evening." It was barely a whisper.

"Keep the camera on Will."

William began with the first story. "Today, climate protesters in Boston blockaded the entrance to the Ted Williams Tunnel. Our Kimberly Nash was there."

The red light in the studio went out, letting Mary and Will know they were no longer on air. The TV screens on the far wall showed the protesters making a human chain across the tunnel's entrance. Mitchell raced out of the control room to Mary's side. He placed a hand on her shoulder and looked her directly in the eye. "You can do this."

Her heartbeat was so fast and erratic that she pictured her fifty-four-year-old self trapped inside her body, pounding on her chest and trying to break free. The room started to spin. Her vision clouded.

Kimberly appeared on the television screens, wrapping up her story. Time was running out. Mary and Will would be back on air in seconds. She took fast, shallow breaths.

"Can you do the show?" Mitchell asked.

Yes, I can, Mary thought, but it was as if the protesters in Kimberly's story had blockaded her mouth, preventing any words from getting out. The light in the studio turned red. Next to Mary, Mitchell crouched below the anchor desk so he couldn't be seen on air.

"Cut to commercial," the voice in Mary's ear said.

"Thank you, Kimberly." Will smiled at the camera. "We'll be right back."

The show broke for an advertisement.

"I think I'm going to throw up." Mary jumped off her stool and rushed out of the studio, through the newsroom, and out the door to the parking lot.

Gulping in air, she didn't notice Carl leaning against the building, smoking, until he spoke. "The anchor chair's much more comfortable when the cameras aren't on." He dropped his cigarette to the ground and crushed it with the bottom of his shoe. "It was hard to watch your meltdown."

Your meltdown. The words knocked the wind out of her. She'd annihilated any remaining chance of getting the job on the national *Morning Show*—no matter how minuscule it might have been—and returning to her family. She was stuck in this life without her daughter and without Dean. Her throat and eyes burned. She was on the verge of tears, but she knew if she started to cry, she would never stop. She, Carl, and the entire news crew would drown in a flood of her tears. All she wanted was to go home to her house in Hudson, but she could never go there again. Instead, she'd go to the apartment in Framingham and crawl into bed, wanting to stay there for the rest of her life.

Carl sidled up beside her. He put a hand on her back. His touch was so unexpected that she flinched. The tips of his ears pinkened, and he stuffed his hands into the pockets of his jeans. "It's not so bad," he said. "Maybe anchoring just isn't your thing, but you're a great reporter."

If Carl was being nice to her, it must be really bad. She had to get away from the news station now, but her car keys and phone were inside. "Do you mind getting my bag for me? It's in my bottom desk drawer."

"What am I, your personal assistant? Get your own bag." If she had paid attention to only his words and not heard his gentle tone or seen his sympathetic expression, she would have thought he had reverted to his grumpy self. "You're going to have to face everyone at some point. Might as well get it over with now." He tilted his head toward the door. "I'll come with you."

She sucked in a deep breath. She could do this. After all, in a world without her husband and daughter, this might be the easiest thing she ever did. With his hand on the small of her back, Carl guided her inside.

As Mary entered the newsroom, the chitter-chatter quieted; the clitter-clatter of fingers tapping keyboards came to an abrupt stop; her coworkers swiveled in their chairs, their eyes burning holes in her back as she cut across the room. Determined not to let them know how humiliated and devastated she felt, she kept her head high and shoulders back.

"What are you all looking at?" Carl barked.

Before lowering herself to her chair, Mary turned to stare back, one hand on her hip. Some of her peers looked away, others flashed sympathetic smiles before returning to their work, and a brazen few stared back with smug looks that conveyed they never would have blown their chance the way she had detonated hers—and they didn't know the half of it.

As she drove home, Darbi phoned. Mary sent the call to voicemail, still angry at her cousin for getting her into this mess. At home she played the message: "We saw what happened tonight. My heart breaks for you. It seems like the promotion is a long shot now." Mary winced. She didn't need Darbi reminding her of her failures or spelling out the consequences. She deleted the message without listening to the rest of it.

Chapter 34

The ringing phone woke Mary from a restless sleep on Saturday morning. James's name flashed across her screen. Groaning, she hit the ignore button and pulled the sheet over her head. Seconds later, the ringing started again. This time she answered.

"Just making sure you're coming to the pub tonight," he said. "Seeing your face in the crowd keeps me calm. Without you there, I'll get stage fright."

Stage fright. The two words brought back all Mary's humiliation from the night before and reminded her that she was never going home. She felt an ice-cold sensation in her chest, as if her heart were freezing over.

"You there?" James asked.

"You're on your own tonight." She couldn't bear to watch him singing in that tiny pub at a golf club located in a town no one had ever heard of. He was supposed to be performing on famous stages in big cities all over the country. She'd stolen that from him. Now, they were both stuck in this world.

"No, please. You have to—"

She disconnected the call, burying her head in her hands and feeling bad she'd hung up on him. She'd ruined so many things for so many people, not just herself.

Needing fresh air, she dressed and went outside. She didn't have the energy to walk, so she sank down and sat on the top step. Cars whizzed by on the street. Everyone had someplace to go except for her. There was nowhere she wanted to be except home in Hudson.

Her phone rang again. Guilt got the better of her. She picked up, ready to apologize to James for hanging up, but it was Carl.

"I'm at the station. Thought you'd want to know there are a lot of emails from sympathetic viewers hoping you'll get another chance to anchor."

They probably wanted to see her self-combust on air. "I don't care about anchoring. I just want to . . ." She stopped herself from saying *go home*. "I'm never going to get the promotion now."

Carl was quiet. Downstairs, a door opened and closed, and Brady, RaeLynn, and Frank appeared on the driveway. With the hand that wasn't holding Frank's leash, Brady waved up at Mary. He had a sympathetic look on his face that made her certain he'd been watching the news last night.

"I wouldn't say never," Carl said. "Get Amato to talk to you, and you're back in business." He paused before adding, "Maybe."

A few minutes ago, she'd had no hope. Now she had at least some. She went back inside and fired up her laptop, determined to think of a way to convince Dean to agree to the interview. She found the Dunlop tire commercial on YouTube and watched it along with old interviews of Dean. Seeing him working to put all the reporters at ease reminded her how he couldn't stand to be the bad guy. Ever. Once he'd even convinced the entire executive team to take a pay cut to avoid company-wide layoffs, and she was always the one to discipline Kendra because he couldn't stomach being the heavy. If she could find a way to appeal to his need to be a good guy, or at least not the bad guy, he'd do the interview.

She knew he'd told James that he would be at the pub tonight, so she called James back and told him that she'd changed her mind. She'd be there tonight. At this point, she had nothing left to lose.

~

Mary thought Dean might be more likely to agree to the interview if more people knew she was asking him for one—just maybe, his need to be a good guy would make him reluctant to say no in front of others. She called Darbi first.

"Didn't he just say no to you?" Darbi said.

Mary, frustrated with her cousin, tightened her grip on the phone. "I can't just give up."

"I don't think you should hound him. Let some time pass before you ask him again."

"I'll go without you." She hung up without saying goodbye, bewildered again by Darbi's refusal to help her.

Looking out the window, she saw RaeLynn and Brady walking Frank and decided to ask them. Just before she opened her door to call down to them, she thought of Kimberly, who had experience asking people for interviews and might be able to offer suggestions. Mary feared Kimberly might not want to go, because ultimately, she'd be helping Mary get the promotion, but she called her anyway.

Kimberly didn't hesitate. "I'm so glad you asked," she said. "We should be helping one another." Mary felt her face heat up with shame, because she didn't think she would have helped Kimberly had the circumstances been reversed. She also asked Carl to come in case she needed him to record an interview. She was getting this done tonight. It was the only chance she had left.

At 8:45, the three of them sat at a long table at the Bunker, the pub at Addison Heights. While Kimberly and Carl watched James, Mary kept her eyes trained on the door. A large group of men entered. She scanned their faces, but Dean wasn't part of the crowd.

"I guess he's not coming." Her voice cracked. She didn't even try to hide her emotion. In this version of her life, everyone would talk about how sad she was. She'd be known as "morose Mary." She didn't care.

"He'll be here," Kimberly said. "And we'll convince him." Mary knew her friend was being optimistic to support her, and she had a new appreciation for the girl. Kimberly was putting her own chance at the promotion at risk to help Mary, and she was doing it cheerfully. Somewhere within Mary, the realization clicked: friends should help each other, not compete against one another. "In the meantime, enjoy the music."

James sat on a wooden stool at the front of the bar, strumming his guitar and singing "Sister Golden Hair," a song Mary was certain no one in the bar except for she, Carl, and James knew.

Carl visited the bar and returned with a beer for himself and mojitos for Mary and Kimberly.

James finished the song and announced he was taking a break. He approached their table and plunked down in the seat next to Carl. Carl slapped him on the back. "Hey, boss, there are like five decades of music more recent than the junk you're playing."

Mary imagined her James responding with a quick witty remark, but this James had no repartee. He stayed silent, face flushed. Mary glared at Carl. What was wrong with him? James needed someone to build up his confidence, not tear it down. "Your voice is amazing," she said. "And I love the old songs."

"I saw what happened on the news." James looked at a spot above her head as he spoke. "I'm sorry."

"What happened?" Dean's voice came from behind Mary. He held a bottle of beer. Anthony stood by the bar, talking to Jessica. Somehow, Mary had missed them arriving. She'd never been so happy to see anyone as she was to see Dean, and she beamed up at him. Even if he hadn't realized it yet, he wanted to help her. Why else would he come to her table?

"She was anchoring, and she forgot how to talk," Carl said.

Mary shot him a look, not wanting Dean to know how she'd messed up. She wanted him to think of her as a talented professional so he'd do the interview.

Kimberly wrapped a protective arm around Mary's shoulders. "She got a little camera shy."

"Complete meltdown," Carl said.

Dean gave Mary a sympathetic smile. "Everyone has a bad day once in a while."

"Exactly," Kimberly said.

Mary nodded. Maybe she could use this to appeal to his need to be the good guy.

"This one will go down in infamy," Carl said.

His break over, James went back to the stool and played the opening chords of a John Mayer song. Mary tried to remember its name but couldn't.

"How bad could it have been?" Dean asked.

"Her career as an anchor is finished," Carl said, kicking Mary under the table to let her know he didn't mean it. He was trying to convince Dean to help. "She'll have to stick to reporting."

Mary tapped her phone, trying to bring up the video, but there was no signal in the pub.

"It's nothing that can't be fixed," she said, silently praying that Dean would want to help.

"She'll do better next time," Kimberly said, sipping her drink.

"There won't be a next time," Carl said.

"There could be, if I score a big interview." Mary flashed her best smile at Dean. "Will you help?"

"Good try."

"Mr. Amato," Kimberly said, and Mary startled, aware for the first time of the age difference between her and Dean now. "There are people out there who think you intentionally cheated. Don't you want to clear that up? Tell your side of the story?"

"People can think what they want."

The pool table opened. Carl pointed at it, and he and Kimberly went to play, presumably leaving Mary alone to talk to Dean.

"You'll get another opportunity." Dean had that know-it-all tone that men often had when talking to women, especially those younger than them. It infuriated her that he thought this, because it would make him less likely to help.

"A lot more than my career was at stake," she said, needing to make him understand.

He rolled his eyes and reached for a fistful of pretzels. She waited for him to tell her to stop being ridiculous because that's what her Dean always told her. Instead, he asked, "Like what?"

Everything she wanted to tell him about what had happened when she had her wisdom teeth removed flashed through her mind. She imagined how he would react. How he would look at her as if she were insane or incredibly drunk. She took another sip of her mojito, her third of the evening. Maybe she *was* incredibly drunk. Telling him was a horrible idea. She bit her tongue and reached again for the minty rum drink.

Dean took a pull of his beer, something she'd seen him do countless times in the past, but seeing him do it now mesmerized her. So often, they'd enjoyed drinks together, engaged in conversations about their daughter: Where do you think she'll go to college? I'm not sure I like that boy for her. What should we get her for her birthday?

Sitting at this table now, having to pretend he was barely more than a stranger, was eating her up. He had to feel the connection between them, even if he didn't understand it.

James sang the lyrics to the chorus. The name of the song popped into Mary's head: "Say."

Dean placed his beer down on the table with the label facing away from him. As soon as he noticed, he'd turn the bottle 180 degrees. "Well?" He twisted the bottle, just as she knew he would. For more than half her life, this man whom she knew so well had given her a shoulder to lean on. There was never a time she needed his support more than she did right now.

James sang the chorus of "Say" again. She took it as a sign that she should say what she wanted and tell Dean why he had to agree to the interview. "In another version of our lives, I'm fifty-four. We're married and have a beautiful daughter."

Dean had been lifting his beer for another swallow. The bottle froze in his hand by his neck. He placed it back on the table with a thud, his eyes big.

"We named her Kendra, after your friend Ken Idleman."

Dean paled. "Who told you about Ken?"

"You did. In our other life. He passed away when you were in high school. Cancer. It's why you always donate to the Jimmy Fund."

The dazed look on Dean's face suggested the ghost of Ken had sat down at the table with them. "How could you possibly know that?"

In all the research she'd done on Dean, Mary had found no mention of Ken in any interview or article. With tears streaming down his face, he'd told her on what would have been Ken's twenty-fifth birthday, and she had held him until they saw the early-morning light, listening to stories about his and Ken's antics together throughout their childhood.

"The same way I know the reason your dad golfed, the same way I knew Michelle was your high school sweetheart. It's why I know all the lyrics to the old songs."

Dean pointed to her drink. "How many of those have you had?"

He was trying to make light of her words, but she could tell by the way he kept shifting in his chair and the way his olive complexion had turned Casper white that he didn't know what to think. She was finally reaching him.

"You and I met right here at Addison Heights. Well, not here in the pub, but in the main banquet room. I was there for a bridal shower, and you were playing in a charity tournament for Ken. You walked into the wrong function room and helped yourself to cake. Chocolate with raspberry filling."

Dean licked his lips as if tasting the cake again. "The groom looked like a tall Dustin Hoffman," he mumbled. Then he vigorously shook his head as if trying to clear his mind.

"Exactly. You remember." Her voice burst with excitement. She had to use all her restraint to keep from running around the table to hug him.

"No." Dean said the word with force, as if trying to convince himself.

She could tell by his expression that she'd made him uncomfortable. He didn't want to, but he believed her. She had to make sure there was no doubt in his mind, keep telling him stories. He peeled the label off his beer bottle. "Quite the imagination. I didn't expect that from you."

"You planted a maple tree beside the house the day Kendra was born. We lived in Hudson, Massachusetts."

Dean took a long swallow of his beer and glanced toward Anthony and Jessica at the bar as if he hoped they'd come over and save him from this conversation. "Nice town. Did you and"—he paused—"Kendra come on tour with me? Cheer me on?"

He was playing with her, and her excitement ticked down a level. "You weren't a golfer. You played, but as a hobby, not professionally. You were a chief revenue officer for an insurance company."

"Insurance? Could there be anything more boring? And chief revenue officer? Is that really a thing?"

Her stomach twisted. If insurance bored this version of Dean, her Dean couldn't have enjoyed his job, yet he'd never complained about it. He always put on a smile and went to work to support their family. How had she not realized that? She shifted in her seat. "You set goals for the sales team and play a lot of golf with other executives."

"I like the golf part." His bored tone suggested he was losing interest.

She had to pull him back before it was too late. "But here's the problem." Mary paused for a sip of liquid courage. Dean stared, waiting, his eyebrows scrunched up. She explained Mulligan magic to him, why she'd wanted to be young again, what had happened to Kendra, and what the letter from Uncle Cillian said. As she confided in him, the weight of the secret she'd been carrying lightened. Even this alternate version of him was easy to talk to, just like her Dean. Her fear of getting stuck in this alternate life lessened. He'd never let her down before. He wouldn't now.

He listened, narrowing his eyes and tilting his head from time to time. His expression reminded her of the way he used to look when toddler Kendra told them long, rambling tales that had no point. He'd be fully engaged at the beginning and checking his watch by the end. Mary had to wrap up.

"So, I need to get the promotion so I can get back to my other life and our family." With her story finished, she reached for her mojito, but Dean pulled the drink away and slid a glass of water toward her.

"What you're saying is that I was such a crappy husband that you decided not only to erase everything about our life together but also to take a mulligan on the last thirty years of your life." He poked her arm, again getting shocked. "Probably would have been easier to just divorce me."

She shook her head. He hadn't caused her unhappiness. She had. "My wanting to leave had nothing to do with you."

He was playing games with her, the same way he'd played along with Kendra when she told them she'd seen Santa coming down the chimney or the tooth fairy flying around her bedroom. But he also had a look on his face that let her know he was trying to figure out how she'd known about Ken and Michelle, and why his dad had started playing golf.

"I know it sounds crazy, but it's true," Mary said.

He smiled, but it was a sad smile, as if he felt sorry for her. "It's the most creative way anyone has ever tried to convince me to do an interview. I'll give you that."

She sat up straighter, leaning across the table toward him, her hand on her head as she racked her brain. There had to be a story he'd told her that she would have no way of knowing that would convince him, or keep him here talking to her, before he walked out of her life for good. "The night you got your license, you took Michelle to a restaurant called Tom Foolery's in Westborough. Before you ordered your food, your uncle walked in, holding hands with a woman who was not your aunt." She spoke as fast as an announcer in an ad for medication, listing all the side effects at the end. "You and Michelle snuck out so your uncle wouldn't see you. You went to Papa Gino's, and you never told anyone but me what happened, not even Anthony."

Dean rolled his eyes. "Obviously you spoke to Michelle at the fundraiser."

"Why would she tell me that? Okay, here's something people don't know about you: you wet the bed until you were six."

The tips of Dean's earlobes reddened. "Damn Anthony for telling you that."

"You have a birthmark that looks like the boot of Italy on your right butt cheek." Would she ever see that birthmark again, tease him about tattooing *100% Italian* under it, or would it just be a memory that would torment her forever?

"Plenty of women could have told you that." He winked and stood. "While I appreciate the effort you've put into coming up with this story and the details you've inexplicably learned about my life, there's not going to be an interview. You need to accept that."

Telling the truth hadn't worked. She'd run out of ideas. The realization that she was stuck in this life without her family shattered her heart into a billion jagged pieces. She'd destroyed everything she loved.

Pulling his keys from his pocket, Dean watched Carl and Kimberly make their way back to the table. He bobbed his head in Mary's direction. "She's not driving, right?"

"I'm the driver," Carl said.

Dean met Mary's eye. "Drink lots of water, and take some ibuprofen before going to sleep."

She wanted to run after him, fall to her knees and beg him, but she didn't have the strength to move. She slumped onto the table, wishing the roof would crash down on top of her and put her out of her misery.

Chapter 35

Back in her apartment later that night, Mary sat on the bathroom floor for what seemed like hours with her head hanging over the toilet. When she thought she had nothing left to throw up, she thought of Dean and Kendra and her stomach lurched again, causing her to dry heave. She would never be with them again. They were gone. Not exactly dead but definitely not alive—and it was all her fault. Kendra's hug goodbye at the airport and Dean's small wave at the dentist's office played on an endless loop in her mind. On both occasions, Mary had been miserable, feeling sorry for herself, yet she'd never be anywhere near that happy again.

Somehow she made it to the living room and curled into a fetal position on the couch, staring into Belli's bowl. Oh, how she wished she could trade places with Belli, because fish only had a ten-second memory. At least that's what she'd learned from a television program. If she kept remembering her life with Dean and Kendra—and she most definitely would—she'd never have the will to leave the sofa. Was there a way to forget?

She and Dean had once seen a movie about a couple who erased each other from their memories after their relationship failed. Was there a real procedure that erased memories? Her laptop sat on the table next to Belli's bowl. She reached for it and googled *how to forget*. Nothing she read helped, so she switched courses and skimmed through articles about Dean again. She even read about the women with her daughter's name. Her stomach twisted, and she folded over in pain. She would never find any information about her Kendra.

At four in the morning, she dragged herself to bed, wearing the sundress she'd worn to the pub. Staring up at the ceiling, she wished on one of the star decals that she'd wake up back in her other life.

She must have managed to fall asleep, because she woke up just past eight to the sound of Frank Sinatra barking.

Hoping that Dean had changed his mind, she checked her messages. There were two texts. The first was from Brady, telling her he'd heard her getting sick the night before and had left a jug of Gatorade by her door. The second was from Darbi, asking her what had happened with Dean. Mary couldn't bring herself to call or text with an answer. If Darbi really cared about what had happened, she would have been there last night.

In the living room, she watched videos of her young self reporting. She hated the girl she saw, knowing what she'd traded for that stupid job. She slammed the laptop shut and flipped on the television. She found a *Modern Family* marathon and settled in to watch it.

Later, there was a knock on her door. Startled, she looked at her watch, surprised to see that it was almost five. She didn't know where the time had gone and couldn't recall what had happened in a single episode she'd watched.

"Mary?" Darbi's voice called.

She said nothing, hoping her cousin would go away.

"I'm coming in." The lock clicked, the door swung open, and Darbi stepped inside carrying a jug of bright-yellow Gatorade. "This was on the ste . . ." Her mouth twisted as her eyes landed on Mary balled up on the sofa in her soiled sundress. She swallowed hard and cradled the bottle to her chest. "I take it Dean said no."

"I'm stuck here." Mary's voice was weak. "I'll never see Kendra or my husband again."

Darbi licked her lips. "No." She managed to communicate a world of sorrow in the one syllable. She disappeared into the kitchen. A few seconds later, she sat on the couch next to Mary, handing her a drink.

"I thought I would come here, fix my mistake. Take the promotion and return a famous newscaster," Mary said, her voice thick with emotion.

Darbi's face crumpled in anguish. "What did I say that gave you that idea?"

Mary took a long sip, the liquid soothing her dry throat. "It wasn't what you said. It's what I wanted. I should have listened to you."

"It's impossible to believe until it happens to you." Darbi placed her hand on Mary's thigh. "You have to make the most of being here, though, or you'll have sacrificed everything for nothing."

Mary's jaw tensed, and her grip on the glass tightened. "Nothing I accomplish here will have been worth the sacrifice."

"No, but you owe it to Dean, Kendra, and even to yourself to live your best life possible." Darbi stood. "Right now, we're going to get you in the shower. You smell worse than a dumpster." She led Mary to the bathroom and turned on the water. "I'll make you something to eat while you're in there."

Mary did as told, suspecting Darbi wouldn't leave otherwise. After she choked down a half bowl of soup, Darbi left, and Mary crawled into bed, pulling the covers over her head.

~

At ten the next morning, Brady let himself into Mary's apartment, Frank Sinatra on a leash by his side. Mary silently cursed herself for forgetting to lock the door after Darbi left yesterday. He sat beside her on the sofa, placing a bag with bagels and a coffee on the table in front of her while Frank sniffed around the living room.

Mary was wearing the same shorts and T-shirt she'd changed into yesterday, and her hair had twisted into half-formed curls because she'd never combed it out after washing it.

Brady's forehead furrowed. "What's going on? You still hungover?"

"Dean won't help me. I'm stuck here." Her voice was hoarse from crying so much.

"Stuck in your current job?"

Mary shook her head. "Stuck in this life." She. Was. Never. Going. Home. She got that ice-cold feeling in her chest again.

Brady scratched his head. "You're a great reporter. Your stories make people happy. Keep doing them, and good things will happen."

Nothing good would ever happen in her life again.

He stood and reached for Frank's leash, pulling the dog to the sofa. "I need a favor. Have to work a double, and RaeLynn is out of town. Can you watch him?" He scratched Frank's neck. "He needs a walk." Brady dropped the leash in Mary's lap and headed toward the door. The dog nudged her with his nose.

"I can't take him." She sounded frantic. She didn't want to see people, except for Kendra and her Dean.

"The fresh air will do you good." Brady slipped through the door, and a minute later, she heard the sound of tires on gravel.

Frank jumped up on her, resting his two front paws on her thighs and bathing her cheek with wet sloppy dog kisses. He must have been to the groomer recently because he smelled like a combination of lavender and mint and had a bright-red bandana tied around his neck, the perfect complement to his neatly trimmed shiny black hair.

When she nudged him off of her, he ran to the door and spun in circles. She sighed, then slipped into her sneakers and slapped on a hat.

Outside, Frank trotted beside her on the sidewalk as they made their way down the street toward the bike path. Every now and then, he looked up at her with his puppy dog eyes. The trust and love she saw in them reminded her of the way baby Kendra had looked at her, and she fought the urge to drop to the ground and curl into a ball.

An older couple waved from their front porch. She'd always thought she'd grow old with Dean. Now they were both on track to grow old alone. She hated herself a little more.

On the bike path, Frank pulled Mary to the edge of the woods bordering the trail. As he sniffed the trunk of a tree, Mary's phone rang, a number she didn't recognize with a 904 area code. She didn't pick up, and the caller didn't leave a message.

When Mary and Frank turned around at Route 30, two women approached from the opposite direction. "Excuse me," the taller of the women said. "You're that girl on the news, Channel 77."

"Yes, Mary Mulligan." This was exactly why she hadn't wanted to leave her apartment. How she missed being able to take a walk or go shopping without being recognized.

"I saw that story on the veteran," the woman said.

Mary nodded.

"That dress you were wearing, it wasn't at all flattering, and the cut made you look chunky."

"Chunky!" Mary's breath hitched, and tears welled in her eyes. Today was not the day to mess with her. In fact, it never would be again. "How dare you," she spit. "Do you really have nothing better to do than insult other women?"

The women rushed off, but it was too late. Mary had reached her breaking point. She started to shake, thinking about all the things she disliked about being a journalist—viewers believing they had the right to critique her appearance, the constant exposure to heartbreaking stories, and news that made you question the decency of mankind. These were the things that had driven her away from the job the first time, not Dean or Kendra. She'd willingly left her job at Channel 77 to raise her daughter. Why had she tried to blame it on Dean?

"Are you okay?" a man walking the other direction asked.

Mary's phone rang again with the same 904 number. She nodded and blinked back her tears. The man kept staring at her, so she turned her back and answered the phone.

"It's Dean Amato."

At the sound of his voice, the tears she'd been fighting rolled down her cheeks, but they were happy tears. She was so relieved to hear his voice. It was the most beautiful sound she'd ever heard.

Dean cleared his throat. "Your friend Kimberly sent me the video." He paused, and Mary wondered why Kimberly would do that. "When you told me about what happened on air, I didn't understand that you never went back to the anchor desk."

Mary didn't want to think about what had happened in the studio, because that was the moment her chance to get back to her other life had started to slip away. She reached down to pat Frank. "I'm trying to forget about that."

"Yeah, it was bad," Dean said.

"You didn't need to call to tell me that. I'm aware."

Dean chuckled. "The thing is, I know a thing or two about cracking under pressure, and your friend told me about the promotion. So I've called to let you know I've reconsidered. If the person you're competing with is willing to help, I figure you must deserve it."

Kimberly had built her up in Dean's eyes and made her seem deserving, not caring that she was hurting her own chances by doing so. Mary's own competitiveness against her friends sickened her. She wished she'd been helpful to Kimberly and realized she should have been more gracious toward Liz. Someone else succeeding didn't mean she was a failure.

"Are you saying what I think you're saying?" Her lower lip trembled. Hope bubbled up inside her frozen heart. She closed her eyes, picturing Dean sitting next to her on the sofa in their house in Hudson, his phone on the coffee table and Kendra on speakerphone. If she understood him right, it was all within reach. Frank leaped to his feet and barked, bringing her back to the moment.

"I'll do the interview," he said. "But I have two conditions."

Chapter 36

Dean's first condition was that he would not do the interview until after Mary had had the chance to anchor again. His demand surprised her because there was nothing in it for him. He'd requested it solely to help her get the promotion. He said it was the same reason he'd agreed to the interview, but she couldn't help but wonder if even a little piece of him believed her story about their life together, and that's why he was helping.

Mitchell was reluctant to let Mary behind the anchor desk, but an interview with Dean was too enticing to pass up. So two days later, Mary stood next to the stool behind the anchor desk, stealing quick glances at Alex, who fiddled with the microphone clipped to her blouse. In less than a minute, they were going on air, coanchoring the six o'clock news. If she did a good job tonight and with the interview tomorrow, she'd have a chance to get back to her old life. Mary heard her heart pounding and felt pressure in her temples. No, no, no. She would not let a panic attack derail her now. She remembered one of the many exercises to stop an attack that Dean had taught her long ago. Looking around the studio, she named three things: the camera, the mural of the Boston skyline, a small platform that Alex sometimes stood on. Her heart slowed, and her breathing returned to normal.

She pictured Dean in the pro shop at Addison Heights, staring up at the television with both fists clenched. He was definitely rooting for her tonight. He'd even texted her earlier in the day, telling her to break a leg tonight. There was a genuine kindness in him, regardless of whether he was her husband Dean or professional golfer Dean.

"We're on in thirty seconds," a voice in her ear said. She could do this. She had to do this. For Kendra. For her and Dean. She wiped her sweaty hands on her skirt and slid onto the stool.

Alex touched Mary's shoulder. "You're going to crush this."

"Thank you," Mary said, grateful Alex was sitting in the chair next to her tonight and not Will, whom she'd heard hadn't stopped talking about her on-air meltdown since Friday.

"We're on in five, four, three, two, one."

"Good evening, I'm Alex Mason."

Mary's coworkers in the newsroom peered through the glass sliding door, watching her. Kimberly smiled and formed a heart with her fingers. Seeing her friend cheering her on strengthened her resolve. She took a deep breath in and pasted on her best smile. "And I'm Mary Mulligan, filling in for William Casey." Her introduction was as good as any she'd ever heard Liz do. She could do this. "We start tonight in Marshfield, where another case of eastern equine encephalitis has been diagnosed. So far three deaths have been linked to the virus in the state's worst outbreak of the mosquito-borne illness in decades. Kimberly Nash has the latest." The red light went off. Mary could have sworn she heard the entire news station exhale.

∼

Dean's second condition for doing the interview was that it had to take place on the course at Addison Heights. Mary didn't care where it happened. It just needed to happen. While he strapped a bag of clubs to the back of the golf cart, she slid into the passenger seat, the excitement building within her. If she did a good job with this, she could wake up as her fifty-four-year-old self in the next day or two. One of the first things she planned to do was convince Dean they needed to take a vacation. Time away together would do them good. They could visit romantic cities like Paris, Venice, and Amsterdam, and of course they'd start the vacation in London, visiting Kendra. Boy, Uncle Cillian better have been right about how to get back to her old life.

A loud bang interrupted her thoughts. Standing beside her, Carl loaded his camera gear into another cart. "Let him play a hole or two. Then stay parked by the green and start the interview. Don't ask him questions while you're moving. Got it?"

Mary nodded.

Dean climbed into the seat next to her, sighing as if he was resigned to getting the interview over with. "Let's do this." The cart beeped as he backed it out of its spot. Mary's entire body tingled. This was the most important thing she'd ever do in either life. She had to get it right.

They drove to the first hole without speaking, the only sound the clanking of Dean's clubs behind them. He parked next to the tee box and pulled his driver from his bag. While Carl positioned the camera, Dean took a few practice swings. His hips rotated effortlessly as the club whooshed through the air. When he finally struck the ball, it sailed more than three hundred yards over a brook and down the fairway, landing about forty yards from the green. He finished the hole with a chip and putt. Mary watched, silently, looking at the scenery, the flawless green grass, the gentle rise and fall of the slopes in the fairway, the pine and maple trees off to the side, the flowers by the tee box. It was all beautiful, peaceful. She understood why Dean enjoyed spending time here.

She waited for him to slip his putter back into his bag and climb behind the steering wheel before asking her question. "Why did you insist on being interviewed here?"

Carl stood next to the cart, pointing the camera at Dean.

Dean cleared his throat and slid his sunglasses off his baseball cap and over his eyes. "I feel most at home on a golf course." He rotated his wrist. "The weight of the club in my hand, my spikes sinking into the fairway, the kerplunk of the ball rolling into the hole. They all put me at ease."

His answer lined up with what she'd just been thinking, but she was surprised to hear that golfing put him at ease. The Dean she knew always appeared at ease, and she understood now that golfing was how he worked off his stress. Maybe if she'd had a hobby she'd loved as much, she wouldn't have been so unhappy.

Carl cleared his throat. She turned toward him, and he widened his eyes as if to say *Let's go*.

She addressed Dean again. "You haven't talked to the press for over three years. Why is that?"

Dean squeezed his hands into tight fists and then released them. "I spent my entire career talking about finishing second. I had nothing more to say about it."

"Why talk to the press now?"

"You're persuasive." He laughed. "No, I saw an opportunity to help someone who's working hard to make their dream come true. I know what it's like to come close and"—he paused, looking off in the distance—"to come close and then blow your opportunity. It's a hard thing to live with."

"How do you live with it?" She hadn't planned to ask the question. As soon as the words had slipped out, she realized she was asking for his advice on how she'd ever live if she got stuck here.

He exhaled loudly. "Life isn't about winning. It's about being in the moment and enjoying it. Even playing my worst round, I was happy being on the course." He gestured with his hand as if to say *Look at all the beauty here*.

Mary swallowed hard, thinking about how she never would have ended up in this alternate world if she'd had that attitude.

Dean stepped on the accelerator, and the cart rolled forward. He played the next two holes, scoring eagles on both. When he pulled up next to the tee box at the fourth hole, she asked another question. "In your own words, what happened at the US Open?"

Dean had been about to step out of the cart, but he settled back in his seat. He chewed on his lower lip. Mary thought he would say that the officials had made a bad call and cheated him out of a win. He swallowed hard and removed his sunglasses. "I didn't realize it was a bunker. It was like no bunker I'd ever seen before, and I've been playing my entire life."

"So you agree it was a bunker?"

"The officials said it was a bunker."

He swung one leg out of the cart.

"But what do you say?" She wanted to see what kind of person this version of Dean was. Would he blame it on the officials, or would he take responsibility? Her husband would shoulder the blame.

Dean exhaled loudly. "From the moment I saw the official approaching me on the green, I realized I'd screwed up." He spoke with his back to Mary, but Carl stood beside him, pointing the camera in his face. "I should have known, or I should have asked."

"There are a lot of people who say it wasn't a bunker, and the win was stolen from you."

Dean shook his head. "No. It was my fault. I broke a rule, and I was rightly penalized. I was mad at myself for making such a stupid mistake." He lowered his voice as if he was confiding in her. Carl leaned closer with the camera. "That's why I didn't want to talk to the press."

Mary swallowed hard, proud of him for owning up to his mistake and admiring his integrity. He was a good man, in both versions of her life. Of course she'd known that about her Dean, but she'd never really thought about it after they'd been together for so many years. Somewhere along the way, she'd started to take all the reasons she'd fallen in love with him for granted.

Dean pulled a club from his bag. He took long, uneven strides to the tee box. Instead of being smooth like all his other swings, his practice swing was jerky. When he lined up next to the tee and took a real swing, he whacked at the ball as if he were trying to exorcise it of demons. It soared high to the left, heading toward the fairway of another hole.

"Fore!" Dean screamed.

The ball sailed toward a group of trees, bounced off a pine, and whizzed toward an oblivious man preparing for his shot.

"Fore!" Dean's voice was frantic. The man on the other fairway covered his head and ducked. The ball landed mere inches from him.

Dean sighed in relief, his face pale. He gave an apologetic wave and climbed back into the cart. "Haven't hit one that bad in a long time."

Her line of questioning on the US Open had made him uncomfortable. She wouldn't ask any more about it. "If golf hadn't worked out, what do you think you would have done with your life?" Did he have a backup plan before he met her, or had he not entertained the possibility that he might fail?

The corners of his mouth ticked upward, and his eyes sparkled. "Probably would have been a chief revenue officer for an insurance company." He winked.

Mary choked down a laugh, but she knew then that somehow she had reached him, that he believed her. Their connection was strong enough to extend into this alternate life.

She followed up with questions about his favorite moments on the tour, and about his relationship with his brother and parents. Their conversation was more like a back-and-forth between friends than a reporter interviewing a star. It reminded her of their first dates, when they were getting to know each other, and reliving the experience gave her the same heady feeling of falling in love with him all over again.

Dean's smooth swing returned, and he scored birdies and eagles on the next few holes.

At the eighth hole, they had to wait for the foursome in front of them to move off the fairway. Mary turned to him, ready to ask a question she'd been curious about ever since learning he was a professional golfer and single. "Why is it you never married?"

Dean's eyes widened. He picked up a ball from the console and rolled it between his palms. "I never met someone I loved more than the game." He nodded as if pleased with his answer.

Mary's stomach fluttered as she connected the dots on what he'd said. *He's never met someone he loves as much as he loved me.* Her eyes stung with unshed tears. She didn't know if she was happy or sad. Both. She hadn't realized he had loved her so much that he'd willingly given up this game he obsessed over.

Needing a moment to compose herself, she reached for her water bottle and took a large sip before asking her next question. "Do you ever wish there was someone waiting for you at home?"

Dean appeared to be choosing his words carefully. He kept his eyes trained on the fairway in front of them so that Mary had a view of the side of his face. How often she had looked at that profile while sitting next to him on the sofa or in the car. The slope of his nose, the jut of his chin, and the freckle on his earlobe were etched on her heart.

"Do I ever wish there was someone waiting for me at home?" he repeated. He was buying time just as she had, she knew.

"Do you ever get lonely?"

Dean tossed the ball he'd been fidgeting with back into the console. "I've never thought someone was the one who got away, if that's what you mean." He picked up the ball again. "Of course, I wish I'd met someone that I wanted to share my life with. I just didn't, though."

Mary heard in the sadness of his voice and saw in the slump of his shoulders that this was something he did not like to think about. She imagined that if he did allow himself to think about what a life with a wife and children would be like, he did it while sipping from a heavy crystal rocks glass filled with scotch.

"Are you happy, Dean?"

She leaned closer to him. Of course she wanted him to be happy. At the same time, she wanted to know that she had made his life better, not worse.

He scrubbed his jaw and let out a loud sigh. "Happy enough."

Chapter 37

That night after Mary finished editing the video, she drove from the station straight to her cousin's. The sun was just setting, and the sky was a fiery red. Darbi and Jacqui sat at the patio table, sharing a pizza.

"I did it!" Mary shouted. "I interviewed Dean."

"Oh my!" Jacqui jumped from her seat and wrapped Mary in a tight embrace. "I'm so happy for you."

Darbi sat deadly still, her face a sickening shade of green.

"Darbi? Are you okay?" Mary asked.

"I'm just . . ." Darbi stopped and gulped down water. "I wasn't expecting that."

"It's a wonderful thing. That means Mary may be able to get back."

Darbi swallowed hard. "Well, if she gets the promotion, yes."

"Why are you being such a killjoy?" Mary snapped. "I thought you'd be excited."

Darbi shredded her napkin; little white pieces fluttered to the ground. "I'll save my excitement for when you actually get the promotion."

Mary glared at her cousin, tired of her lack of support. She was starting to suspect Darbi wanted her to remain stuck here. The thought terrified her, because the only reason Darbi would want her to stay here was if she'd changed things in her real life. Nope. She wasn't going to think about that.

Jacqui waved a dismissive hand toward Darbi. "Never mind her. When will the interview air? We should have a viewing party."

"A week from tonight. In prime time on all ICNN stations. Can you believe it?"

"Oh, honey, congratulations." Jacqui embraced Mary again. "Invite your friends over. We'll have a barbecue and watch on the outdoor TV."

Darbi rose from her seat as if in a stupor. "Excuse me. I'm not feeling well." She rushed toward the sliding doors.

"Told you the pepperoni wouldn't agree with your stomach," Jacqui called after her.

~

The sound of the blender crushing ice blasted through Darbi and Jacqui's backyard. Kimberly's fiancé, Tyler, tended bar, tossing bottles in the air and catching them like Tom Cruise in the movie *Cocktail*. Kimberly sat on a stool, sipping a piña colada. In the pool, riding on Brady's shoulders, RaeLynn shrieked. Darbi and Jacqui set bowls of salad, corn on the cob, coleslaw, and chips on a table covered with a red-and-white-checkered tablecloth. Carl manned the barbecue, charring pineapple and grilling burgers, steak tips, and chicken.

With Frank Sinatra curled up on the ground next to her, Mary sprawled in a lounge chair, looking up at twinkling fairy lights strung over the fence. They reminded her of chasing fireflies around the backyard in Hudson with Kendra. Tomorrow morning, Mitchell would announce who was receiving the promotion. Mary smiled at Kimberly, wishing they could both get promoted.

"Food's ready," Darbi said. She'd had a pained expression ever since Mary arrived.

"We need to put the TV on," Kimberly said.

"Remote's in the top drawer behind the bar," Jacqui called.

Kimberly switched on the television and turned the station to Channel 77. An episode of *The Big Bang Theory* played. The special prime-time news show with Mary's interview of Dean was scheduled to start in ten minutes.

Everyone gathered in front of the food table to make up their plates. Mary and Darbi stood at the end of the line. Soon they were the only two remaining. Darbi pointed to Mary's overflowing dish. "That's a lot of food."

Mary smiled. "I might come back for more." She leaned closer to her cousin and lowered her voice. "The calories don't count. I might be back in my old body by this time tomorrow."

Darbi's sunburned face paled, and she rubbed her peeling nose. She picked up the tongs for the pineapple, but her hand shook so much she wasn't able to grab a piece. In frustration, she threw the tongs back into the bowl and used her fingers, knocking the ketchup to the ground with her elbow in the process.

Mary bent over to retrieve the bottle. "Is everything okay? You seem on edge."

"I'm afraid you're counting your chickens before they're hatched. You need to remember what we talked about, making the most of your life if you can't go back." Darbi said it gently.

Mary froze. "I feel like you're rooting against me every step of the way, like you want me to stay here."

"Th-that's the l-last thing I want," Darbi stammered.

"Mary, Darbi, come sit down," Jacqui called.

"I just don't want you to be disappointed." Darbi's chin dropped to her chest. Her shoulders slumped as she walked across the patio to join the others. Mary trailed behind, breathless with dread.

"It's on." RaeLynn gestured toward the bar, where the television hung on the back wall.

On TV, Mary stood in front of the clubhouse wearing a red top and gray skort as if she were about to play a round of golf. "Three years after a penalty stripped him of victory at the US Open, retired PGA golfer Dean Amato finally breaks his silence and talks about what happened," TV Mary said. "I accompanied him on a round at Addison Heights

Golf Club, where he's been volunteering this summer as a favor to his
brother, who's the head pro there." The shot changed to Dean hitting
off the first tee.

"He's hot," RaeLynn said.

"Yeah, for an old guy, he's all right," Kimberly agreed.

Old guy. Mary frowned. Funny how when she was in her twenties
the first time, people in their fifties seemed ancient, but now she understood that fifty wasn't old. There was still a lot of life left to be lived, new
dreams to chase after, lots to look forward to. Anyway, age was more an
attitude than a number. People in their fifties could be just as young as
those in their twenties. The key was to take advantage of all life had to
offer and not to take it for granted.

The image on the television screen morphed from Dean golfing to
Mary asking him why he'd wanted to be interviewed on the golf course.
Conversation at the table stopped, and everyone turned toward the bar.
Darbi's leg bounced up and down under the patio table as she watched.
Every now and then, she fiddled with her silverware. Mary's sense of
dread grew as she watched her cousin, fearing Darbi knew something
she wasn't saying. The others all sat still, not speaking. Even Frank
Sinatra seemed to be mesmerized. He sat on a lounge chair, looking
up at the television with his head tilted and his tongue hanging out of
his mouth.

When the interview ended, Carl clapped, and the others joined in
the applause.

Brady stood behind Mary's seat. "Our own Savannah Guthrie's
making her move."

Before Mary knew what was happening, Brady had her in his arms
in the fireman's carry and was working his way toward the pool.

"No, no, no!" She banged her fists against his back, laughing. "Put
me down."

Frank Sinatra jumped off his seat, barking, and ran along next to
them.

"One. Two. Three." Brady flung Mary from his arms into the deep end.

She sank to the bottom, water filling her nostrils. She surfaced, sputtering and laughing, and pulled herself from the pool. RaeLynn wrapped her in a towel. "Bless his heart. He's like an annoying big brother to you."

The pool deck spun. Mary got that same lightheaded feeling she'd had before a memory came crashing through. She closed her eyes and saw herself sharing a bottle of wine with Brady while binge-watching *Ozark*. At the end of the night, when he'd gotten up to leave, she'd grabbed his shirt. Ever since she'd moved into the attic apartment, they'd been spending time together, but their relationship, or whatever it was, was purely platonic. She needed clarity, and the wine she'd drunk had made her bold. "You should stay," she'd said.

Brady's body went rigid.

"You must know I have the biggest crush on you."

"I'm flattered, and I think the world of you." He'd glanced toward the door as if he couldn't wait to be on the other side of it.

Mary hugged a throw pillow to her chest, wanting to use it to deflect the word "but" she knew was about to shoot out of his mouth.

"But you're like a sister to me," he'd said.

Standing on the pool deck next to RaeLynn now, Mary felt an overwhelming sense of relief. She hadn't cheated on Dean. If she made it back to her old life, she'd have one less thing to feel guilty about. The chlorine from the pool made her skin itch. She had water in her ears. "I need to change."

~

Mary came out of the bathroom to find Darbi pacing the hallway, the horrible scent of patchouli clouding the hallway.

"We need to talk." Darbi led Mary to the guest room in the back of the house and shut the door.

Mary's body tensed, afraid of what Darbi would say.

Darbi took a deep breath in and pushed her shoulders back. "If you get the promotion, don't turn it down."

Mary glared at her cousin, fed up with her strange behavior and lack of support. "Why do you want me to stay in this alternate world?"

Darbi wrapped her arms around herself, rocking back and forth. "The letter's not real."

Darbi's words replayed through Mary's mind. She shook her head. Clearly she had misunderstood. "What?"

"The letter's fake. I wrote it."

"No way." Mary leaned against the wall, needing something solid behind her to keep herself upright. She knew what Darbi's writing looked like. All the letters leaned left. "It wasn't your writing."

"The neighbor next door helped. I told him what to write, explained the letter was part of an elaborate prank."

Heat crept up Mary's neck. Her stomach turned rock hard. She balled her hands into tight fists. She'd relied on Darbi's guidance in this strange new world, and her cousin had betrayed her. "Why would you do that?"

Darbi's shoulders slumped, and her spine curved as if she were folding in on herself. "You were so broken up about being stuck here. Moping around in your living room, doing nothing. Destroying your career. Ruining your life. I know nothing can ever replace your family, but you're here now. You have to make the best of it. For you and for them."

"So then why did the letter tell me to turn down the promotion? It makes no sense. Unless it's real."

"I didn't know what to write, and it made sense to me that if you made the same decision, you'd end up back where you were. I was trying to buy time to work up the courage to tell you that you can't go back."

Mary slid down the wall to the rug and buried her head in her hands. This couldn't be happening. Moments ago, she'd been almost certain she was going home to Dean and Kendra, and now she knew she was stuck here forever. She wanted to jump in the pool, sink to the bottom, and stay there forever. "You let me believe I was going back to my old life."

"I didn't know what to do. You were so sad. I was afraid of what you might do."

"I'm stuck here in a world without my family."

"You are, and it breaks my heart every day."

Mary would never see Kendra again. Dean wouldn't be a part of her life anymore. She wouldn't be able to trust Darbi, the only family she had left. She'd be by herself, living hell on earth, all because she'd wanted to feel like she mattered. She'd wanted people to know who she was, but getting recognized by strangers on the street who thought they knew her or felt they had the right to criticize her was annoying. She wanted no part of that anymore. Being Dean's wife and Kendra's mother was what was important—being loved by her family and loving them back. How had she not seen that? The burger and steak she'd eaten for dinner bounced around her stomach, threatening to come back up.

She heard footfalls in the hallway and then a knock on the door. "Why are you two hiding back here?" Jacqui asked. "Everyone's waiting for you for dessert."

"Does Jacqui know?" Mary asked.

"Know what, honey?"

"There was no letter from Uncle Cillian. Darbi wrote it."

Jacqui's hand flew to her mouth. "Oh, Darbi, please tell me that's not true."

Darbi covered her face with her hands. "I was in an untenable position. I didn't know what to do." She took a deep breath in and slowly released it. "I was trying to keep you happy, let you live a life with meaning for as long as I could."

Chapter 38

Darbi and Jacqui returned to the backyard to tell everyone Mary wasn't feeling well and wouldn't be coming back outside. Mary stayed where she was, on the floor of the guest room, staring at the wall in front of her but seeing nothing. Her mind and body were both numb. Out front, engines started and cars drove off. A little later, she heard Jacqui and Darbi arguing. Mary couldn't make out the words but knew the fight was about Darbi's lie.

With her stomach in knots, she slipped out of the house into the backyard. Just a few minutes before, it had been lively and she'd been full of hope. Now it had the ambience of a funeral parlor, and she felt as if she was there to pay her last respects to Kendra and the version of Dean she had loved. A fresh round of uncontrolled sobs racked her body, and she bent over, heaving. Soon, she felt a hand on her back, rubbing in small circles. She looked up and locked eyes with Darbi, the heartbreak on her cousin's face matching the way Mary felt. Darbi pulled her into her arms, and the two stood, holding each other tight, Darbi's tears soaking Mary's shoulder as waves of grief rolled through her as well.

"This is all my fault. I didn't appreciate the life I had, and I didn't listen to you. How will I live without them?"

"I don't know," Darbi said. "I hope in a way that honors them."

~

Despite Darbi and Jacqui pleading that Mary spend the night in their guest room, she went home, surprised when she pulled into her driveway because she had no recollection of driving across town. Brady's Jeep wasn't there, and the house was dark. She dragged herself upstairs and collapsed on her bed, crying harder than she'd ever cried in either life.

She couldn't wrap her head around the fact that she would never see Kendra again. Her daughter didn't exist because she'd been too self-absorbed to appreciate all the good in her life. She'd wanted more and ended up with nothing. She'd thought she'd been unhappy, but she'd be nowhere near that happy again. Being Kendra's mother and Dean's wife had left her unfulfilled, but without them, she'd never be fulfilled. She cried so hard for so long that she got a massive headache.

While digging through her bag for aspirin, she noticed a text message from Dean. Her breath hitched as she tapped on it.

Dean: Glad that's over with. Let me know if you get the promotion. I'm cheering for you.

Mary stared down at the message until the words all blurred together. In their other life, she and Dean had let each other down. He hadn't paid enough attention to her, and she'd blamed him for being bored with her life. If she could return to her fiftyish self, she would talk to him about what was troubling her. He would listen, and they would fix it, because in the end, they'd loved each other deeply. She understood that now.

In this alternate world, he'd been there for her when it mattered most. He hadn't let her down, and she wasn't going to let him down either. He'd done an interview he didn't want to do so that she could get ahead in her career. It didn't matter that she didn't care about being a journalist anymore—if she got the promotion, she'd take it. She owed that to Dean the golfer. She would make the most of the career and make him proud. There would not be a better journalist than Mary Mulligan. She owed that not only to golfer Dean but also to the Dean she'd left behind. And to Kendra. Her breath hitched again at the thought of Kendra. The absence of her daughter would leave a big hole in Mary's soul. She'd never get over the loss. Darbi was right, though. Mary couldn't just sit around feeling sorry for herself. She'd left behind a family she'd loved to be here in this world and have a chance to be a broadcaster. While the sacrifice she'd made would never be anywhere close to worth it, she couldn't let it be for nothing.

~

Blurry eyed and heartbroken, Mary entered Mitchell's office the next morning. She knew by the way he smiled at her that she was getting the promotion, but she didn't want it anymore. Kimberly deserved it more. Without her help, Dean might not have ever agreed to the interview.

Mitchell's chair squeaked as he rolled it backward to stand. His expression reminded her of Dean's when he'd told six-year-old Kendra they were taking her to Disney World, like if he kept the news inside him for another second, he'd burst. She forced the thought of her daughter and husband out of her mind. Otherwise, she'd break down again.

"The ratings were through the roof last night. For ICNN stations all over the country," Mitchell said. "Congratulations—the job at the *Morning Show* is yours."

Thank you for the opportunity, but I'm going to pass. That's what she'd said all those years ago, and the words were on the tip of her tongue now, just to see if she'd be whisked back to her old life. "Thank you." She swallowed the rest of the sentence, knowing there was no way back. This was her life now.

Mitchell's smile flatlined. "I thought you'd be more excited."

If that letter had been real, she would have exploded with excitement, self-combusted and somehow ended up back in her old life. "I'm tired." That was true. She hadn't slept. "I also need you to know I wouldn't have gotten the interview without help from Kimberly."

"I have some exciting things in mind for her," he said. "But let's focus on you for now. The higher-ups want you in Chicago next week."

Mary nodded. She'd leave today if she could. Her only hope of coping in a world without her family was to get to a place that didn't bombard her with memories every time she turned a corner. Not that she'd ever forget them. They'd be her first thought every morning and her last thought every night, not to mention the countless times she'd think of them throughout the day. Memories of them would make her miserable, but never as miserable as she deserved to be for leaving them.

"Go home and get some sleep," Mitchell said.

As Mary left the building, she couldn't believe she'd ever thought a career at a news station would fulfill her. Only the love of her family and friends could do that. As she cut across the parking lot, her phone pinged with a text. When she saw it was spam, she jabbed at the delete button until the message disappeared. Dean's text from last night returned to the top of her list. In her car, she started to respond to let him know she'd received the promotion but stopped herself, wanting to tell him in person instead. The only time she'd felt comfortable in this do-over life was during the times she'd spent with him, and she might never have the opportunity to see him again. When he congratulated her, his smile would light up her soul. He'd hug her, and she'd breathe in his distinct Dean scent and relax in his arms. For the last time in her life, she'd feel connected to something that really mattered.

~

Mary circled around the lower lot at the golf course but couldn't find an empty space. Today was the Club Championship, and all the members were competing. If she were in her real life, her husband would be taking part, but former PGA golfer Dean was not allowed to participate. In the upper lot, she pulled into the last available spot next to a white Volvo with a bumper sticker that read MY OTHER CAR'S A GOLF CART.

The scent of fresh-cut grass hung in the humid air as she made her way toward the clubhouse. On the pub's patio, groups of men and women eating lunch and drinking pints sat under umbrellas, laughing while recapping their morning rounds. In her other life, she'd never had an appreciation for the golf club, but after coming here several days over the past week, she saw the appeal. She understood why her Dean had enjoyed being here. A summer camp–like vibe oozed from the place. Spending all day here playing a game several times a week might have been a way for him to fight getting old—or at least feeling old. Her eyes felt hot and gummy. If only she'd realized that while they were together, she could have aged with him. Oh, how they would have spoiled their grandkids. She pictured her Dean here, his hair completely gray, teaching their grandson with the British accent to play golf. She blinked away the tears building in her eyes and quickened her steps.

Inside the pro shop, Anthony manned the counter, checking in a couple who appeared to be in their late fifties or early sixties and were playing the par three course. The man wore navy blue shorts and a gray shirt, while the woman had a gray skort and navy blue shirt. To Mary, their color coordination suggested they were the best of friends, making her heart ache for what she and Dean should have been.

"We have dinner riding on this afternoon's round." The man smiled as if he were posing for a picture.

"Potato-encrusted haddock special in the pub," Anthony said. "I hear it's out of this world. And pot de crème for dessert."

The woman wrapped her arm around the man's waist. "After I win, I'm having both." Her smile matched her husband's.

The man swiped his credit card. "But you're not going to win."

A feeling of sadness enveloped Mary as she watched the couple leave. If she'd shown more interest in the game he loved so much, if he'd given her more of his attention, maybe she and Dean could have spent more time together and been as happy as that couple seemed. Then she wouldn't be in this mess.

Anthony grinned at her. "Well, well, well. If it isn't our budding Barbara Walters. Great job interviewing Dean. You really got him to open up. Congratulations."

Mary version 1 would have been thrilled by Anthony's words. Today, his compliment rolled off her. Her interview with Dean hadn't accomplished what she'd wanted it to. It hadn't sent her back to her other life.

"What can I do for you?" Anthony asked.

"Is Dean around?"

Anthony nodded. "At the driving range, teaching a lesson."

She trekked up to the range, stepping to her right every time she heard a golf cart motoring behind her. At the top of the hill, she saw Dean standing behind the second bay, watching a teenage girl hit balls. "Is it fair to say about fifty percent of your weight ended up on your front leg at the end of your swing?" he asked.

The girl nodded.

"Remember what we talked about? That's not enough. Shift your weight so that over ninety percent ends up on the front foot." He took the seven iron from the girl and demonstrated. When he finished and returned the club to her, his eyes landed on Mary. "I'll be over there." He pointed in Mary's direction. "Remember, most of your weight should be on your left foot at the end of your swing."

He stuffed his hands in his pants pockets as he approached Mary. "My phone hasn't stopped ringing since the story aired."

"Told you people wanted to hear from you."

He raised his eyebrows. "So, did you get the promotion?"

Her stomach sank, thinking of all she'd lost for that meaningless promotion. She forced herself to smile, not wanting him to see how miserable she was after all he'd done to help her. "I did."

He beamed at her, the way she'd known he would, lighting up her entire being. She stared at him, savoring the moment and trying to imprint his smile on her soul.

"Congratulations."

She stepped toward him, thinking he'd hug her, but his hands remained tucked in his pockets, and she felt herself deflate.

"I'm surprised to see you. I thought you'd be returning to your other life with Kendra. I'm a little disappointed I won't get to be a husband and father." He winked.

Mary's breath caught in her throat. Again, he was making a joke about what she'd told him. Weren't all jokes based in reality? He'd believed her. "Hey, that story helped get me the interview with you." She reached out to Dean, resting her hand on his arm. Again, a spark shot through the air. "It's not too late for you to have a family. You'd make a great husband." She wanted him to be happy, even if it wasn't with him. Her throat burned, and she felt that cold sensation in her chest again, her heart freezing over.

"Would I, though?" he asked in a teasing voice. "I'd probably love golf more than my wife. She would wish she'd never married me and end up in an alternate universe where she was thirty years younger."

His words knocked the wind out of her. She heard Darbi in the restaurant asking her, *Would you choose Dean again?* How she wished she could go back and explain to the woman she was how miserable she'd be without him.

In front of them, the girl in the second bay hit a ball to the hundred-yard marker. "Great job, Brittany," Dean yelled.

"What I didn't tell you," Mary said, her lips quivering, "is that while in the alternative universe, your wife comes to appreciate all the great things about you and realizes she made a terrible mistake by leaving." Her voice cracked. There was an ache in her chest that would be there forever.

Dean pushed his tongue against the inside of his cheek. She knew her show of emotion was making him uncomfortable. "Maybe someday she'll make it back to her other life, and they'll do better by each other." He said it gently, reminding her again of how kind he was.

If only that could be, but there's no way now. She felt too exhausted to stand any longer and eyed the grass beneath her, wanting to collapse onto it and never get up. "I hope so."

"I enjoyed meeting you, Mary Mulligan. You're an old soul and the breath of fresh air I needed." He ran a hand through his hair. "See you on the *Morning Show*," he said as he walked away from her.

Tears rolled down Mary's cheeks. She wanted to run after him, grab hold of his legs, the way Kendra had done to her on the first day of kindergarten. Instead, she turned back toward the parking lot. Halfway down the hill, she looked back up at the driving range. Dean already seemed to have forgotten all about her. He was in the first bay, swatting one ball after the other. They soared high into the air and disappeared in the metal-gray sky. She never saw them land.

With a hollowness inside her, she continued down the dirt path, wishing she and Dean could be friends. In the time they'd spent together, he had made life in this world without Kendra almost tolerable. Why hadn't she realized her life with him had mattered? They'd created an amazing daughter. Mary had been a loving mother. She'd been a good friend, too, encouraging James and Jenni. She'd even helped create a broadcaster America could trust, Liz. Mary Amato had made a difference in the world. She had mattered.

"Fore! Fore! Fore!"

Mary turned back toward the driving range, where Dean was frantically screaming. A white blur barreled toward her at a breakneck speed. Before she could react, the ball smacked her right between the eyes. Her world went black, and she crumpled to the ground.

~

"Can you hear me?" Brady's voice came from far away. She might have even imagined it. She lay flat on her back on a dirt path, something sharp sticking into her shoulder blade. The gums over her wisdom teeth felt as if someone were striking them over and over again with an ice pick.

A clammy hand wrapped around her wrist; three fingers rested on her pulse point. She forced her eyes open. Brady's face came in and out of focus. She blinked hard, trying to clear her vision. Brady, dressed in his uniform, knelt beside her. A fire truck and ambulance with flashing red lights idled in the parking lot behind him.

"Welcome back," he said.

"What are you doing here?" Where was Dean? Hadn't she just been talking to him? "What happened?" Her voice sounded low, slightly hoarse. She cleared her throat.

"A golf ball hit you in the face," Brady said. "You lost consciousness."

"And you're my savior?" She laughed, remembering the white blur coming at her, full speed ahead. "Big brother to the rescue." Her voice still didn't sound right.

Brady frowned. "Are you dizzy? Lightheaded?"

"I feel like I've been hit by a truck." She winced as another sharp pain streaked through her mouth.

"You probably went down hard when you fell. We'll get you checked out."

A crowd had gathered around them. From somewhere in the back, Dean's voice called out: "Excuse me." He fought his way through the mob, pushing people or yanking them by the arm when necessary, and rushed to her side. His shoulders quaked as he crouched by Mary's side. "Are you okay?" His chin trembled and his eyes glistened. "I was on the twelfth hole, and Anthony called to tell me you were hurt." His voice cracked. "Said they had to call 911." He reached for her hand. There was no shock when he touched her, but she could feel he was shaking. At that moment, she was certain he cared about her, really cared about her. The realization broke her heart, because it reminded her of how lonely he was in his world as a professional golfer and how lonely she'd be without him. She'd ruined his life, Kendra's, and her own. The ice picks kept hacking away at her gums, the pain more severe than before she'd had her wisdom teeth removed.

"What are you even doing here?" Dean asked.

Mary blinked hard. "I came to tell you about my promotion." She pointed toward the driving range. "We talked. Remember?"

"Remember? What promotion?" He adjusted his baseball cap.

Something about the gesture niggled at Mary. She couldn't tear her eyes away from the hat.

"Did you finish your les . . ."

The hat was beat up and royal blue. In her mind, she saw Dean sitting on their deck on Father's Day years ago, unwrapping a gift Kendra had given him. The image was clear, right down to the green golf carts on the wrapping paper and the smudge of chocolate above Kendra's lip from the cake she'd just eaten. Dean had pulled a hat out of the box, a royal blue baseball hat. He'd folded its bill before placing it on his head. "Exactly what I needed," he'd said. "A good luck cap."

"The hat Kendra gave you." She shot up to a sitting position and snatched it from his head. "You're wearing the hat Kendra gave you." Halle-freaking-lujah! Somehow, she'd made it back. The attack on her gums stopped. She was pain-free.

Dean chewed on his lip. "I always do in a tournament. You know that."

Mary tipped her head back and turned her face to the sky. "Kendra exists. She gave you a hat. I made it back." The words came rushing out, leaving her breathless.

Dean looked side-eyed at Brady, who leaned closer to Mary's face to study her pupils.

"I thought I was stuck in my other life without you forever." She assessed her body. The legs that only days ago a man on the street had called "sexy" were bruised with varicose veins. She could see bulges in her stomach beneath her baggy shirt. A diamond band encircled the slightly arthritic ring finger of her left hand. She grinned and threw her arms around Dean. He felt solid in her embrace, real, reliable, someone she could depend on. Someone she loved who loved her back. "I'm not twenty-four anymore. You're my husband again."

Brady rubbed his hand over his razor stubble. "Head injuries can be tricky," he said.

"I have never been better." She felt her smile from the tip of her toes to the ends of the hair on her head. She pointed at Brady. "Good to meet you here in my real life."

Brady raised an eyebrow. "We need to get her to the hospital to get checked out."

Using Dean's shoulder for leverage, Mary pushed herself up from the ground, musing that mere minutes ago, she would have been able to lift her young body without needing any type of assistance. It was a price she was more than happy to pay to return to her life with Dean and Kendra.

Kendra! She needed to call her. Right now. She bent to retrieve her bag from the ground, almost falling over, but Dean got it first.

Brady shot to his feet and wrapped an arm around her waist. "Ma'am, let's be on the safe side."

Ma'am? Usually she hated being called that, but hearing the word now overjoyed her. She was once again someone hot twenty-somethings would never notice. She was back to her beyond-middle-aged self.

Brady motioned to another paramedic to bring the stretcher over.

"I need to talk to my daughter."

"Let's get you checked out first," Dean said.

Brady and the other paramedic carried Mary down the dirt path to the parking lot. Dean walked along beside them, holding tight to her hand. He climbed into the back of the ambulance and sat next to her, with his hand still wrapped around hers. Before Brady closed the door, Mary called to him: "Take good care of Frank Sinatra, and treat RaeLynn well."

Brady blinked fast. "How do you know about them?"

"Who are they?" Dean asked.

"My dog and girlfriend."

"And Belli, don't hang him from any more ceilings."

Brady's mouth fell open. Mary winked, laughing without a care in the world and with a brand-new appreciation for her real life.

~

As Mary sat on a bed in the emergency room waiting to see a doctor, Dean handed her his phone.

"Mom."

Mary's body trembled, and she burst into tears. She thought she'd never hear her daughter's voice again. Nothing had ever sounded as sweet. Dean sat next to her, taking her free hand into his. *This must be what it's like to go to heaven and see your loved ones again,* she thought.

"Are you okay? Dad told me you got hit in the head by a golf ball."

There were voices outside Mary's room. Somewhere down the hall, a machine beeped over and over again.

"I'm the best I've ever been." No words had ever been truer. She'd never loved her daughter or husband more. She was a lucky woman, back from the dead. "How are you? How's London?" Mary wished she could jump through the phone and hug Kendra. Why wasn't teleporting a real thing?

Kendra laughed. "I'm fine, Mom. What were you doing at the club?"

"I miss you so much."

"I miss you too. And I'm sorry we haven't had a chance to talk."

"We're talking now. That's all that matters." Mary meant it. Her irritation at Kendra had contributed to her losing her family. How absolutely foolish she'd been.

"The thing is, I wasn't really sure I wanted to move here, but I wanted to try it. And I knew you don't want me to live here. I was afraid I wouldn't give it a real chance, and I'd just end up coming home because I didn't want to disappoint you."

"You could never disappoint me." The curtain to Mary's room opened, and an Indian woman in a white lab coat stepped inside.

Dean stood and reached for the phone. "Time to hang up."

"Are you happy living there?" Mary asked.

"I am," Kendra said.

"That's all that matters. We're going to fly out to see you." She paused, remembering Dean's "smothering" comment. "If that's okay?"

"Come soon," Kendra said.

"I love you," Mary said.

The doctor approached the bed. "I'm Dr. Khatri."

Dean grabbed the phone. "We'll talk to you later. The doctor needs to examine your mom."

"Tell Mom I love her." Kendra said it loud enough for Mary to hear across the room, and Mary felt so light she could have sworn she was floating above the bed. Having people to love who love you back: that's what mattered in life.

Chapter 39

The next night, Mary and Dean sat at the patio table eating salmon and sweet potato planks that Dean had grilled. The sun had started to set, and the sky showcased beautiful shades of pink and purple. Eating outside in the fresh air gave Mary so much joy, especially here on the deck in their backyard, a place they'd spent so much time together as a family. She glanced toward the putting green and imagined six-year-old Kendra learning how to play, and then she saw twenty-four-year-old Kendra competing against Dean. They had a lifetime of memories here, and so many more to come.

A strong breeze sent her napkin fluttering across the deck. Dean jumped from his seat to chase it down. "Do you need anything while I'm up?" He'd been keeping a watchful eye on her ever since bringing her home from the hospital, barely leaving her side. The doctor had diagnosed her with a grade three concussion and prescribed rest. For the most part she had taken the advice, exerting herself only to plan a three-week vacation to Europe, with the first stop in London to visit Kendra and a surprise stay in Scotland so Dean could play at Saint Andrews. With the napkin in hand, he returned to his seat.

"I'm going to book our flights and hotels tomorrow," Mary said. "Are you sure you can take the time off?"

Dean reached for the water pitcher. "I put it on my calendar when you mentioned it this morning."

She extended her glass toward him so he could fill it. "I think this trip will be really good for us. Give us a chance to reconnect."

"What do you mean by reconnect?"

She paused to take a sip. "I feel like we don't spend enough time together lately. You spend so much time on the golf course, and I'm here by myself, lonely." Just admitting that to him was a huge relief.

Dean's eyes widened. "Lonely? I didn't realize you felt that way. I'm sorry."

"I understand you love to play."

He shook his head. "I don't need to golf every afternoon, and when I do, you could meet me at the club for dinner."

"I'd like that." Mary swallowed a bite of sweet potato, the smoky, sweet flavor of cinnamon exploding in her mouth. "It will be nice to spend time together."

He reached across the table and squeezed her hand. "I agree."

Mary felt the same thrill she had at the beginning of her alternate life at the prospect of spending more time with her husband of over twenty years.

"When we get back, we should have date night once a week. Get dressed up. Go to dinner. See a show or something."

"That would be nice." Dean's phone rang. He pulled it from his pocket and hit the ignore button. "That reminds me, I saw James is playing at Foxwoods in November. I got tickets, for Rick and Jenni too. To make up for missing him last time."

An image of James in his postal uniform popped into Mary's head. She couldn't wait to see the real version of him again. "Wonderful."

They ate in comfortable silence for a minute or two.

"There's something I've been thinking about that I want to run by you," Mary said.

Dean put down his fork, giving her his full attention.

"I want to work. Do something that makes a difference."

"For a charity?"

"I was thinking of pitching a weekly segment to Channel 77 where I covered good news, happy stories about people helping each other. Or I could start my own YouTube channel or post the stories to Instagram." She braced herself, expecting Dean to laugh at the idea.

"That's a great idea. The world needs more happy stories," he said. "My assistant is a whizbang at that online stuff. He could help."

"You really think it's a good idea?"

Dean nodded, chewing on a piece of fish. Mary beamed at him. In the things that mattered most, he'd never failed to support her, both here and in the alternate world, where he hadn't owed her anything. Their love for one another really was tattooed on their souls.

She stood to clear the dishes. Dean reached for her arm. "I'll do it. You're supposed to be resting."

She sank back to her chair.

"Anything come back to you about why you were at the golf course yesterday?" he said.

He'd asked last night and again this morning. Both times she'd told him that she didn't remember. "Nothing."

Dean rocked back and forth in his seat, the wrinkles in his forehead more pronounced. "The doctor said your memory should return. We should call to find out why it isn't."

Mary reached for a wedge of lime and squeezed it into her water glass. He wasn't going to let this go. If she told him the truth, he would think she was hallucinating and insist on taking her to the emergency room right now. She had to come up with something.

The wind blew. Below the deck, the flags on the putting green fluttered. She closed her eyes, remembering that she'd promised herself that if she made it back to this version of her life, she would try to develop a love for the game he loved so much.

"I wanted to see about taking golf lessons," she said. "Now that Kendra's not here, I thought I could play with you from time to time."

Dean's entire face lit up. "Really?"

"Yes, really." Her smile matched his.

"You don't need to sign up for lessons. I can teach you. I want to teach you."

This little thing made him so happy. She should have suggested it long ago. "Okay then, you'll give me a lesson."

His cheek twitched. "That reminds me. I had the weirdest dream last night."

"Was I in it?"

Dean pointed his fork at her. "You were a TV reporter just starting out, and I was a retired PGA golfer. You wanted to interview me."

A shiver ran down Mary's back.

"Hello, is anyone home?" Darbi's voice called out from inside the house. The door to the sunroom slid open, and she stepped onto the deck. "Mary, are you okay? Kendra called. Told me what happened to you on the golf course."

Darbi was sunburned and her nose was peeling, just as it had been the night of the viewing party. Mary studied her cousin for a clue that she remembered everything that had happened. All she noticed was that the tension that had tightened Darbi's face in the alternate world was no longer there.

"I'm fine. Dean was just telling me about this weird dream he had where he was a professional golfer. I was a young reporter, and he was giving me golf lessons." She said it to see how Darbi would react.

Darbi gasped and looked pointedly at Mary. They held each other's eyes. By the way Darbi's mouth hung open, Mary knew she remembered everything.

Dean cocked his head. "I didn't say anything about the lesson. I mean, I did give you a lesson in the dream, but I hadn't told you that yet."

Darbi looked away and pointed at the small piece of remaining fish. "That looks amazing. Can I have a bite?"

"I'll get you a plate in a minute," Dean said, his gaze never leaving Mary's face.

Mary reached for his empty dish and piled it on top of hers. "I was speaking too fast. Meant to say you were telling me about your dream and also that you're going to give me golf lessons so we can play together. Two separate, unrelated things."

"Okay, sure." Dean reached for the dishes Mary had stacked and brought them inside.

"I'm so relieved to see you here." Darbi motioned to Mary's house, her eyes welling up.

Mary felt a surge of love and empathy toward her cousin. She'd felt responsible for Mary being in the alternate world, and it wasn't her fault. "I understand why you faked the letter. I'm sorry for blaming you."

Darbi reached for Mary's hand and squeezed it. "It was an unbelievably stressful time for both of us."

Dean returned with a plate and silverware for Darbi. "I'll clean while you two catch up."

Mary waited for him to leave before speaking again. "I don't know how I got back or what happened while I was gone."

"I suspect it will be like what happened before. Memories will fill in as you need them."

"What do you think brought me back?"

Darbi wiped her mouth and reached into her bag. She pulled out a beat-up envelope with a return address in Limerick, Ireland.

"What's this?" Mary asked.

"A letter from Uncle Cillian. A real one. I finally found the stack right before Kendra called. In the storage closet inside the old pressure cooker. Jacqui is scared to death of that thing. I must have hidden it there because I knew she'd never use it."

My dearest Darbi,
I'm delighted to hear that you're happy in your new life in
America and that you've found the love of your life. She sounds

like a lovely lady and I do hope to make it back to the States to meet her someday.

I sincerely doubt that you will ever wish to return to your former situation. However, if you do, I want to reassure you that you have the power within you to get back. All you need to do is to develop a genuine appreciation for the life you left behind, warts and all. Truly, let go of your regrets. No thinking the grass is greener. That, my dear, is no easy task. We tend to want it all and romanticize that which we don't have.

In every life, dearest Darbi, there are hurdles to overcome and periods of great sadness. My hope for you is that the good times make the bad times worth it and that the blessings in your life outweigh the curses.

Fondly,

Uncle Cillian

Mary folded the letter and returned it to Darbi. She felt a bit like Dorothy in *The Wizard of Oz*. She'd had the power to get home all the time within her. She also knew that if she hadn't lived in the alternate world, she would have continued to be unhappy here in her real life. "I do appreciate my life. It's more meaningful than I ever imagined."

"We never truly know the impact we have on others," Darbi said. "A smile, a kind word, positive feedback can change a life."

"I see that now."

"So, no more regrets?" Darbi asked.

Mary's gaze flickered to the sunroom, where Dean was carrying paper plates and a carrot cake. He'd been gone for less than a minute, but her heart leaped at the sight of him making his way toward her to sit at their table on the deck of the house where they'd raised their daughter. These were the meaningful moments in life. "Just one," she said. "I wish I hadn't had to learn to appreciate my life the hard way."

Chapter 40

One year later

Mary and Dean sat at a high-top in the pub at Addison Heights after their round of golf. Above the bar, all the televisions were set to CBS, where Liz Collins was anchoring the evening news. "We'll be right back with a heartwarming story about Gasper, a golden retriever in Massachusetts," Liz said.

Dean beamed across the table at Mary. "My wife's story is coming up next," he announced.

A commercial for a candidate running for president came on the television. Mary swayed impatiently, not believing her story was about to be on *CBS Evening News*. She'd written to Liz months ago, telling her she'd started a YouTube channel that covered only happy stories. Liz had called immediately, delighted to hear from Mary after all these years. "I'll do whatever I can to help," she'd promised. "Our time together at Channel 77 put me on my path." Mary had felt a lump of regret in her throat, thinking about how she'd begrudged Liz her success. She'd learned a valuable lesson about supporting others from Kimberly, who was getting national attention for her work on ICNN's *Morning Show*.

The commercials ended. The bartender turned up the television's volume. Liz was back: "This story comes from a former colleague of mine, Mary Amato, who has a YouTube channel, Mary's Miracles, with the good news stories we all need."

The screen switched from Liz's face to a dark-red golden retriever wagging his long tail and Mary's voice. "Ten months ago, the Cornell family's trip to Maine to view the foliage took a sad turn when their dog, Gasper, bolted from a hiking trail chasing a squirrel and went missing."

On television, Mary squatted so that she was eye level with a seven-year-old girl and a five-year-old boy. The golden retriever stood on all fours between the two kids, each child with an arm around him. The dog's thick red tongue hung out the corner of his mouth, and his tail swished back and forth. His ribs were visible through dark-red hair, but he otherwise seemed healthy and happy.

"Tell me what happened," Mary said.

The camera focused on the girl. "I couldn't believe it. I went outside to play on the swing set. The slide is really fun." The little girl's two front teeth were missing, giving her words a whistle-like quality. "Gasper was just lying there. Somehow he found his way home. I don't know how." She shrugged with her arms extended and her palms facing up. "It's a miracle." She wrapped her tiny arms around the dog and kissed him on his snout. Gasper wrapped his front leg around her calf as if he were hugging her back. "I missed him so much."

"Looks like he missed you too." Mary smiled.

The story ended. Dean clapped, and soon all the patrons in the pub were joining in.

Mary paid no attention to the applause. She was too busy thinking about that determined dog covering all those miles through rough terrain to get home to his family. She understood exactly how miserable he'd been without them and how happy he must have been to make it home.

ACKNOWLEDGMENTS

The first people I need to thank are my editors, Alicia Clancy and Tiffany Yates Martin. Alicia, thank you for believing in this book from the start, when it was only fifty pages long. I so appreciate that you took a chance on this story and then connected me with Tiffany. Tiffany, thank you for helping me make this story shine. Your comments and questions were incredibly insightful and really helped me infuse the story with emotion. The book is so much stronger thanks to your comments and Alicia's.

To the team at Lake Union, I'm happy and grateful to be working with you on a second book. The experience for my first book—editing, proofreading, marketing, working on the cover design, and everything else—was absolutely exceptional. Thank you for doing such a great job.

Liza Fleissig, Lake Union was my dream publisher, and you made it happen. Thank you for always believing in me and encouraging me. My query letter to you is still the most important thing I've ever written. I can't imagine being on this journey without you.

Brittany McHatten, the best part about writing this book was the time I spent in Maine at WABI Channel 5, shadowing you at work and hanging out with you, Tyson, and Daniel. Thank you for answering all my texts and emails with questions and letting me see you in action. You are a true professional, and I still burst with pride from watching you anchor and report the news. I took some fictional liberties with what I learned from you, but hopefully Mary seems like a real reporter.

Alexandra Devane, thank you for inspiring Belli and always making me laugh with your stories.

Steve, I love you. Thank you for all your support while I worked to meet deadlines and for your holiday heroics, which allowed us to host Christmas last minute while I was working on edits.

My writing group at the Hudson Library—Tiana, Neville, Steve, Amanda, Maureen, Sam, Betsey, Jeanette, and Scott—thank you for all your feedback and for the opportunity to read/critique your work.

Michele Lugiai, my WFWA critique partner, thank you for your feedback on early versions of this story, and Lidija Hilje, thank you for your comments and enthusiasm early on as well.

Dad, Mom, and Susan Devane, thank you for being my biggest fans and best marketers. I love you. Love you, too, Michael and Maria, but I'm still waiting for the invite to your book clubs. ☺

Susan Timmerman, thank you for reading an early draft and providing spot-on feedback! And thanks for all your support and interest in my writing journey.

Karen Vivenzio, thank you for taking the time to read my manuscript and for your enthusiasm for it.

I'm sure I will get teased for this, but thank you to Golden Boy (a.k.a. Oakley) for keeping me company by resting under my desk as I wrote this and for reminding me when it was time to take a walk. And thanks for all the hugs!

To all the bloggers and reviewers who post pictures and help me publicize my books, thank you. Your enthusiasm is so important in helping me spread the word about my stories.

Thank you to everyone who takes the time to read my novels, and especially to those who leave reviews. Your support means everything.

ABOUT THE AUTHOR

Photo © 2023 Shannon Graham

Diane Barnes is the author of *All We Could Still Have*, *More Than*, *Waiting for Ethan*, and *Mixed Signals*. She is also a product market manager in the health-care industry. When she's not writing, Diane can be found at the gym, running, or playing tennis, trying to burn off the ridiculous amounts of chocolate and ice cream she eats. She and her husband, Steven, live in New England with Oakley, their handsome golden retriever. She hopes you enjoy reading her books as much as she enjoys writing them.